A Simple Prayer

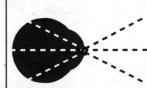

This Large Print Book carries the
Seal of Approval of N.A.V.H.

A SIMPLE PRAYER

AMY CLIPSTON

THORNDIKE PRESS

A part of Gale, Cengage Learning

GALE
CENGAGE Learning·

Farmington Hills, Mich • San Francisco • New York • Waterville, Maine
Meriden, Conn • Mason, Ohio • Chicago

GALE
CENGAGE Learning®

LIBRARY OF CONGRESS CATALOGING-IN-PUBLICATION DATA

Clipston, Amy.
   A simple prayer / Amy Clipston. — Large print edition.
      pages cm. — (Hearts of the lancaster grand hotel ; book 4) (Thorndike Press large print christian romance)
   ISBN 978-1-4104-7945-7 (hardback) — ISBN 1-4104-7945-5 (hardcover)
   1. Amish--Fiction. 2. Large type books. I. Title.
PS3603.L58S56 2015b
813'.6—dc23   2015008896

Published in 2015 by arrangement with The Zondervan Corporation LLC, a subsidiary of HarperCollins Christian Publishing, Inc.

Printed in Mexico
1 2 3 4 5 6 7 19 18 17 16 15

*For my mother, Lola Goebelbecker,
with love, appreciation, and admiration.
You're my rock and my best friend.
Thank you for all you do for our family.*

GLOSSARY

ach: oh
aenti: aunt
appeditlich: delicious
Ausbund: Amish hymnal
bedauerlich: sad
boppli: baby
brot: bread
bruder: brother
bruderskinner: nieces/nephews
bu: boy
buwe: boys
daadi: granddad
daed: dad
danki: thank you
dat: dad
Dietsch: Pennsylvania Dutch, the Amish
  language (a German dialect)
dochder: daughter
dochdern: daughters
Dummle!: hurry!
Englisher: a non-Amish person

fraa: wife
freind: friend
freinden: friends
froh: happy
gegisch: silly
gern gschehne: you're welcome
grossdaadi: grandfather
grossdochder: granddaughter
grossdochdern: granddaughters
grossmammi: grandmother
Gude mariye: Good morning
gut: good
Gut nacht: Good night
haus: house
Ich liebe dich: I love you
kapp: prayer covering or cap
kichli: cookie
kichlin: cookies
kind: child
kinner: children
kumm: come
liewe: love, a term of endearment
maed: young women, girls
maedel: young woman
mamm: mom
mammi: grandma
mei: my
mutter: mother
naerfich: nervous
narrisch: crazy

onkel: uncle

Ordnung: The oral tradition of practices required and forbidden in the Amish faith.

schee: pretty

schmaert: smart

schtupp: family room

schweschder: sister

Was iss letz?: What's wrong?

Wie geht's: How do you do? or Good day!

Willkumm: welcome

wunderbaar: wonderful

ya: yes

Hearts of the Lancaster Grand Hotel

Family Trees
Glick Family

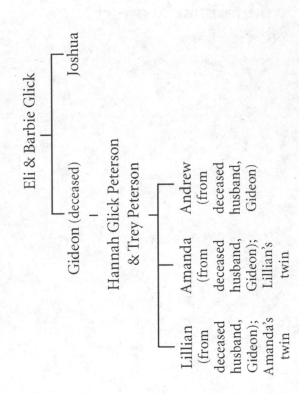

Eli & Barbie Glick

Gideon (deceased)

Joshua

Hannah Glick Peterson & Trey Peterson

Lillian (from deceased husband, Gideon); Amanda's twin

Amanda (from deceased husband, Gideon); Lillian's twin

Andrew (from deceased husband, Gideon)

Lapp Family

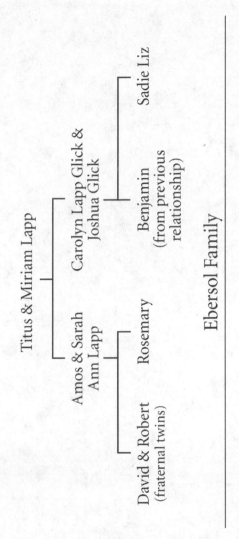

Titus & Miriam Lapp

Carolyn Lapp Glick & Joshua Glick

Amos & Sarah Ann Lapp

Rosemary

Benjamin (from previous relationship)

Sadie Liz

David & Robert (fraternal twins)

Ebersol Family

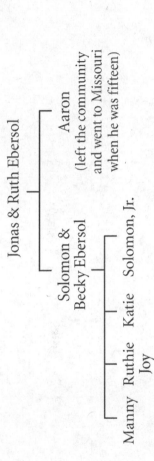

Jonas & Ruth Ebersol

Solomon & Becky Ebersol

Aaron (left the community and went to Missouri when he was fifteen)

Manny   Ruthie   Katie   Solomon, Jr.
Joy

Beiler Family

Saul Beiler (wife deceased)

———

Emma

Smucker Family

Marcus & Sylvia Smucker

———

Esther

Stolzfus Family

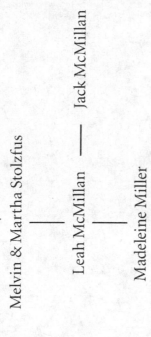

Melvin & Martha Stolzfus

Leah McMillan —— Jack McMillan

Madeleine Miller

NOTE TO THE READER

While this novel is set against the real backdrop of Lancaster County, Pennsylvania, the characters are fictional. There is no intended resemblance between the characters in this book and any real members of the Amish and Mennonite communities. As with any work of fiction, I've taken license in some areas of research as a means of creating the necessary circumstances for my characters. My research was thorough; however, it would be impossible to be completely accurate in details and description, since each and every community differs. Therefore, any inaccuracies in the Amish and Mennonite lifestyles portrayed in this book are completely due to fictional license.

ONE

Memories flashed through his mind as Aaron Ebersol steered his pickup truck through Paradise late Tuesday afternoon. When he saw the old schoolhouse, he pulled over and thought about the years he spent learning with his peers in the one-room building. He took in the place, wondering if his brother had any children still attending there. Had Solomon's family grown during the past seventeen years? He was certain it had.

Aaron put the truck in gear and drove to his parents' house. His pulse pounded as he slowed to a stop in front and took in the property. Their house looked the same — an average-size, two-story white house with the green window shades typical in Lancaster County Amish homes.

His brother's house, behind their parents' home, was more substantial. When Aaron left, the house was already framed, so he knew the two-story home was nearly twice the size of his parents' house. He remembered the plans included six bedrooms, a spacious kitchen, and two bathrooms. Solomon and his wife, Becky, wanted what every Amish couple dreamed of having — a place of their own to raise a large family.

Solomon had always seemed so certain of himself and his future. He was confident and serious, the opposite of Aaron. Solomon never doubted where he belonged in life or what path he should follow. Eight years Aaron's senior, Solomon had joined the church when he was eighteen, married his childhood sweetheart when he was twenty, and started a family when he was only twenty-one. Solomon had figured everything out at a young age — not only would he help his father with the dairy farm that would one day be his, he would raise his family in the Amish church.

For a long time, the two brothers were close. Solomon was the best older sibling anyone could ask for. But then Aaron started getting into trouble with behavior his by-the-book brother couldn't understand. How could he, when following all the rules had made his own life so perfect? By the time Aaron left, they seemed more like strangers than brothers.

Aaron spotted a man walking out of the largest of the red barns. He was sure it was Solomon, though he supposed it could be his son, Manny, who'd be nineteen by now. He considered climbing from the truck. Instead he sat still in his seat, unable to move. Something had kept him away from his family all these years, and he wasn't sure he was ready to see any of them now. Not today.

He watched Solomon saunter toward his parents' house for a moment longer and then drove off before he'd be noticed. He was going to the Heart of Paradise Bed & Breakfast, where he had reserved a room for his stay. He'd found the place by searching for hotels close to his parents' home, and it was only three and a half miles away.

He parked in their driveway and grabbed his duffle bag from the backseat. The crisp January air seeped through his coat and caused him to shiver as he climbed the front steps leading to the three-story, clapboard house. Just as the website had boasted, the building had a large, wrap-around porch with a large swing and was peppered with rocking chairs. A wooden sign with old-fashioned letters boasted the name of the place: Heart of Paradise Bed & Breakfast. He knocked on the front door, and in a minute or so it swung open, revealing a tall man with short sandy-blond hair and a matching goatee. He looked to be in his mid-forties.

"Good afternoon," Aaron said. "I'm Aaron Ebersol. I'm going to be staying here for a while."

"It's nice to meet you. We've been expecting you. I'm Trey Peterson." Trey shook Aaron's hand and then swung the door open and motioned for him to enter. "My wife, Hannah, and I own this bed-and-breakfast."

Aaron followed him into a sitting area sparsely decorated with antiques and a few plants. "This is nice."

"Thank you." Trey pulled out a book and flipped through it. "Let me see where we have you staying." He reviewed a page and then looked up. "Oh, yes. I remember. You said you don't know how long you'll be here, so we'd like to have you pay for a week up front. Does that still sound okay?"

"That will be fine." Aaron slid his wallet from the back pocket of his jeans and pulled out his credit card.

Trey ran it through the machine and Aaron signed the receipt. Trey handed him a set of keys, explaining that one was his room key and the other was the key to the front door. Aaron followed him up the stairs to the second floor and down a hallway to the last door on the right.

"Here we are." Trey opened the door and stepped inside.

Aaron stood in the doorway and surveyed the room. It had a double bed, a dresser with a flat-screen television on top of it, a small desk with a chair, and a nightstand. He could also see a small bathroom with a shower through another open door and what was probably the closed door to a closet. A stack of towels sat in the middle of the bed. The walls were white, and a small mirror hung in one corner next to a flowered wreath. A painting of a farm landscape adorned the wall above the bed, and another wall had a big window.

It was all he'd need for his visit.

"It's perfect," Aaron said.

"We'll provide fresh linens every day." Trey picked up a piece of paper next to the television. "We have basic cable, and this is a list of channels."

"Thanks, but I don't watch much television." Aaron dropped his duffel bag next to the bed with a thud.

"Breakfast is included with your stay, and it's served at eight. The back stairs we passed lead right to the kitchen. We don't have a formal dining room. One authentic Amish meal is also included, and you can choose what day you want that meal."

Trey paused, looking as if there were something else he wanted to say.

"Mr. Ebersol," he finally said, "I didn't want to ask when you called, and I didn't say anything to my wife for fear I'd get her hopes up, but . . . are you Ruth's son? She and my wife are friends."

"Yes, I am. But if you don't mind, could you not tell anyone I'm here? My family doesn't know anything about me being here. Not yet."

"Of course. But I know from what Hannah has told me that Ruth will be thrilled to see you. They worked together at the Lancaster Grand Hotel. Well, welcome back."

"Thank you. And please call me Aaron." He was surprised his mother had had a job outside the home. Inwardly, he winced. Had the farm not adequately supported his family over the years?

Trey moved to the doorway before adding, "Do you have any questions before I go?"

"No. Everything is great." Aaron smiled. "Thank you."

"You're welcome. Just let me know if you

need anything." Trey tapped the door frame and then walked down the hallway.

Aaron took off his coat and sat down on the edge of the bed, which creaked under his weight. He didn't know what to do first. He stared out the window, considering his options. He had to go see his parents, but something was holding him back. Was it his pride or was it something more like fear — fear of their continued rejection?

Shaking those thoughts from his mind, he unpacked his clothes, placing his shirts and undergarments in the dresser and hanging his jeans and trousers in the closet. Besides, his family members were not the only people he wanted to see.

Aaron's childhood friend Saul was the one who'd contacted him a little over a week ago to tell him his mother had suffered a massive stroke. He even indicated she was asking for him. Aaron had been both shocked and saddened by the news, but also surprised. He hadn't heard from anyone in his family for seventeen years. Still, he had decided before they had even finished talking that, if his mother wanted him, he'd go.

He tied up loose ends at the construction company he co-owned in Missouri and headed to the community where he'd been born and raised until he left at the age of fifteen.

It was difficult to believe he was here.

After freshening up in the bathroom, Aaron grabbed his coat and started down the back stairs to the kitchen. He found Trey flipping through a cookbook.

Aaron knocked on the door frame and then leaned against it. "Hi, Trey, I was wondering if you could help me."

Trey looked over at him. "Sure. What do you need?"

"I want to visit a friend, but I'm not sure where he lives these days. His name is Saul Beiler, and he owns Beiler's Cabinets somewhere in Paradise. Do you know him by any chance?" Aaron asked.

"Oh, yes, I do know where that is. It's only a few blocks from here." Trey pulled a map out of a nearby drawer, grabbed a pen, and drew a line. "We're here, and his property is over here. It will only take you a few minutes to get there. You can't miss the sign advertising his business. You can see it clearly from the road. There's a small house in front of his property, and you'll drive up the rock driveway past that house to Saul's place behind it."

"Thanks." Aaron took the map and stuck it in his pocket.

"We don't serve lunch," Trey said, "but are you hungry? I have some lunch meat and rolls if you'd like to make a sandwich. I think there's some potato salad in the refrigerator."

"Oh, no, thanks. I'm fine. I had a late lunch on the road." Aaron pulled on his coat.

"Well, that's probably for the best. I'm not much of a cook, but I do what I can now that my wife has to take it easy. She's expecting our first child in the spring. But we hired a part-time person to help, and she's a great cook. Her name is Linda, and she'll be here tomorrow morning."

"Sounds good. I'll be back later. May I use this back door?"

"Sure. Have a good visit with your friend," Trey called after him as Aaron stepped out onto the back deck.

Using Trey's directions, Aaron easily found his way to Saul's place. He spotted the sign with Beiler's Cabinets on it and steered his pickup up the rock driveway, passing the small, one-story house as Trey had advised. A larger house was surrounded by several other small buildings.

Aaron parked near one of the larger buildings and climbed from the truck. He heard whirling from inside and assumed Saul was working in there. He pushed open the door and stepped into a woodworking shop.

The smell of wood dust filled his senses. The soft yellow light from lanterns perched around the large former barn illuminated the shop. A tall man with dark-brown hair and a matching beard stood at a workbench and sanded a cabinet while a diesel generator hummed. An array of tools cluttered a line of surrounding workbenches. A pile of wood sat in the corner beside cabinets in various stages of development.

Aaron knocked on the door frame and then stepped into the shop. "Hello?" he called over the noise.

The man stopped working and turned toward Aaron. He shut off the generator, and his brow furrowed as he stared at him. "May I help you?"

"Saul?" Aaron took a step toward him.

Saul's eyes widened. "Aaron Ebersol? Is it you?"

"*Ya,* it's me," Aaron said. "I made it."

"Praise God!" Saul clapped his hands. "I'm so glad I didn't have to go out to Missouri and fetch you."

Aaron shook his head. "No, that wasn't necessary. When we talked last week I told you I'd get out here as soon as I could. My business partner, Zac, is taking care of things so I can stay here for a while if my family wants me to. I arrived in town about an hour ago." He paused. "You didn't tell anyone I was coming, right?"

"No. I didn't want to get anyone's hopes up in case, well, in case you changed your mind or got held up. If you just got here, I take it you haven't see your *mamm* yet?"

"No, I . . . I wanted to talk to you first." Aaron glanced around the shop. "You have a nice setup here." He pointed toward the door. "I saw you have other buildings as well."

"Ya." Saul wiped his hand on a shop rag. "I bought this property from Mel and Martha Stoltzfus. They owned all this land, including that smaller *haus* by the road. Soon after I bought the farm, I converted one of the large barns into this shop, and I added two more buildings a couple of years later. I stain the wood in one of the other buildings, and the third shop is the showroom."

"This is great." Aaron shoved his hands in his pockets while glancing around at the workbenches full of tools. "I take it you've been successful."

"Ya, I have. The Lord has blessed me with a *gut* business. I'm thankful." Saul leaned against the workbench behind him. "You've

27

been blessed with a successful business as well, *ya*?"

"Yes, it has been successful. When the economy tanked, so did some of our business, but it's starting to pick up again. We're actually beginning to see a decent profit." Aaron shoved his hand through his messy curls. "When I moved out to Missouri, my friends and I all went to work for a construction company. The owner was also a former Amish man. He taught us everything he knew about the business, and I met my friend Zac. His mother had left the Amish community and married an *Englisher*. Zac and I moved up in the company, and seven years ago, we took out a loan and started our own business."

"That's great," Saul said.

"Thanks. It's grown a lot since we started," Aaron continued. "We have quite a few employees, and we hire former Amish workers too. It's sort of our way to give back to the community. We help other young Amish find their way in the *English* world. It's worked out well. The phone rings off the hook some days. We do very little advertising. It's mostly word of mouth and referrals."

Saul's expression hardened slightly. "Do you think it's right for you to help former

Amish find their way in the outside world? You're leading them astray instead of leading them back to the community."

Aaron could tell he'd hit a nerve with Saul, but he didn't want to argue with him. After all, Aaron had left when he was fifteen, and he had help adjusting to the *English* lifestyle. "People leave for different reasons, Saul. It's not my place to judge them. It's up to them to decide if they belong in the Amish community or in the modern world. I simply offer help to those who need it."

Saul moved to a cooler and pulled out two bottles of water. "Would you like some water?"

"Thanks." Aaron opened the bottle Saul handed him and took a long drink.

Saul watched Aaron for a moment as if he were considering his words. "Does Timothy work for you?"

"Timothy?" Aaron tilted his head in question and then recognition flashed through his mind. "You mean Timothy Esh." He knew Saul's wife, Annie, had abandoned him and their daughter, filed for divorce, and moved to Missouri to be with Timothy, who had been her first boyfriend.

"Ya." Saul's expression was grim.

Aaron nodded. "Yes, he does. I guess you remember he and I left the community

29

about the same time."

Saul's gaze moved to the floor, and Aaron struggled with what to say. He knew Annie had died in an accident nearly two years ago, and he was certain it was still a loss for Saul despite his painful past with her.

"I'm sorry about Annie," Aaron said.

"Danki." Saul cleared his throat as he looked over at Aaron. "I'm *froh* you made it here."

"Thank you." It was time to stop stalling. Aaron had to move from the small talk to the reason he was here. "How's my *mamm*?" His voice hitched on the word *mamm*.

"Apparently her stroke was fairly severe." Saul sat down on a stool. "She spent a few days in the hospital until her condition stabilized, and now she's home. The doctors only agreed to skipping a stay in a rehab center because she'll have so much support at home. Nurses come to help care for her, and both a physical and speech therapist come. Her right side was markedly affected, and she needs to learn basics like how to dress and feed herself, as well as speak more clearly. Her words are a bit garbled, and she has problems getting out what she wants to say."

All this new information weighed heavily on Aaron's chest, stealing his breath. He inspected the toe of his work boot.

"I'm sorry, Aaron. I had hoped there would be better news when you got here."

Aaron sipped more water and then cleared his throat in hopes of restraining his surging emotion.

"The good news is that she can get all this therapy at home." Saul studied him. "She asks about you constantly, Aaron. That's why I called you. It's *gut* that you're here. Maybe it will help with her frustration."

"What do you mean by frustration?" Aaron held his bottle a bit tighter.

"Because she has a difficult time speaking, she gets upset. She's often agitated and lashes out at people, even your *dat.*"

Aaron shook his head with disbelief. "I don't ever remember my *mamm* lashing out at my *dat,* my brother, or me. She sounds like someone I don't know."

"The stroke has changed her. It's been difficult on your *dat,* but the community has pitched in to help. Becky helps the most, but some of the women take meals and help clean and do laundry too." Saul paused to drink more water. "There's more, Aaron. She's lost her mobility."

"She can't walk?"

Saul hesitated. "No, she's in a wheelchair. But with therapy . . ."

31

Aaron blew out a sigh. "This is a lot to take in. In my mind, I still see her as the mother I left when I was fifteen. She was still young and strong. I knew she would grow older, but I never imagined she'd have a stroke and change into someone I don't know."

"I think Ruth is still the same person. She's just going through a rough time. But things have changed, Aaron. You've been gone a long time."

"I know I have. Is my *dat* still healthy?"

"*Ya,* but even with all the help, this is taking a toll on him."

"Where did the stroke happen?" Aaron asked.

"It was the Sunday before last. We were all surprised your parents weren't at church. Your *mamm* hadn't been feeling well for a few days. When she woke that morning, she wasn't able to get out of bed or communicate. Your *dat* called an ambulance, and they took her to the hospital. She'd lost her speech and mobility overnight. It happened that quickly."

"Will she even know who I am?" Aaron asked.

Saul nodded with emphasis. "I believe she will. She knows everyone else. I've told you, she asks for you constantly. She will know her own *kind.*"

Aaron finished his water while the truth of his mother's condition soaked through him. It all felt like a bad dream. He'd missed his family for so long and wondered why his mother hadn't answered his letters. Why hadn't his father contacted Aaron? He hadn't shared his contact information with anyone else in Paradise, but he always included his phone number in the letters in hopes his mother would call him.

"I was so shocked when you called that I didn't even ask. How did you find me?"

Saul placed his bottle on the workbench behind him. "Timothy wrote to tell me about Annie's passing, and he sent the letter in an envelope that had Paradise Builders printed on it. That's why I thought he probably worked with you. Anyway, I remembered you once said you wanted to open your own construction business and call it Paradise Builders."

Aaron was stunned. "You remember that? We were only kids when I said that."

"I remember it clearly," Saul said. "We were at a youth group gathering and someone asked what we wanted to do when we grew up. We were all sitting around in a field after playing volleyball."

Aaron smiled. "That's amazing, Saul. I'm

stunned that you remember that so well."

"It came to me when Madeleine asked me if I knew a way to get in touch with you."

"Who's Madeleine?" Aaron asked.

"She lives in the house out by the road." Saul pointed toward the front of the property. "Madeleine works at the Lancaster Grand Hotel where your mother worked before the stroke. When Madeleine asked me that, I remembered the envelope and we searched the Internet for Paradise Builders."

Aaron shook his head as the burning question that had bothered him since Saul's call echoed through his mind. "If my mother was asking for me, why didn't my father or my brother call me?"

Saul looked bewildered by the question. "You left, Aaron. No one knew where you were."

Aaron lowered his body onto a stool. "I had no choice. Things had gotten so bad at my parents' house that it only made sense to leave."

"Was it really that bad?" Saul looked skeptical.

"You have to remember all the trouble I was in. My friends and I went from sneaking out and drinking to playing with matches, which resulted in torching the

34

bishop's barn." Aaron grimaced with embarrassment. "My *dat* and I were already having problems. We argued all the time, and I knew it was tearing my *mamm* apart. After the barn burned down and I took the blame, my parents were left to pay for the damage. I felt so bad about it, and there was no peace at the house. I also doubted I could ever live up to the ideal Solomon had set for a son. Moving to Missouri sounded like a good idea. I didn't want to bring any more shame to my parents."

Saul's eyes were full of sympathy.

Aaron fingered the bottle while he gathered his thoughts. "I didn't cut off my family completely. I wrote my mother nearly every week for a few years, and then I wrote her monthly. I sent checks to pay my parents back for the money they spent rebuilding the barn, but I never heard back from *Mamm* or anyone else in the family."

"You wrote to your mother?" Saul looked surprised. "Ruth has always made it sound like you left and never contacted her."

"I wrote her for years, but no, I never heard back from her. And the checks were never cashed. They treated me like I didn't exist. It's as if they forgot about me as soon as I left."

"That doesn't sound like your parents. I

would understand them being upset and hurt that you left, but I don't think they would treat you as if you didn't exist." Saul looked unconvinced. "Your parents love you, Aaron."

"If they loved me, then they would've acknowledged my letters. My family chose to ignore me, and I don't really understand why they would need me now."

"Aaron, you need to think beyond yourself." Saul shook his head. "Your *mamm* suffered a debilitating stroke. Of course she needs you now. You need to stop feeling sorry for yourself and go see her."

Aaron stood, crinkling the plastic bottle in his hand. He needed to turn the subject to something less painful. "Do you have time to give me a tour of your property?"

"That sounds like a *gut* idea." Saul started for the door and motioned for Aaron to follow him. "*Kumm.* You can meet my daughter, Emma, too."

Aaron slipped into bed and under the heavy quilt. He stared up at the ceiling and considered the day. It had been his first time in his hometown in seventeen years, and he felt like a stranger, maybe even a tourist with no ties to the community. His thoughts were stuck with Saul, who had been more like an acquaintance than a close friend when they were young. Like Solomon, Saul had always been on the straight and narrow, never running with the wild boys. And now Saul had a successful business and a lovely daughter. Aaron had a successful business, too, but he'd give anything for a family, a real family that loved him and needed him.

He rolled onto his side and stared through the darkness at the wall. He had to find the courage to face his mother, and he had to do it tomorrow. He closed his eyes and sent a prayer up to God, asking him not only to grant him the courage but also to open his family's hearts toward him. He fell asleep wondering how his mother would react when she saw him. Would she even recognize him after all these years?

Linda Zook rushed around the Hearts of Paradise Bed & Breakfast kitchen, preparing the morning meal. The spacious kitchen was painted a warm yellow color, reminding her of lemonade, and it had a long table with eight chairs to accommodate a full house of guests. Colorful paintings of farmland scenes, along with decorative plates, a calendar, and a clock bedecked the walls. Unlike her kitchen in the cottage she shared with her uncle, this kitchen had electricity and modern appliances, such as a microwave, toaster oven, dishwasher, refrigerator with an ice and water dispenser on the front, a coffee machine, and a fancy mixer for baking.

For the past week, Linda had enjoyed working at the bed-and-breakfast and learning how to use the modern appliances. She was grateful Hannah had asked her to help her and Trey with the business. Since Linda worked only part-time at the Lancaster Grand Hotel, she could help Hannah at the bed-and-breakfast and also earn extra money. As an added bonus, she hoped the extra income would help her finally earn her uncle's respect.

The aroma of bacon, freshly baked bread, and eggs filled Linda's senses as she dumped the pan of scrambled eggs onto a platter and then began breaking more eggs into the bowl. According to the reservation book, only one couple was staying at the bed-and-breakfast, along with a guest named Aaron Ebersol. That was not an unusual name among the Amish, but she still wondered if somehow her friend Ruth's family had located her son. Linda didn't know why he wouldn't be staying at Ruth's house, but she also didn't know why he had stayed away all these years.

She only had fifteen minutes until the clock would strike eight. The table was set with the best dishes, utensils, and glasses, along with a bowl of fruit salad, the freshly baked rolls, butter, a variety of jams, and orange juice.

She turned to place the platter on the table and gasped when she found a man standing in the doorway watching her. Her hand flew to her mouth as she tried to slow her heart, which was pounding with shock.

"I'm sorry." He smiled, and the corners of his bright-blue eyes crinkled. "I know I'm a bit early, but I didn't mean to startle you. I guess I assumed you heard my work boots on the stairs."

"It's quite all right." Linda's eyes widened as she stared at him. Not only did she recognize his warm smile, but she also recalled his dark-blond curls that fell in a jumbled mess to his collar. Although his face and hair were familiar, he was now taller, much taller than she remembered. When they were fifteen, he had been only a couple of inches taller than she was. Now he stood a full foot taller than she did. She estimated he was about six-foot-two. His shoulders were broad, and his wide chest filled his button-down, collared blue shirt. He was also dressed like an *Englisher* with his tight blue jeans.

"Are you all right?" he asked while his gaze probed hers.

"Aaron," she finally said. "You're Aaron Ebersol."

"Yes, I am." His eyes filled with questions as he nodded.

Now that she realized their guest was Ruth's Aaron, Linda's lips formed a thin line as frustration filled her. Assuming he was here because of his mother's condition, why had he waited over a week to come? Ruth was in a fragile state, and she had been asking for Aaron since the day of her stroke. Ruth was desperate to see Aaron and reconnect with him. He had walked away from them seventeen years ago.

"And you are . . . ?" he asked.

Her frown deepened. Aaron didn't remember her. The realization gripped her with sadness to replace her frustration. She seemed to be just as insignificant to him as she believed she was to almost everyone.

"Linda Zook," she finished his sentence. "We went to school together."

"Oh, Linda. It's nice to see you again."

She studied him, taking in his phony smile. He didn't recall her, and now she felt disgust for him. Aaron had no regard for his family or his community. He'd forgotten his schoolmates along with his family. She hoped he didn't disappoint Ruth when he went to visit her. Ruth mentioned Aaron constantly whenever Linda visited her, first in the hospital and then at home. It would be a tragedy if Aaron managed to break Ruth's already fragile heart with his arrogant demeanor and blatant disregard for his former community.

"Please have a seat. Help yourself to some eggs and rolls." She placed the platter of eggs on the table and then turned toward the stove, where the bacon sputtered and sizzled. "The bacon is ready too."

"Thank you. Everything smells delicious."

She drained the bacon, slid it onto a platter, and quickly set it on the table, doing her best to avoid conversation with Aaron. She couldn't possibly be friendly with this man after he'd hurt his mother so badly. Ruth was her dear friend, and Aaron had broken Ruth's heart when he left and never bothered to contact her.

"How long have you worked here?" he asked.

"Only since last week." Turning her back on him again, she filled one side of the sink with hot, soapy water for washing and the other side with plain hot water for rinsing,

41

then began to wash the pan she'd made the eggs in.

"Oh," he sounded interested, but she knew he was only being nice. He didn't remember her, so why would he care about her life? After all, he obviously didn't care about even his mother's feelings.

"Do you still live in Paradise?" he asked.

"*Ya,*" Linda said, scrubbing the pan harder and harder. She knew it was rude to keep her back to him, but she couldn't stop thinking of Ruth and her broken heart.

"It hasn't changed much in the past seventeen years, has it?" he asked.

"It has changed a bit," she said. "There are more stores and more traffic, but the town is still somewhat the same. After all, the Amish community does what it needs to in order to stay separate from the *Englishers.*"

He was silent as she continued her work. She hoped the other guests would join them in the kitchen soon so she didn't feel so self-conscious.

"This jam is amazing," he said. "Did you make it?"

"No," Linda responded as she rinsed the thoroughly cleaned pan. "I believe Hannah and her *dochder* made it."

"It reminds me of my *mamm*'s strawberry

jam," he said.

She couldn't stop herself from turning around. "You know, it does taste like Ruth's." The comment popped out of her mouth.

He tilted his head in question. "You've had my *mamm*'s jam?"

"*Ya.*" Linda wiped her hands on a dish towel. "She brought a jar of jam and some *brot* to share at lunch one day at work."

"You work at the hotel where my *mamm* worked?" he asked.

"*Ya,* I do." Had he been to see his mother yet? If so, had his mother's heart mended after missing him for seventeen years? Had his visit helped her heal? She hoped his being back would help Ruth recover from her stroke instead of setting her back.

They stared at each other for a moment, and her cheeks nearly burst into flames. She wasn't used to men noticing her. She quickly turned her attention back to the sink. She wished she could look at Aaron without feeling so awkward and self-conscious. Linda never outgrew the shyness of her youth. Instead, she was forever stuck in a painful, awkward stage.

Footsteps and voices echoed in the stairwell, and Linda was thankful the other couple was joining them for breakfast.

"Good morning," an older man with graying hair said as they entered the kitchen. He took a seat across from Aaron. "Everything smells magnificent."

"Hello." His wife sat beside him and picked up the jar of jam Aaron and Linda had just discussed. "Oh, good. I love this jam."

Linda nodded at them as she continued cleaning up the counter and stove. Guests quickly got used to the informality of an Amish kitchen. In fact, Linda had noticed they all seemed to love it.

"How are you doing today?" the man asked Aaron.

"I'm fine, thank you," Aaron said. "I can tell you that breakfast is wonderful. Linda is a fantastic cook."

"Oh, yes, we know," the woman agreed. "You should have her barbecue meat loaf with boiled potatoes. We had it last Wednesday night, and it was wonderful."

Linda wished her cheeks would stop burning. She worried her face might spontaneously combust!

"I'll have to try that," Aaron said as he stood.

"I highly recommend it," the man chimed in.

Aaron crossed the kitchen and handed

Linda his plate. "Thank you for breakfast."

"Gern gschehne," she said softly. She gazed into his eyes and found sadness there. She longed to ask him where he'd been for seventeen years and why he chose to stay away from his mother, who loved him deeply. It was none of her business, and it didn't matter. After all, he was probably going to visit his family and then go home.

"I'll see you later," Aaron said.

She nodded as he left the kitchen and went back up the stairs. Somehow, the frustration and disgust she felt for him had melted away.

TWO

Aaron contemplated Linda Zook as he drove to his parents' farm. He could see the recognition in her eyes as soon as she looked at him, and he felt guilty that he didn't remember her. Her name was familiar, but he couldn't place her, which surprised him since she was attractive. Linda had the most striking, bottomless brown eyes and clear, ivory skin. She seemed terribly bashful, though. Or maybe she just didn't feel comfortable around him.

She intrigued him, though, especially when she said she worked with his mother. He'd wanted to ask her if she knew any more than Saul had about how his mother was doing, but the subject was too painful to bring up. He feared he might get emotional in her presence, and that would have been awkward for both of them. Although when he mentioned his mother, Linda had stared at him as if she had something she wanted to say to him too. He wondered what she was thinking, but she turned away from him before he worked up the courage to ask her what was on her mind.

He parked his pickup truck in front of his parents' house and stared at the front door. His heart thumped in his chest and he grasped the wheel. He had to face his fear and make his way to the front door. If his family rejected him, then he'd pack up and go back to Missouri with the satisfaction of knowing he'd tried once again to reach out to them. Only this time, he had traveled a long way instead of writing a letter.

Aaron rubbed the bridge of his nose. He knew he wouldn't handle the rejection that easily; his heart would be broken, especially if his mother turned him away. Saul said she had been asking for him, but he also wondered if that was merely some result of the stroke.

Just do it, Aaron. Go face your mother. His inner voice pushed him to risk seeing his family despite a possible painful outcome.

He killed the truck's rumbling engine and stuffed his keys in his coat pocket. He wrenched the door open and walked toward the front porch. His heavy boots crunched the frozen ground, and he shivered even though it was warmer than most January days. Aaron glanced toward the barns and knew his father and brother were busy caring for the animals. He remembered all those freezing winter days when he'd spent hours mucking the stalls. Since the animals spent more time inside the barns during the cold months, there was more shoveling and hauling to do than during the warm months.

Aaron climbed the front steps, stopped on the porch, and instantly felt transported back to his childhood. After taking a deep breath, he knocked and waited for someone to answer.

The door swung open and a young woman dressed in light-blue scrubs appeared.

"May I help you?" she asked.

"Hi," Aaron said, suddenly feeling self-conscious and out of place. "I'm Aaron Ebersol. I came to see my mother."

Her expression lit up. "You're Aaron? I'm her nurse, Jocelyn — the nurse who'll be here most days. It's nice to meet you. She talks about you nonstop — even with the difficulty she's having trouble speaking."

"She does?" He was stunned by that. He truly thought Saul had said that to make him feel better.

"Yes, she does. Please come in." She opened the door wide and he stepped into the small foyer. "Mrs. Ebersol is sitting out on the back porch. I have her well covered, but it's not too cold today. It's the only place that seems to calm her down when she's upset."

She paused. "If it's all right with you, I'd prefer to let her know you're here before you see her. She's quite fragile, and I don't want her to be shocked when you walk in. If anyone else in your family knew you were coming, they haven't mentioned it to her or to me."

Aaron elected not to explain that he hadn't yet told anyone in the family he was here. "How has she been agitated?" he asked.

Jocelyn paused again, and he wondered if she was censoring her words. "Mrs. Ebersol becomes very frustrated when she can't communicate. She knows what she wants to say, but she can't put it into words. It all stems from the damage done by the stroke."

"Oh." Aaron jammed his hands into his pockets. He hoped he had the strength to face how the stroke had changed her.

"I'll go tell your mother you're here and then come and get you when she's ready. Her moods have been unpredictable. If your visit is too overwhelming for her today, then you may have to come back."

He frowned. "I hope it isn't too much for

her. I drove a long way to get here, and I'm eager to see her." He felt ashamed now that he hadn't come in the day before.

"I'll see what I can do. Just give me a few minutes." Jocelyn headed toward the back porch.

Aaron sighed. He couldn't be forbidden from seeing his mother after coming so far both physically and emotionally. He couldn't turn back now.

He stepped into the family room and a chill passed over him. The house was exactly as he remembered it. The furniture he recalled clearly from his childhood was still there, though looking more worn. The same tan sofa, brown wing chair, oak end tables and matching coffee table sat in the exact spots they were in when he was a young boy. Two propane-powered lamps decorated the end tables. The walls were painted plain white and sparsely decorated, with only two shelves that held candles. He clearly remembered his parents sitting across from each other after supper every evening. Once again he felt as if he'd stepped back in time and had never left home.

"Mr. Ebersol?" Jocelyn asked from the doorway. "Mrs. Ebersol is ready to see you."

Aaron's stomach flip-flopped and he stood cemented in the middle of the family room.

The moment of truth had arrived. He'd anticipated this moment ever since receiving the message from Saul. What if things didn't work out the way he'd hoped? What if his mother rejected him? *What if* Mamm *isn't happy to see me after all*?

The nurse tilted her head in question. "Is something wrong? Her mood is fine. She's eager to see you."

"Great." Aaron rubbed his hands together, and his heart pounded. He still couldn't move.

"Are you okay?" the nurse asked as she approached him. "Mrs. Ebersol is waiting for you."

"I don't know what to say," he admitted, sounding more like a little boy than a full-grown man. "It's been so long since I've seen her."

"Just be yourself," Jocelyn said gently. "She's overjoyed that you're here after all these years. You really don't have to say anything. Just be there with her. Hold her hand and tell her that you've missed her." She motioned him to follow her to the kitchen, and he did.

When the nurse reached the door to the mudroom leading to the porch, she said, "I'll give you some privacy. We were working on her exercises, but she can use a

51

break. I just don't want her to overdo it."

"Thanks," Aaron said softly.

His steps were bogged down with the weight of his anxiety as he crossed the mudroom floor. His breath hitched when he made it to the doorway and saw his mother sitting in a wheelchair at the far end of the porch, facing the back pasture. She looked so petite and frail instead of tall and self-assured as he remembered from his childhood. She had on a thick shawl, and a blanket covered her lap and legs. Her hair showing from beneath her prayer covering was gray instead of the deep brown he recalled from his childhood. The porch was outfitted the way he remembered, with three rocking chairs and a wooden glider.

He leaned against the door frame as his emotions churned inside him.

"Aa-ron?" His mother called. "You t-there?"

Her voice was weak and her words were garbled, which further caused his heart to feel like it was twisting. He could tell the stroke had stolen the light he'd always seen inside her. When he was young, he believed his parents were invincible. They were the strongest, wisest adults he knew. He felt as if he were watching a television drama about a family he didn't know. This wasn't the mother he remembered.

"A-aron?" His mother struggled to turn the wheelchair with her left hand. "Y-you there?"

Aaron stepped onto the porch and slowly made his way over to her. As he reached her wheelchair, she turned her face toward him. She gasped, and her tired brown eyes shimmered as she looked up at him.

"A-Aaron," she gushed. "Y-ou *k-k-k-um* t-t-t . . ." She closed her eyes and scowled. She opened and closed her mouth several times, and her cheeks flushed bright red.

So this is what the nurse means when she says Mamm *becomes agitated.*

"Mamm." His voice broke as tears spilled from his eyes. "Calm down, *Mamm.* It's all right. You don't have to say anything."

After opening her eyes, she reached her good hand toward him, and he held it.

Regret, love, and anguish drenched him, and he was overwhelmed by the riot of emotions. He dropped to his knees in front of her, and she pulled him close. He couldn't stop the tears that were burning his eyes and streaming down his cheeks as his mother hugged him. He felt like a little boy cradled in her arms.

"*Ach,* A-Aaron," she whispered, tracing her fingers through his hair. "C-curls."

"Yes, I still have them," he said as he sniffed. "There's no stopping them. No matter what I do, my hair is a mess of curls. I've considered shaving my head."

"No, no. No sh-shave." Her words were garbled, but she still sounded like his mother. He could feel her unfailing love, despite the years he had stayed away. "H-home. You h-home."

Aaron sat back on his heels and brushed his hands over his wet cheeks. "Did you get my letters?"

She tilted her head, and her eyebrows pinched up with confusion. "What l-letters?"

"I wrote you twice a week, then monthly, for years, and I sent you checks," he explained. "I paid back every cent you and *Dat* would have to spend on the bishop's barn. I sent you extra money, in fact, but you didn't cash even one of the checks."

"N-no," she said slowly. "N-no."

"You didn't get the letters?" he asked, trying to make sense of her terse responses.

Aaron stood and sat in a rocking chair beside her. "I know I wrote the correct address on the envelopes. I don't understand why you didn't get them. All this time . . ."

She gave him a lopsided smile and placed her hand on his.

He took in her face and noticed the right side seemed frozen. She was partially paralyzed, and it nearly crushed his heart. He thought again about how she was so strong and intelligent when he was a child. She always had good advice and an encouraging scripture verse to share when he needed support. Now she had problems speaking and was sitting in a wheelchair. The reality settled over his soul, tearing at his emotions. He tried to take a deep, cleansing breath but could only produce a puff of air.

His mother seemed oblivious to his shattering emotions as she continued to smile at him.

"I *fr-froh.*" A tear trickled down her cheek as she squeezed his hand.

He patted her fragile hand and cleared his throat, trying to eliminate the knot that swelled there.

"St-stay for lunch. Sup-per too," she said, speaking slowly. "M-must s-see *kinner.*"

"*Kinner?*" Aaron asked. "Are you saying you want me to meet Solomon's *kinner?*"

Mamm nodded.

"How many children does Solomon have?" Aaron asked.

"F-four," *Mamm* said. "Two *buwe* and two *maed.*"

"Four?" Aaron repeated as the information sank in. Solomon had everything he'd hoped to have. He was helping their father run the farm and he had his large family. "That's wonderful, *Mamm.*"

"M-must s-see *Dat,*" *Mamm* continued.

Jocelyn appeared in the doorway. "Mrs. Ebersol, it's time for you to take your medicine and I think you should get some rest. This has been an exciting morning for you. We'll work on your exercises later."

"*Ach,* no." *Mamm*'s face shone with disappointment.

"I know you're disappointed to end your visit, but Aaron can come back later, right?" The nurse gave him an expression imploring him to agree with her. "You're planning to come and visit again soon, right, Aaron?"

"Right," Aaron chimed in. "I'll come back and visit you very soon."

His mother hesitated and then nodded. "*G-gut.*"

"Take care of yourself, *Mamm.*" He leaned over and kissed her cheek. "Thanks for inviting me for a meal, but next time might be better for you."

His mother cupped her hand to his cheek and her eyes glimmered with fresh tears. "*Ich l-liebe d-,*" she whispered, her mouth stumbling over the words.

Aaron blinked back his threatening tears

as his emotions swirled again. She was attempting to tell him she loved him, and watching her struggle to say the words tore him apart. "I love you too, *Mamm,*" he said with a quaky whisper.

As he walked past Jocelyn on his way into the mudroom, she smiled at him.

"I haven't seen her this happy since I started here last week." She touched his arm. "You're like a miracle drug."

Aaron merely nodded since his emotions were still raw. He started to go back through the kitchen, but two Amish women he didn't know were there cleaning and talking in Pennsylvania Dutch. Without his mother seeing, he quickly slipped back through the porch and out the back door. He wasn't ready for church members to pepper him with questions about where he'd been and why he'd left.

Once he reached the safety of his truck, Aaron breathed a deep sigh of relief. The visit had been overwhelming, but he was grateful he'd come. His mother had welcomed him with open arms, but he wasn't certain how his father and brother would react to his return, and he was glad no one else in the family had seen him. He needed to take the visits one step at a time, and this was the most emotion he could face in one day.

His eyes scanned the house while considering his mother's condition. He remembered a job he and Zac had completed last year. They had made a home handicapped accessible for a woman when her elderly father came to live with her. Aaron and his crew built a ramp on the front of the house, widened doorways, and added a large bedroom and bathroom on the first floor. He wondered if his father would allow him to add a ramp to the front and back of his house. Would he consider having Aaron redesign the downstairs bathroom? The smaller one near his parents' bedroom was too small for what he thought his mother needed as she was more able to get around. Ideas and plans rolled through his mind for a few minutes.

His stomach rumbled and he realized it was well past lunchtime. He suddenly had a craving for his old favorite, ham loaf, which he used to enjoy at the Bird-in-Hand Family Restaurant and Smorgasbord. The idea of having a nice, leisurely lunch warmed his soul. He needed to get away from his parents' house and allow all these overwhelming emotions to subside while he cleared his head.

■ ■ ■ ■

Once Aaron was seated in the restaurant, he ordered ham loaf then contemplated his mother's condition as he occasionally sipped his cup of water. He folded a napkin over and over as he recalled his mother's face when she first saw him.

"Aaron Ebersol?"

He looked up to find a pretty Amish woman staring at him. She was holding an infant. Her face was vaguely familiar, but he couldn't place it. She looked to be about his age and was standing with an Amish man and teenage boy.

"Yes?" he asked while trying to recall who she was. Why did he have such a terrible time remembering faces and names? Had he blocked them from his memory to mask some of the pain of leaving his hometown?

"Aaron!" She repeated his name and snapped her fingers and smiled. "I thought that was you." She pointed to her chest. "I'm Carolyn Lapp. Actually, I'm Carolyn Glick now, but I used to be Carolyn Lapp. We went to school and youth group together. And we worked at the Philadelphia Market together."

"Carolyn!" Recognition flashed through

59

him. *Praise God!* He remembered her! "How are you?"

"I'm well, thanks." She gestured toward the man and boy. "This is my husband, Josh, and my son, Ben." She then turned the infant to face him. "And this little angel is Sadie Liz."

Aaron stood and shook their hands. "It's nice to meet you all."

"This is Ruth's son," Carolyn explained to her husband. "Could you give me a minute to talk to him?" Her husband nodded, but his expression was stoic, almost accusing.

"Of course. We'll go sit." Josh tapped the boy's arm, and he and Ben ambled to the other side of the restaurant.

"Have you seen your mother?" Carolyn asked while bouncing the baby.

"Yes." Aaron frowned. "I just left her house."

"I'm glad you came," Carolyn continued. "She's been asking for you."

"That's what I've heard." Aaron crossed his arms over his chest.

"Linda Zook and I were just saying last week that we hoped your family would locate you. Ruth was so adamant about seeing you. She needs you to be here with her."

At first, he was surprised to hear she knew

Linda, but he quickly reminded himself how small and tight-knit the community was. He was bewildered by how much he missed being a part of that community.

"I was shocked when I saw her. I had no idea what to expect, but I was still really stunned by how much she has changed and how frail she is. She's not the person I remember at all. And she can barely speak. It was painful watching her try to pronounce words."

"I'm sorry." Carolyn's eyes were full of empathy. "I know it was difficult for you. The stroke took a lot out of her."

Aaron sighed. "That's very true."

"Listen, I want to ask you something." Her expression was hesitant, and she lowered her voice. "I heard when you left that you went with the others from our youth group."

"That's right. A group of us went together."

"Did —" She stopped as if the words were too difficult to say. "I don't know if I should even ask."

"What do you want to ask me?" he gently questioned her.

"Did Paul go with you?" After she said the name, her cheeks blushed bright red. "I know he left around the same time you did."

"Paul Bender from the Philadelphia Market?" he asked.

She nodded, but her expression was a mixture of embarrassment and apprehension. "Please don't tell anyone I asked about him. It's been a long time, and I don't want anyone to think wrongly of me."

"I know he was in Missouri with us for a while, but he left several years ago."

"Oh." She smiled and seemed relieved. "*Danki.* I had wondered what happened to him because I never heard from him again. He was gone in a hurry, and only left me a cryptic note." She glanced across the restaurant toward her family. "I better go before they eat without me. They both were complaining they were hungry."

"Enjoy your lunch," he said.

"You too. I'm glad you came back to the community." Then she walked away.

The server brought Aaron his lunch as he considered his conversation with Carolyn. He was stunned she'd recognized him, but he was also thankful to talk to her. The community truly cared about his mother, and that warmed his worried heart. He just couldn't figure out why she didn't get his letters. Had she really not received them? Or had she forgotten about them due to her stroke? Yet Saul didn't seem to think she had ever received them.

When he finished his lunch, he drove back to the bed-and-breakfast. As he climbed the front stairs to his room, he heard the hum of the vacuum. He walked slowly down the hall and found Linda propelling the vacuum cleaner back and forth in his room.

She was focused on cleaning and completely unaware that he was standing in the doorway. When she looked up, she gasped, cupping her hand to her mouth, mirroring the same reaction she'd had to seeing him that morning. She flipped the vacuum cleaner off, and her cheeks glowed a bright pink.

"I'm sorry." He couldn't help but smile at her adorable expression. Her deep-brown eyes were wide, like a child seeing fireworks for the first time. "I've startled you yet again. I honestly didn't mean to."

"No, I'm sorry." She trained her gaze down on her apron. "I didn't mean to get in your way. I was just finishing up." She pointed to a pile of towels on the chair by the desk. "Your clean linens are there. Please let me know if you need anything else."

She seemed to deliberately avoid his gaze, and he wondered why she was so shy. Had she always been this self-conscious? He longed to remember her. She lunged and unplugged the machine from the wall. After winding the cord around the handle, she pushed the vacuum toward the door, and he stepped aside so she could move past him. She was so petite and thin that he felt like a giant next to her.

"Wait. Don't leave on my account." He felt bad for interrupting her. "I can go downstairs until you're done."

"No, really, I was just finishing up." She started to push the vacuum cleaner toward the room next door and then suddenly stopped and faced him. "Did you go to see your *mamm*?"

"Ya." He sighed and leaned against the door frame.

Her eyes were full of sympathy. "You were shocked by how she looked."

It was more of a statement than a question, and the compassion in her expression caught him off guard. Although her cheeks were still slightly pink, her eyes were focused on him, eagerly awaiting his response.

He nodded as emotion churned anew within him. He didn't want to get emotional in front of her. What would she think of him if he shed a few tears in her presence? No self-respecting man would reveal that kind of sentiment in front of a woman he barely knew.

"I was stunned when I first saw her too," Linda continued. "But it will get better. Hold on to your faith. God won't abandon Ruth." Her expression was determined, and he knew she believed those words.

"I know." He cleared his throat. "I just never expected her to be so weak and frail. When I was a kid, she was always the strongest woman I knew. And now, she has to use a wheelchair." He felt a lump swelling in his throat, and he stopped speaking and regained his composure. "She was so astounded that I'd come. I could see it in her eyes."

Linda nodded. "I know she was. Still, she's prayed for this for a long time."

"But that's what I don't understand," Aaron said. "I wrote her many times. After I moved to Missouri and got settled in a job, I wrote her every week, and I even sent her checks. But she had no idea what I was talking about when I asked her if she got the letters and the checks. None of the checks were ever cashed, which didn't make sense to me."

Linda tilted her head and squeezed her eyebrows up. "She never mentioned any letters to me."

Aaron felt his frustration swelling. "I don't understand that. How could all my letters get lost in the mail? Maybe she did get them and never mentioned them to anyone. Did she lose her memory at all when she had the stroke?"

"No, I don't think she lost her memory." Linda's eyes were steady and focused, showing her certainty. "She talked about you all the time at the hotel. I think she would've mentioned the letters if she'd received them."

"She talked about me all the time?" His voice hitched on the last word. He couldn't help but question that every time he heard it.

"*Ya,* she did. Well, actually she still does talk about you." Linda looked confused again. "Why does that shock you?"

"I figured she forgot about me."

"You can't possibly believe that, Aaron." Linda's expression became incredulous. "I've never had any *kinner,* but I'm positive a *mamm* would never forget a *kind.* Ruth shared many times that she worried about where you were, whether you were warm and had food, if you were *froh.* She didn't know where you were, so I know she never received those letters."

"I don't understand it," he repeated as he

66

slapped his thigh with frustration. "It doesn't make any sense at all."

"I think all that matters now is that you're here. In her mind, her prayers have been answered." Linda's expression was full of sympathy again, and her kind expression calmed his growing frustration.

"I know you're right, but that doesn't excuse the years she had to worry about me. I'd feel better if she had received those letters," he insisted. "I feel bad, but I had tried to reach her."

Linda's expression hardened. "Saul and I are both friends with Madeleine Miller, and he had already told her you were back. When she came by to see how Hannah is this morning and I mentioned you were here and had left to see your family, she and Trey both realized they didn't have to keep quiet about you being here now. Madeleine explained how Saul tracked you down. They just didn't tell anyone in case you changed your mind about coming and Ruth would be crushed."

She paused a moment before going on. "I'd just like to know, if you were going to come home, why did it take you so long after Saul called you?"

Aaron blanched at her direct question. "I came as soon as I could. I own a business, so I had to make sure things were handled before I could come."

Linda nodded, but she looked unconvinced. "It's none of my business, but after the stroke, Ruth became more upset and worried about you than ever. She told my friend Madeleine that she had to see you right away, which is why Madeleine helped Saul find you on the Internet. Business or no, I can't understand why you didn't jump in your fancy pickup truck and drive here the day after Saul called you."

Aaron crossed his arms over his chest and sighed. "You're right, Linda. I should've come the next day. The truth is that I was a coward. I was afraid my family would reject me, and I was also upset that my mother had never answered my letters. I felt as if they'd shunned me, even though I can't technically be shunned since I never joined the church. I'm an awful person for not coming right away, but I was scared. Now I feel bad knowing that she's worried about me all these years."

Linda's expression softened again. "I imagine she's forgotten all of that worry now that she knows you're okay." She turned her attention toward the room next door. "I better get back to my cleaning."

As he watched her walk away, a memory

of the school playground flashed through his mind. He was about ten years old and standing up to bat during a softball game. He glanced toward a big tree across the playground and saw a little brunette girl sitting alone underneath it. She was small for her age and shy. And, he remembered now, she was almost always alone. That was Linda. She was a wallflower, never talking much or contributing in class. But he suddenly remembered those captivating eyes.

"Linda, wait," he called after her.

She stopped in the doorway of the room next door and gave him a curious expression.

"You were raised by your *onkel* Reuben and *aenti* Verna, right?"

She paused, her eyes assessing him. "So you do remember me."

"Of course I do," he tried to stave off the awkwardness, but he could feel it filling the air between them. "How are your *onkel* and *aenti*?"

Her expression softened slightly. "*Mei aenti* passed away several years ago. *Onkel* Reuben is the same."

"Oh." He did a mental head slap. *Great job, Aaron. More awkwardness.* "I'm sorry about your *aenti*."

She gave him a stiff nod. *"Danki."*

She pushed the vacuum cleaner into the room, and he wondered why she was still single when it seemed most members of the community their age had married and started families. He didn't remember seeing her at any youth group gatherings. Did she prefer being alone?

Soon the vacuum roared to life and he was left alone with thoughts of his mother. He needed to find out what had happened to his letters, but Linda's encouraging words echoed through his mind. He had answered his mother's prayer by coming home, but would the rest of his family welcome him as his mother had?

THREE

Solomon couldn't prevent his scowl while sitting at his parents' long kitchen table that evening. His family ate meals with them a lot more often now that Becky and their daughters were helping out with some of the cooking. He chewed the pot roast slowly, and, although it smelled delicious, it tasted like sawdust in his mouth while he listened to his mother haltingly detail her visit with Aaron.

He still couldn't believe the news — Aaron had returned. His irresponsible, inconsiderate, reckless, thoughtless younger brother had returned to the community after seventeen long years. It was too much for him to process. His appetite had vanished, and he dropped his fork onto the plate with a loud clatter.

Becky, who was sitting beside him, jumped.

"I'm sorry," Solomon muttered before

wiping a napkin across his mouth.

Becky leaned over and lowered her voice. "Is there something wrong with the pot roast, *mei liewe*?"

"No." He lifted his glass of water. "It's *gut*."

"Why aren't you eating?" she pressed on.

"I'm letting my food settle." He knew it was a sin to lie, but he couldn't admit the truth to his wife — he was furious that his brother had come back and given their mother the false hope that he would actually stay. And he hadn't even had the decency to face the rest of the family.

"He . . . t-tall," *Mamm* said, struggling with every word.

"Really? He's tall? Taller than *Dat*?" Solomon Jr. asked with amazement. "I know I'm only eleven now, but I want to be really tall when I grow up."

"Will we get to meet him?" Katie asked, ignoring her little brother. "*Onkel* Aaron left four years before I was even born, but I've always wondered about him."

Ruthie Joy looked over at Solomon. "And I was born a year after he left, so I'm really curious too. We'll meet our *onkel*, right, *Dat*?"

Solomon gave her a curt nod, but in his heart, he doubted Aaron would stay around long enough to get to know his nieces and nephews. And that thought irked him. Why was his brother showing up now anyway? Just because the mother he had abandoned was ill? And who had contacted him? That was the even bigger unknown that infuriated him.

"I can't believe it." His father's eyes gleamed with tears as he sat at the head of the table. "What a miracle that Aaron has finally come home. I worried that we'd never see him again and then he just shows up out of the blue when we need him most. I wish he'd come to find me out in the barn."

Solomon gritted his teeth. How could his parents celebrate his brother after he'd been gone for so long? Didn't they resent his absence as much as he did? He felt Becky's eyes studying him, and he busied himself with piling more mashed potatoes on his plate even though he wasn't hungry.

"It's very unexpected." Becky frowned while cutting up a piece of pot roast. "I'm stunned that he's back now after all these years. I never thought we'd see him again either. He left in such a rush that it felt as if he had no feelings for his family. In fact, I didn't think he cared about any of us. Now he's back and it's difficult to believe anything will ever be the same again."

"Did Aaron say where he's staying?" his father asked. "Those bedrooms upstairs aren't even used anymore. I hope he's not paying for a room somewhere when we have more than enough room for him."

His mom stopped struggling to fork a piece of meat with her left hand and shook her head. "N-no."

"Did he say when he's coming back?" Manny asked. At nineteen, his oldest son was one to ask for details.

"*Y-ya.* T-t-o-m-morrow." *Mamm* sniffed as a tear trickled down her cheek. She reached up and touched her prayer covering with her left hand. "H-he . . . c-curls."

"He has curly hair?" Katie's eyes widened. "Are they like my curls?"

"*Ya,*" *Mamm* said.

"Wow." Katie beamed.

"I want to meet him," Manny said.

"I do too," Junior added. "I didn't know I had an *onkel.*"

"*Ya,* you did," Katie corrected him. "*Mammi*'s mentioned *Onkel* Aaron before."

"Not to me," Junior insisted before turning to Solomon. "Why don't you talk about your *bruder, Dat*?"

Solomon felt all the eyes at the table turn to him, and the room fell silent. It was as if

74

he were stuck in a fishbowl. He simply shrugged off their stares. "Aaron left. There was nothing more to say."

"He a-a-sked . . . l-letters . . . ," *Mamm* started to say. She stopped talking and closed her eyes, then her face turned as red as a Red Delicious apple as she struggled to speak.

"Calm down, Ruth." *Dat* touched her arm. "What are you trying to say?"

Mamm glared at *Dat* and shook her head while she tried to think of the words. Solomon couldn't stand seeing her so frustrated.

"You can do it, Ruth," *Dat* patiently encouraged her. "Just take your time and concentrate."

"L-letters. H-he wrote . . ." *Mamm* continued to struggle and then smacked her good hand on the table. "W-wrote m-me l-letters."

"Letters?" *Dat* asked. "Who wrote letters?"

"H-h-e di-did." *Mamm* sighed. "Aar-on."

"Are you saying Aaron wrote letters to us?" *Dat* asked.

Mamm nodded.

Solomon's shoulders stiffened as his parents looked at each other, confused.

"That's so strange," his father said. "We

never received any letters. I wonder how they got lost."

Solomon forced himself to clean his plate during the remainder of the meal while his family continued to discuss Aaron. He tried to tune them out, but their analysis of why Aaron came, how long he would stay, and how miraculous it was that he returned droned on through dessert. Once supper was over, Becky and their daughters began to clean up, and his father pushed *Mamm*'s wheelchair into the family room.

Solomon pulled on his coat and turned toward Manny. "Let's go finish our chores."

"I'll come too." Junior pulled on his coat as well and zoomed out the back door.

Solomon followed Junior as he walked toward one of the barns, shuddering in the crisp winter air.

"Dat," Manny called as he jogged to catch up with them. "Wait a minute. I want to talk to you."

Junior turned back toward them, and Solomon waved him on.

"Go on, Junior," he instructed. "You start checking on the cows, and we'll be there in a minute." He waited until Junior disappeared into the barn and then turned to his older son's concerned expression. *"Was iss letz?"*

"I was going to ask you the same thing," Manny began as they started walking. "You seemed upset during supper."

Solomon fingered his beard while trying to concoct a reason for his behavior. He couldn't possibly tell his son the truth and risk losing his respect. "I'm just concerned about your *grossmammi.*"

"I thought she seemed better today." Manny kicked a stone with the toe of his boot. "She's so *froh* that *Onkel* Aaron came back. Maybe this is what she needs to get better."

Solomon wished his stomach would stop churning at the mention of his brother's name. "I'm concerned she will be disappointed."

"Why would she be disappointed?" Manny looked up at him. "I don't understand."

Solomon fingered his beard and considered his response. He didn't want to speak badly of his brother to his son, but he also didn't want to lie. "Aaron left abruptly once. I'm concerned that he'll do it again, and *Mammi* won't be able to bear it. She's in a delicate state right now."

"I think it's *gut* that *Onkel* Aaron came back." Manny turned and gazed back toward the house. "I can't wait to meet him. I'm sure he wouldn't recognize me since I was two when he left."

Solomon grunted a response. "We have work to do." He started toward the barn. He was tired of hearing about his brother. After all, he was the one who had stayed and taken care of their parents. Aaron had abandoned the family.

After checking on the animals, Solomon told his sons to head into the house and he stayed behind in the same barn. Memories swirled through his mind. He was still stunned that his brother had returned. Was it because Aaron heard about their mother's stroke? How? And why would even that be enough for him to return after all these years?

He still clearly remembered how his mother had sobbed when she discovered Aaron had left. She cried for him for months and begged God to bring him home. Her heartbreak was apparent on her face every time Solomon looked at her. For several months, she couldn't say Aaron's name without tears shimmering in her sad eyes. Aaron's leaving also hurt their father. He didn't cry in public, but Solomon had caught him wiping tears from his cheeks several times while he worked in the barns.

Solomon couldn't understand why Aaron had left. He knew their home life had been tense after the bishop's barn burned down, but it wasn't bad enough for Aaron to just leave. He resented the hurt his younger brother had caused his parents, and he was determined to shield his mother from suffering more pain, especially now.

He stepped into his shop and reached for a locked box hidden under his workbench. He fetched a key from his pocket and opened the box, revealing a stack of envelopes addressed to his mother. He held up the top letter and examined the return address, reading his brother's name written in his perfect penmanship. Ever since he'd been the one to see the first letter, he'd intercepted the mail for years, hiding anything sent from his brother's address in an attempt to allow his parents to heal from the anguish Aaron had caused.

But had they? Had they healed? They seemed so happy to see Aaron, as if they had been broken the whole time he'd been away.

Solomon pushed those thoughts aside. With his mother's stroke, his parents' lives were difficult enough without his brother returning to make a terrible situation even worse. Solomon's heart hurt every time he talked to his mother since the stroke. Every day he prayed, begging God to heal her. He wanted her to return to the strong, vibrant woman she'd been, and he didn't need his younger brother rubbing salt into old wounds. He placed the letters back in the box, locked it, and slipped it back into its hiding place. He'd never even opened and read any of them, and he still didn't care what Aaron had to say.

The key went back into his pocket where he'd kept it all these years.

The sun was beginning to set, and the now-frigid air caused Solomon to shiver again as he exited the barn. He ambled across the frosted ground. He glanced over at his parents' home and spotted his father sitting on the glider on the screened-in back porch, a lantern by his side.

"Is everything all right?" Solomon asked as he climbed the steps and opened the screen door.

"Ya, ya." Dat patted the seat of the glider.

"Why are you sitting out here in the cold, *Dat*?" Solomon sat down beside him. The cold wood seeped through his trousers.

"Your *mamm* is resting. I wanted to step out here for a few minutes to clear my thoughts." He shook his head and rubbed his hands together. "I still can't believe your *bruder* showed up out of the blue today. I would've loved to have seen him, but it

80

sounds like he'll be back tomorrow."

Solomon looked toward his house and scowled. If he'd gone home with his sons, then he wouldn't have been stuck listening to more accolades for his brother.

"It's just a miracle," *Dat* continued. "Your *mamm* was so excited when I came in from working in the barns. When I first saw her, she was crying, and I was terrified that something was wrong, that her condition had worsened. She was so worked up that I couldn't understand what she was saying. When I realized she was saying 'Aaron was here,' I started crying too. Jocelyn filled in the rest for me."

Dat chuckled. "Oh, we were a pair, but it was like a dream come true. For years, she's asked me if I thought Aaron would ever come home. The truth is that I was worried he was dead. I mean, he was only fifteen when he left, and I had no idea if he could find his way in the world without an adult to guide him. I guess he's smarter than I thought he was."

Solomon looked down at his hands. "How did he know about *Mamm*'s stroke?"

"I don't know. I was wondering if you had found a way to contact him and did it as a surprise for your *mamm*."

"No." Solomon met his gaze. "I didn't

81

contact him."

"I wonder what happened to the letters he says he wrote. It's odd that they didn't make it here. How could they all have gotten lost in the mail? I would imagine he remembered this address correctly."

Solomon looked back toward his own house while trying to ignore the guilt that nipped at him. Why should he feel guilty for hiding the letters? He was only protecting *Mamm.*

"I suppose it doesn't matter about the letters now. I'm just *froh* he's back." *Dat* stood and patted Solomon's shoulder. "I'm grateful God decided it was time for our family to be back together. It's freezing out here. We'd better head indoors. *Gut nacht.*"

"Gut nacht." Solomon made his way to his house while silently praying that God would shield his mother from further heartbreak. Surely God wouldn't lead his brother home only to hurt their mother in the process.

But though he trusted God, he didn't trust Aaron.

Later that evening, Linda thanked her driver and started up the rock driveway past her cousin Raymond's large, two-story house to the cottage in the back of the farm where she lived with her *onkel* Reuben. She glanced up at the large farmhouse that sat at the front of the property and wondered if Raymond and his family were already sitting down for supper.

Perhaps it was because Raymond had lost his own parents — her *onkel* Elam and his wife — that Linda's parents had left the place to him and not to her or *Onkel* Reuben. Linda didn't know. She didn't even know why Reuben hadn't inherited as the oldest son instead of her father, Matthew, who had been the youngest of the three brothers. Her *onkel* did not like to talk about anything in the past.

She was nearly thirty minutes later than when she normally arrived home after working at the bed-and-breakfast, but she needed a few groceries for the meal she planned to cook tonight and stopped at the market on her way home.

Even in a glance, her eyes studied the big house, taking in the sweeping wrap-around porch and large windows. For a moment she tried to remember the four short years she'd lived there. It had been nearly twenty-eight years since she'd moved out of the house, and her memories were blurred, like faint whispers caught in the wind. She vaguely remembered sitting on the back steps and watching her mother hanging out laundry. She also recalled holding her father's strong hand while they walked together toward the large barn that still stood behind the cottage where she now lived with her *onkel.* Her happy life with her parents was erased in a cloud of screeching tires and twisted metal, when a semi-truck carrying a load of new cars slid on ice and slammed into the buggy carrying her and her parents. She recalled the powerful impact that sent her catapulting behind the buggy.

When she awoke in the hospital, Linda's right leg was in a cast, and her *aenti* Verna was at her bedside. Although Linda was immersed in a confusing fog due to medications and gripping pain in her leg, she understood when her *aenti* tearfully told her that her parents had been killed on impact. They had been crushed by the truck, while Linda had landed behind the buggy, her right leg mangled in the wreckage. After four surgeries, her leg was repaired and she underwent months of therapy to learn how to walk again.

Her *onkel* Reuben had been named her guardian, and she moved into the cottage behind the farmhouse, where he and her *aenti* Verna lived. Losing her parents changed her life forever. Linda had often wondered why the childless couple agreed to take her in. She supposed because it was expected. Neither had ever shown any real affection toward her. Most of the interaction with her *aenti* was learning how to cook, clean, and sew, and she'd spent a lot of time on her own.

Linda pushed away the memories and balanced two grocery bags in her arms. Making her way toward the cottage, she felt her posture shift as her right leg began to ache. She climbed the porch and wrenched open the front door. As she stepped into the house, her shoulders reflexively hunched, and her left leg favored her right one, giving her a slight limp. It always seemed to be worse when she was at home, tired from the day's work.

Her gaze moved to the left, and she spotted her *onkel* sitting in his favorite chair by the fireplace and scowling at the empty hearth. The small family-room area included a sofa, end table, two propane lamps, a coffee table, and his favorite chair.

"Hello." She crossed to the kitchen area and placed the bags on the counter, then hung her coat on the peg by the back door before returning to put away the groceries. The kitchen was tiny compared to Hannah's kitchen at the bed-and-breakfast. The walls were plain white without any decorations, other than the oak cabinets. The appliances included a propane stove and refrigerator. A small dinette set with four chairs took up most of the free space.

Reuben stared at her, his wrinkly face creased in a frown. In his mid-seventies, he was tall and wide, a giant of a man with a booming voice that matched his more than six-foot stature.

"How was your day?" she asked while putting away the groceries.

"You're late," he barked. "Where have you been?"

Linda breathed a heartfelt sigh, reaching deep inside herself for patience. "I told you this morning that I had to stop at the grocery store on the way home today. Don't you remember?"

"No, I don't remember you saying that. I'm starved. What's for supper?"

"I'm going to make my favorite meat loaf recipe. I'll mix it up right now." She pulled a pan out of the cabinet and began gathering the ingredients from the cabinets and refrigerator.

"That will take too long. I don't want to wait over an hour for it to bake." He shuffled into the kitchen. "We'll have sandwiches and potato salad. You can make the meat loaf tomorrow. I'll get the lunch meat, and you get the bread."

"*Ya, Onkel.* That's a *gut* idea." Linda knew it wasn't any use to argue. After all, she'd disappointed him by not having supper ready on time. No matter what she did, it never seemed to please him.

They brought the food to the dinette set, and he sat at his usual spot, which was at one end of the table, its head. She took her seat to his right. After a silent prayer, they began putting together their sandwiches.

As Linda piled turkey, cheese, and lettuce onto the bread, her mind flickered back to Aaron. When she first saw him, she was upset that it took him over a week to come to Paradise to see his mother, and she was further hurt that he didn't remember her. But then she was struck by the sadness and desperation in his eyes after he'd visited his mother. He truly had believed his mother had forgotten him, and he was stunned to hear she had missed him. His anguish touched her heart. She cautioned herself not to let this emotion affect her too deeply, though. After all, he wasn't Amish, and he wasn't going to stay in the community permanently.

"Do you remember Aaron Ebersol?" she asked.

"Who?" He shook his head. "The name is familiar, but there are probably several men named Aaron Ebersol in the area."

"He's Ruth and Jonas's younger son," she explained while spooning potato salad onto her plate. "He left the community when he was fifteen."

"Ruth and Jonas's *bu*?" *Onkel* Reuben nodded as he piled potato salad onto his plate. "*Ya,* I think I remember him. Why do you ask?"

"He came back to see Ruth. He heard about her stroke, and he's back. He's staying at Hannah's bed-and-breakfast. He went to see his *mamm* for the first time today."

"*Gut.*" He picked up a copy of the *Budget* and began to read the front page.

"I think he's —" She stopped talking when she realized her *onkel* didn't want to hear her story or her thoughts concerning Aaron and his family.

She ate her sandwich, hoping he'd look up from the paper and ask her to finish her story. She wanted him to value her as a person. She longed for him to care about what she had to say.

Instead, he looked at the paper while chewing. He found the stories of other Amish folks from around the country more interesting than his niece, who was sitting across from him. She glanced at the chair where her *aenti* Verna sat at every meal until she'd passed away several years ago. Linda wasn't one to question God's plan, but she realized she missed her *aenti.* Reuben had been less abrasive when Verna was alive. Now it seemed as if he was stuck in a bad mood for eternity.

Linda chewed her sandwich and glanced toward the front window, where she had a clear view of her cousin's house. She imagined he and his family were all sitting down to eat together. Their long table was probably bursting with noise and laughter as they enjoyed their supper. Linda used to enjoy spending time with them, but between caring for her *onkel* after Verna died, her part-time job at the hotel, and now her job at the bed-and-breakfast, there just wasn't time. Besides, she didn't want to intrude on their family life very often.

She wondered what it would feel like to have a real family. A family of her own.

She pushed that dream away. She knew she wasn't worthy of a family. Instead, she was supposed to stay with her *onkel* and care for him. After all, this was God's plan for her. Yet she couldn't stop that tinge of longing that bubbled up inside of her periodically.

Linda sighed, feeling defeated and ignored once again. No matter how hard she tried to share her feelings and thoughts with her *onkel,* he walked away from her. What was she doing wrong? She considered Aaron's reaction when he first saw her this morning. He hadn't remembered her, and that had hurt just as badly as her *onkel*'s disinterest in what she had to say. She was tired of being invisible. Though she wondered what had made Aaron remember her later, when she'd been cleaning his room.

As she finished her supper, she wondered if she would ever find anyone who would love her completely and appreciate what she had to say. But how could that happen? She was convinced that she wasn't worthy of love, and the idea broke her spirit. She wanted a family and a home of her own, but maybe she was meant to care for her *onkel* and then live in this little house alone after he passed away.

The thought echoed through her mind while she finished her sandwich and also while she cleaned up the kitchen and took care of the dishes. Then she headed to her room and sat in her favorite chair next to her bed. She picked up her Bible and flipped to the book of Ephesians, and her eyes fell on a scripture verse that seemed to

90

speak to her. She softly read it aloud: "Be kind and compassionate to one another, forgiving each other, just as in Christ God forgave you."

Linda closed her eyes and began to pray for the Ebersol family, asking God to heal their estranged relationships — and also to mend Aaron's broken heart.

FOUR

Linda pushed her grocery cart toward the produce section at the market. Once there, she examined her list, checked off the items she'd already gathered, and then reviewed what she had left to find.

"Which ones do you like better?"

Linda heard the question and ignored it. Of course the person speaking wasn't addressing her.

"Linda?"

Her head snapped up when she heard her name, and she gasped when she saw Aaron. He was holding two bouquets of flowers.

"Oh, no." He laughed, and she was in awe of how much she enjoyed the warm, rich sound. "Have I managed to startle you again?"

"Hi," she said with a nervous chuckle. "I didn't see you."

She knew her cheeks were red, and she wanted to crawl under her cart. Why did she always blush when a man spoke to her, especially a handsome man like Aaron? She longed to be more confident and comfortable around male acquaintances, but she couldn't seem to overcome her shyness.

"I'm really sorry." He took a step toward her as a woman wove through the crowd of shoppers, threatening to push between them. "You must be tired of running into me, huh?"

"No." She hoped her cheeks would cool down soon. "I was surprised I didn't see you at breakfast. Did you get an early start?"

"Yeah, I did. I have a lot on my mind and decided to take a walk around a local park to sort some things out. It was cold, but I think it helped. I'm heading over to my parents' farm now." He held up the bouquets. "I thought my *mamm* might like some flowers to brighten her day. Which bouquet do you like better? The one with more roses or the one with more carnations?"

Linda looked at the flowers while considering the question. "I think I like the one with the carnations better. I like the pink in it."

He raised an eyebrow. "So you like pink?"

Linda shrugged. "*Ya,* I do. It's pretty."

"Great. Pink it is." He grinned. "I'm glad

I ran into you. You seem to give great advice, and I needed your expertise."

"Danki." Linda was flabbergasted by the compliment. Although she still felt insecure, she enjoyed the positive feedback. "Have you seen your *dat* yet?"

"No." His smile faded. "I haven't."

"What about your *bruder*?" she asked.

"No, I haven't seen him either." Aaron studied the flowers as if he was avoiding looking at her. "I thought it would be easier to talk to my *mamm* alone first, so I left yesterday before either of them came in from their work."

"Don't be afraid to talk to them," Linda said. "I know they will be overjoyed you're home."

"Thanks." He smiled again and then pointed at the contents of her grocery cart. "Well, I guess I'd better let you finish your shopping. Do you need a ride home?"

"Oh, no *danki.* Hannah and I are shopping together, and Trey is next door at the hardware store. He's going to take us home." She clasped the grocery cart handle. "Have a *gut* day. Tell Ruth I'm thinking of her and will come visit her soon."

"I will. Have a great day too." He smiled again and then moved toward the floral display.

94

Linda smiled as he walked away, chose the produce on her list, and then pushed her cart toward the dairy aisle in search of Hannah.

Hannah plucked a package of cheese from the display and placed it in her basket. When she looked up and saw a young Amish woman pushing a cart nearby, she gasped. She was certain it was her estranged daughter, Lillian. After living as a widow for nearly a decade, Hannah had left the Amish community and opened a bed-and-breakfast with her new husband, Trey. When she'd left, two of her children, Amanda and Andrew, had come with her and also become *English*. Lillian, however, had remained in the community with her paternal grandparents.

Hannah had prayed over and over that Lillian would accept her decision to leave the Amish church and forgive her. She longed to have her daughter back in her life, especially now that Hannah was expecting her new baby in the spring.

As she cautiously moved toward Lillian, her heart nearly burst with excitement at the possibility of having a conversation with her. Perhaps this would be the day Lillian would finally talk to her, really talk to her, the way a mother and daughter should. Hannah missed Lillian so much that her heart ached daily.

"Lily?" Hannah called.

Lillian met her gaze, and her eyes widened. Hannah expected her to flee, but instead, she stood still, resembling a statue, while other shoppers guided their carts around her.

Encouraged, Hannah walked to her side. "How are you?"

Lillian shrugged. "I'm all right. How are you?"

"I'm doing well." Hannah smiled. So far, this was already the most pleasant conversation they'd had since Hannah left the community, causing Lillian to feel abandoned. Lillian hadn't instantly backed away, and the tension in Hannah's shoulders lifted slightly, and she rushed to tell Lillian what was on her heart.

"It's really *gut* to see you. Amanda and Andrew talk about you all the time, and we'd love for you to come visit us and see the bed-and-breakfast. I think you'd really like it."

Lillian pushed her glasses further up on the bridge of her nose. "Yes, I know. You've told me all that before. But teaching keeps me very busy. I'm only here to get some supplies for a special project. My assistant is taking care of the class, but I have to get back to the school soon."

"Oh, I understand. The bed-and-breakfast keeps us busy too. We have guests coming and going all the time." Hannah found herself babbling just to keep the conversation with her daughter going. "We have couples visit from all over the United States. You have to come and see how Trey and I have decorated the house. I think you'd agree that it's a nice mixture of Plain and *English.* It's very cozy."

Lillian's eyes moved down Hannah's body and she gaped. "I didn't realize how far along you are."

"I know. It's going quickly. The *boppli* will be here in the spring." Hannah's hand instinctively rubbed her protruding abdomen. "I want you to be a part of our new family. You're still my family, Lily. I miss you."

"I don't know how to be a part of your new family." Lillian shook her head and gripped the handle on her cart. "I just can't. I need to go now. I can't be late."

"Please don't go." Hannah reached for Lillian's arm, and Lillian pulled it away. "It breaks my heart not to have you in my life anymore. We all miss you. Please consider giving me a chance. I left the church, but I never wanted to lose you too."

"You left me," Lillian whispered. "You left me and never looked back."

"You know that isn't true. We've been through this over and over."

"Hannah. There you are!" Linda rushed over and smiled at Lillian. "Hi, Lily. How are you?"

Lillian nodded. "Hi, Linda. I'm fine. *Danki.*" She began to push her cart and turned back to her mother. "I need to go. Give my love to Amanda and Andrew. Tell them I want to see them soon."

"Lily, please," Hannah pleaded with her. "Please consider coming to visit. I'll make tea and a carrot cake, your favorite, and we can sit down and have a nice, long talk. It can be just you and me. Please think about it."

Lillian's lower lip trembled. "I need to go." She nodded at Linda once more and started down the aisle.

"I'm so sorry." Linda touched Hannah's arm. "I interrupted you, didn't I?"

"Oh, no." Hannah smiled. "You didn't do anything wrong. Something felt different this time. I felt like I was reaching Lily because she listened to me. She almost seemed like she wanted to talk to me."

"That's *wunderbaar*. Maybe she's starting to realize how much you want her in your life."

"I hope so. I'm doing everything I can to make her realize I love her and I need her." Hannah sighed. "I'm not going to give up hope. Someday I'll have my whole family again."

Linda smiled. "*Ya,* I believe you will."

Aaron stepped into his parents' house through the front door and said hello to Jocelyn, who had once again answered the door. He thought he heard voices talking away in Pennsylvania Dutch on the other side of the house.

"Does my mother have company?" he asked the nurse.

"Oh, a couple of women are here taking care of the laundry," Jocelyn said. "Someone comes nearly every day to help out around the house. They are so sweet. I think it's amazing how the community comes together to help families. The rest of us should take a lesson from the Amish. They know what community means." She motioned toward the family room. "Your mom is in here." She lowered her voice before going on. "She's been looking forward to your visit. You're all she talks about."

Aaron held the flowers behind him as he stepped into the family room, where his mother sat in her wheelchair, holding a hand weight. "Hi, *Mamm.*"

"A-aron!" *Mamm* beamed as she reached up with her left hand. "*G-gut* to s-see you."

He leaned down and kissed her cheek, then held out the flowers. "These are for you."

"*D-danki.*" She smelled the blossoms and smiled. "So *schee.*"

"May I put those in a vase for you, Mrs. Ebersol?" Jocelyn offered.

"*Ya. D-danki.*" Aaron handed her the flowers and Jocelyn headed for the kitchen.

He sat down on the sofa, which was nearest his mother. "So how are you today?"

"*G-gut.*" Ruth held up a hand weight. "W-w-work." She put it down on her lap and touched his leg. "T-tell me a-b-b-b . . ." She closed her eyes and moved her lips as her face turned red with frustration.

"It's okay, *Mamm.* Stay calm." Aaron pulled off his coat and set it down next to him. "Did you want to hear about my life?" He took her hand in his.

She opened her eyes and nodded as relief covered her expression.

"Okay. Well, I worked in construction when I first moved to Missouri, and then my friend Zac and I opened up our own business about seven years ago. We mostly do home improvement type projects. It was busy for a while and then work fell off when the economy tanked. But things started picking up again. We've been really busy lately, and I'm thankful."

"Oh." *Mamm* nodded slowly. "F-fam-ily?"

"Do I have a family?" he asked, clarifying the question. She nodded, and he said, "No." Aaron folded his arms over his chest.

Mamm's expression fell again. "N-no f-family?"

Jocelyn returned with the vase of flowers and set it on the coffee table in front of the sofa. "Would you like something to drink?" she offered.

"Oh, no thank you," Aaron said.

Jocelyn turned to his mother. "We need to get back to your exercises shortly, okay? Your therapist expects us to keep up with them, and I have to leave in a little bit to visit my other patients."

His mother nodded. *"Ya."*

Jocelyn smiled at him before heading back to the kitchen.

His mother immediately turned her focus back on him. "N-n-no fa-fami-ly?" Her eyes were full of confusion, as if she couldn't fathom the idea that Aaron was alone.

"No, I don't." He ran his fingers over the arm of the sofa. "No family."

"L-lonely?" she asked.

"No. I thought about getting a dog, but my landlord doesn't allow pets." He tried to lighten the mood by chuckling, but his mother continued to stare at him. He could feel her disappointment filling the air in the room. "I work a lot, so I really don't have time to meet many people. I love my work, but it's a very demanding job. I have plenty of things to do, and I don't mind spending the evening at home alone while working on paperwork. Owning a company is a huge commitment, but I enjoy the work. I love the satisfaction when the customer tells me I've done a good job."

"Be-dauer-lich." The word was garbled, but he understood what she was trying to say. Her lower lip trembled, and he hoped she wouldn't cry.

"It's okay, *Mamm.*" He leaned forward and touched her hand again. "I stay busy so I don't even think about it." He was lying to his mother, but how could he admit that sometimes he loathed the lonely nights in his apartment? He didn't want to further upset her. He couldn't stand to see her cry. He needed to change the subject, and his thoughts drifted to his brief encounter with

Linda at the grocery store. "I saw Linda Zook today."

"Oh?" *Mamm*'s eyes lit up.

"Yes, I did. She sends her regards. She was at the grocery store when I stopped to get your flowers. She actually helped me pick these out for you." He gestured toward the vase. "Linda has good taste."

His mother chuckled, and he felt his mood brighten. It was good to hear her laugh, even if she looked and sounded different than he remembered. Saul had been right. She was still his sweet mother.

"She works at the bed-and-breakfast where I'm staying," he said in an attempt to keep the conversation going. "I'm staying at the Heart of Paradise Bed-and-Breakfast not far from here. Apparently Trey and Hannah Peterson own it. Trey said you know them."

"Y-ya," Mamm said.

"They seem like nice people."

"Ya." His mother nodded. "Han-nah . . . A-Amish."

"Hannah was Amish?" he asked.

Mamm nodded. "L-Linda is s-s-sweet *ma-maedel.*"

Aaron nodded slowly. "She seems very quiet and shy."

"Ya." Mamm started to reach for a cup of

water on the coffee table. When she struggled, he handed it to her. She nodded before taking a sip.

"Her parents died in a buggy accident, right?" he asked.

"Ya." She leaned toward the table, and Aaron helped her place the glass back on it.

"That is so sad," Aaron said. "I can't imagine how difficult it was for her to lose her parents that way." Aaron wondered what Linda's life had been like growing up without them.

His mother grew quiet and trained her gaze on her lap, and Aaron felt the need to fill the space between them.

"Let me tell you about some of the projects Zac and I have worked on over the years," he began. "One of my favorites was when we added on a mother-in-law suite for this one family. We had the opportunity to design how the suite would be laid out, and it was really fun. We created an amazing closet that had shelves for shoes and a built-in dresser."

He detailed some of his most challenging projects over the years, and his mother listened with interest as he talked.

Soon Jocelyn returned and announced that his mother had to get back to her exercises. After pulling on his coat, Aaron told her he'd be back soon, and he kissed her cheek. He said good-bye and then made his way through the kitchen toward the back door. He was grateful the women who had been working in the laundry room earlier weren't there. He didn't want anyone asking him how long he was going to stay. The truth was, he had no idea.

But when he stepped out onto the back porch, he saw the women hanging the laundry on the line that ran from the house to the nearest barn. They had their backs to him, which made it easy for him to slip past them. He descended the porch steps and felt again as if he were stepping back in time to his childhood. The line of red barns was just as he'd remembered, and he felt as if he were home. He made his way to the dairy barn and memories assaulted his mind. He recalled running through the fields with friends in the summer and helping his father and brother muck the stalls in the stable. He suddenly missed those days.

Aaron looked toward his brother's house and his thoughts turned to all he'd missed by leaving. He wondered how his life would've been if he hadn't made the mistake of playing with matches and the bishop's barn hadn't burned down. Would he have a family and a home like Solomon's?

He pushed the thought away as he stepped into the dairy barn. The aroma of animals and hay covered him as he looked at the rows of cows. More memories came to mind as he thought back to when he helped his father and brother with the animals.

"Aaron?"

Turning, he found his father standing in the doorway behind him. He looked the same as Aaron remembered, except that his hair and beard had turned from dark brown to gray and he had more lines around his blue eyes. Aaron also stood a few inches taller than his father now, and it felt strange to look down on the man who had raised him.

His father's eyes misted over with tears. "It's a miracle," he said, his voice shaking with emotion.

"Dat," Aaron said, his voice also thick with emotion.

His father rushed over and hugged him. "I couldn't believe it when your *mamm* said you'd come to visit. It was like a dream. Our prayers were finally answered." He smiled and wiped his eyes. "You're taller than your *bruder* and me. I can't believe it. And we thought you'd never make it to my height."

"I shot up the summer before I turned

seventeen." Aaron cleared his throat. "You look well, *Dat.*" He thought of his mother. "*Mamm* is struggling."

"*Ya.*" His dad blew out a heavy sigh. "It's all been such a shock. The stroke came out of nowhere, and now we're trying to adjust. We're hoping she'll regain her strength and learn to walk again. The physical therapist is trying to help strengthen her legs, and another therapist is working on her speech."

"I always thought *Mamm* was so strong and nothing would ever happen to her." A lump constricted his throat. "I just can't believe she's so frail now."

"I know." *Dat* touched Aaron's arm. "She'll be all right. The Lord will take care of us." He suddenly smiled. "I can't believe you're back. We were so worried about you. We feared something bad had happened to you."

"I wrote to you," Aaron said as frustration boiled again within him. "I wrote probably close to a hundred letters, telling you all about my life. I own a construction business now, called Paradise Builders. My company is finally starting to take off, and things are going well for me."

"That's *wunderbaar.*" His father smiled and brushed his hand over his eyes again.

"Even when I was working for someone

else, I sent checks to pay you back for the cost of the bishop's barn. I tried to make things right. I felt so bad that you were left with that bill, and I wanted to make it up to you and *Mamm*. I sent you more than enough money to cover the cost of the barn, but you never cashed the checks. I wanted to show you that I'd changed. I wasn't the same immature and reckless boy. I know my actions brought shame on this family, and I wanted to show you how sorry I was. How sorry I still am."

"We forgave you, Aaron." His father's expression was consumed with sympathy. "You should have never doubted we would."

"So then why didn't you answer my letters?" Aaron demanded. "Why didn't you let me know you forgave me? I thought you had forgotten me."

"We never got the letters," his father said, throwing up his hands. "I don't know why they didn't arrive, but I'm telling you the truth when I say we didn't get them."

Aaron raked his hands through his curls and grimaced. "If you didn't get the letters, then why didn't you try to find me?"

His father looked stunned by the question. "You left us. We didn't know how to find you. As far as I know, none of the young men who left when you did contacted their families again either. I hoped you would contact us or come back."

"How could you not have gotten my letters? It doesn't make sense."

"I told you, I don't know." His father looked dejected. "I don't know how to explain what happened to your letters, but I'm grateful you're here now. You're home, and that's all that matters to our family."

"Right." Aaron's emotions swirled, filling him with a mixture of frustration, anger, and regret. He had to bolt. He had to escape all the memories that were crashing down on him before he suffocated. "I have to go."

"You have to leave?" His father looked bewildered. "Why? You just got here. I want to talk to you and find out more about your life. You haven't seen Solomon and his family yet. And we want you to stay with us. We have plenty of room."

"We'll talk soon. I just need to go." He started to walk toward the door. "I'll be back. Give my love to *Mamm*."

Aaron left the barn and stalked toward his truck, not caring if the Amish visitors saw him. He looked at his parents' house and was overwrought with thoughts of all he'd lost by running away from his problems. He missed being a part of the community; he missed being part of a family. He hadn't realized how much he'd needed his family until he'd returned to the farm he'd once been so desperate to leave.

As he drove to the bed-and-breakfast, he felt himself drowning in the regret of all he'd done to hurt his parents, and he had no idea how to make it subside. He begged God to help him sort through all the emotions that plagued his heart and soul.

FIVE

Linda pulled sheets out of the dryer and began folding them in the large laundry room next to the bed-and-breakfast kitchen. She would never understand why *Englishers* liked to use fancy electric dryers and expensive laundry detergent when nothing could replace the natural fragrance of laundry that had dried on a line outside.

She was folding the last sheet when she heard the kitchen door slam so hard that it shook the laundry room wall. She dropped the sheet into the basket and rushed out to the kitchen to see who had come in. She found Aaron leaning against the sink and staring out the window at the field behind the house.

"Aaron?" She took a hesitant step into the kitchen.

He looked over his shoulder at her, and his normally bright eyes were dull and stormy until he connected his gaze with

111

hers. "Did I scare you — again? I'm sorry. I didn't mean to slam the door that hard."

"Was iss letz?" She walked over to his side.

"What's wrong?" He turned to face her, and his eyes clouded again as he gave a sarcastic snort and leaned his tall body against the counter behind him. "I don't even know where to begin. Everything is wrong."

She assessed his pained expression, taking in the frustration and hurt she found there. "Did something happen at your parents' *haus*?"

He nodded.

Linda pointed to the kitchen table. "Sit. You need a cup of coffee."

Aaron draped his coat over the back of a chair and sat down.

She started the coffee machine and then brought a plate of cookies, two mugs, and cream and sugar to the table before sitting across from him.

Aaron somberly examined the cookies. "*Mei mamm* always said *kichlin* could solve any problems."

Linda grinned when she heard the word *kichlin*.

When he met her gaze, he lifted an eyebrow. "Why are you smiling at me?"

"I'm sorry." Her cheeks heated. "I think

that was the first time I've heard you say a *Dietsch* word other than *mamm* and *dat,* maybe *ya.* I was beginning to wonder if you remembered how to speak *Dietsch.*"

"Of course I remember." He sat up straighter. "I'm offended by that remark." His lips twitched, and she knew he was teasing her. "Most of my employees are former Amish folks, so there's a lot of *Dietsch* conversation at the job sites."

"Your employees?" She took a chocolate chip cookie from the plate. "You own a business?"

"I do." He picked up an oatmeal raisin cookie and broke it in half. "I own a construction company called Paradise Builders."

"Paradise," she repeated. "You named it after your hometown."

"That's right."

"Do you only hire former Amish workers?" She found this point fascinating.

He shook his head. "No, but I seem to attract them. My business partner and I help former Amish adjust to the *English* life. Someone helped me do that, and we know how important it is."

"Was your business partner Amish?"

"No, but his mother was. She moved to Missouri and married an *Englisher.*" He bit into the cookie and moaned. "These are *appeditlich.*" He grinned as he said the word, and she enjoyed seeing his smile again. "See, I can still speak *Dietsch.*"

"I'm not convinced yet, but I'm getting there." She made the joke and realized she felt comfortable with Aaron Ebersol now. He was the first man she'd ever joked with, and it felt good. Why did she feel comfortable with someone she hardly knew?

"Did you make these?" he asked.

"*Ya,* I did."

"They are *wunderbaar.*" He finished the cookie and then took another one.

The aroma of coffee filled the kitchen, and she stood to retrieve the coffeepot from the machine.

"Well, do you still think I forgot *Dietsch*?" he asked.

"*Ya,*" she teased as she filled his mug.

"*Danki,*" he said, enunciating the word.

"*Gern gschehne.*" She filled her own mug and then returned the pot to its base. "So why were you so upset when you came in?" she asked as she sank back into the seat across from him. "What happened when you went to your *mamm*'s *haus*?"

His expression darkened again as he stirred cream into his mug. "I visited with my *mamm* and then saw my *dat* for the first

114

time since I got back."

"That's *gut, ya*?" She wanted to encourage him.

"I had a good visit with my parents, but I still don't understand why they didn't receive my letters. It doesn't make any sense." His eyes shimmered with a mixture of pain and regret. "My *dat* said they hoped to hear from me, and when they didn't, they were afraid I was dead. I asked him why he didn't try to find me, and his answer was that I had left without leaving any word where I was going to be and all they could do was pray I'd come back or at least contact them. So they were hoping I'd come back while I thought they had forgotten me."

Linda shook her head while wishing she could relieve the pain in his eyes. "I already told you your *mamm* never forgot you. She was heartsick that you had left. She told me she worried about you all the time. Even though she knew you had grown up, she wanted to know if you had a place to live, enough food to eat, and clothing to keep you warm. It's only natural for parents to worry about their *kinner*, no matter where they are or how old they are. How could they forget their son?"

Aaron's eyes searched hers, and she felt

115

heat radiating up the back of her neck. No man had ever looked at her the way Aaron did. She'd always felt invisible around members of the opposite sex. His attention made her self-conscious.

"I never stopped loving my parents," he finally said. "I never stopped missing them. In fact, I realized today how much I miss being a part of the family."

She nodded slowly, intrigued by the honesty in his eyes. "I understand."

"I thought I was satisfied with my life, but nothing can replace family. Going home to an empty apartment and working on paperwork until late into the night . . . well, being off on my own isn't as fulfilling as I thought it would be when I was fifteen."

"I can understand feeling that way." She wanted to tell him she was lonely, too, but it was too personal. She couldn't risk sharing her most private feelings with Aaron, who wasn't much more than a stranger. Yet she felt a connection forming between them. Did they have more in common than she first thought?

He broke their gaze and then took another cookie from the plate. "Do you know why I left?"

"No," she said before sipping her coffee.

"Do you remember when Elmer Smucker's barn burned down?"

"*Ya*, I do."

"It was my fault." He fetched a napkin from the wooden holder in the middle of the table and began to fold it like an accordion.

"It was entirely your fault?" she asked with shock, and he nodded. "But I thought some other boys were involved. What happened?"

He paused and drank more of his coffee. "I'm sure you know I ran with a wild group back then."

"I remember." She cradled the warm mug in her hands. "I heard stories about you and your friends getting caught sneaking out at night and drinking alcohol."

"Yeah, that happened more than once." He grimaced, appearing embarrassed. "I'm not proud of what we did, but I'm not going to lie either. We were irresponsible and disrespectful. My *dat* and I argued all the time back then. I fought him on everything, and he didn't know what to do with me. I didn't want to work on the dairy farm, so my *dat* let me work at the market in Philly with my friends. Of course, I still had chores on the farm as well, but I wanted to be with my friends all the time. I caused a lot of grief for my parents, and burning down the barn was the last straw for my *dat*."

Linda took in his face, astounded by the way he was pouring his most private thoughts out to her. She felt privileged that he would share his feelings with her. Did he consider her a friend?

He paused and ate another piece of cookie. "That night my friends and I met at Elmer Smucker's farm because it was sort of in the middle of where we all lived. One of my friends brought some cigarettes and matches, along with the beer. We were goofing around, and I was playing with the matches. We'd had a bad drought that summer, so the idea of playing with matches was just completely reckless. I thought it would be funny if we made a little bonfire, and I lit it too close to a pile of dry leaves. And poof!" He held his hands up like an explosion. "The barn went up like that." He snapped his fingers for effect.

Linda shook her head. "You must've been so scared."

"Yeah, I was more stunned than scared." Aaron sighed, resting his elbow on the table and his chin on the palm of his hand, the remains of his cookie left on the folded napkin. "My friends said we should all share the blame, but it was my fault. I was the genius who came up with the idea for the bonfire, and I lit the matches. So I did what

I knew was right and took all the blame. My parents were so upset. I think what hurt the most was when my *dat* said he was disappointed in me. He had every right to feel that way, but I realized then that I was totally out of control. I'd brought shame on my family, and I also hurt them financially. The dairy farm was having a tough year, and it took nearly all of my parents' savings to pay for the damage to the barn."

"I'm so sorry," Linda said, her heart shattering for his suffering.

"Thanks, but I'm the one who should be sorry," he said simply. "I couldn't face my *dat* after that. He's a *gut,* hardworking man. I knew I'd really messed things up for him. I realized that I'd done everything wrong. I wasn't the son *Dat* deserved, and I certainly wasn't like Solomon."

He seemed to analyze the coffee in his mug while gathering his thoughts. "My *bruder* was the opposite of me. He joined the church when he was eighteen, married his girlfriend a couple of years later, and started a family right away. He built a *haus* on my parents' property, and he was going to take over the dairy farm. He was the perfect son, and I was the one who messed up. My parents deserved a son who was better than I ever was. They didn't deserve all

119

the stress I brought to their home."

"Everyone follows a different path," Linda insisted. "You made mistakes, and you learned from them. Even then, you saw what you'd done wrong. You and your *bruder* are different people, but that doesn't make you wrong and your *bruder* right. Your *bruder* matured sooner than you did. He's older."

"It's more than that, though. My *dat* couldn't even look at me when he found out I had been the one who caused the fire, and I couldn't blame him. It's a miracle no one died in that blaze. Even the animals were spared. It could've been so much worse. But still, I brought shame and financial problems on my family."

She couldn't stand the pain in his eyes, and she was determined to ease some of it. "But you were forgiven, Aaron. You didn't need to leave."

He stared at her for a moment. "My *dat* said the same thing today, but I didn't forgive myself."

"You need to forgive yourself. God has forgiven you, and your parents have too. That's our way."

He looked unconvinced as he took up the rest of his cookie.

"Did you ever apologize to the bishop?"

she asked.

He shook his head. "I'm embarrassed to admit I never faced him. I was too afraid to say anything to him."

"Why don't you go visit him and tell him you're sorry?" she suggested. "That seems to be the most logical way for you to let go of the guilt. If you talk to him, then you'll feel better."

He smiled, and her stomach fluttered. "You are one *schmaert kichli.*"

He held up a piece of cookie and waved it toward her. His smile was adorable and the gesture was so goofy that she began to laugh. Soon they were laughing together.

One question still remained in her mind.

"So what made you decide leaving was your only option?" she asked. "You were only fifteen."

"It wasn't my idea exactly." He ran his fingers over the top of his mug while he spoke. "One of my friends suggested it. They were all tired of the restrictions, and they'd heard there was a former Amish community in Missouri where we could go. It wasn't a good decision, but I was trying to run away from my problems, which, of course, never works. A group of us went, and a couple of the guys were over eighteen. They acted as our guardians." He met her gaze, and she was stunned by the humility in his eyes. "Thank you for listening to me. Now it's time for me to be quiet. Tell me about your life."

Linda was speechless for a moment. She'd never expected him to want her to talk about herself. No man had ever asked her about her life. "There isn't much to tell. I live with my *onkel* Reuben, and I work part-time here and at the Lancaster Grand Hotel."

His eyes probed hers, and she felt self-conscious again. What was he thinking about her?

"You were always shy and quiet, weren't you?" he asked.

"Ya." He hadn't just finally remembered her, but had noticed her all those years ago?

"Why?" he asked.

She looked down at her half-full mug to avoid his intense gaze. "I guess I was never comfortable in groups." She ran her finger over her placemat. "Losing my parents was difficult. It's not my place to question God's plan, but it hasn't been an easy road for me."

"I'm sorry."

She looked up and found sympathy in his warm eyes, and she could only nod in response as her next words were stuck in her throat. She'd never expected someone like him to care about her. His concern was overwhelming, and also confusing.

"I told my *mamm* that you sent your regards to her, and she looked happy," he said. "She didn't say, but I could tell she thinks a lot of you."

Linda smiled. "*Danki.* That's very nice. Your *mamm* and I worked together at the hotel. She's one of my dear friends. I think a lot of her too. She's like a *mamm* to me."

"I'm sure it was hard on you when you lost your parents. Do you remember them?"

"*Ya,* I remember little things, here and there," she said as the memories flickered through her mind. "I remember sitting on the porch and watching my *mamm* hang out laundry. She was smiling and humming and the sun was warm on my face. And I remember holding my *dat*'s hand as we walked together toward the pasture. He was like a giant next to me. He was tall and strong. I felt so safe with him. But that all changed in an instant."

"Do you remember the accident?" he asked gently.

"*Ya,* I remember some of it." She took a deep breath as the memories swept over her. "We were on our way home from Sunday service. It was sleeting and the roads were treacherous. I was playing in the back of the buggy. I had a book and a doll with me. A semi carrying new cars lost control on the ice and slammed into the buggy. I remember the squeal of brakes and the smell of rubber. The buggy jolted and then rolled, and I was thrown. Someone was screaming, but I don't know if it was my *mamm* or maybe it was even me." She paused and took a deep breath. "I woke up in the hospital, and *Aenti* Verna was at my side. She told me my parents were gone, and I was going to live with her and *Onkel* Reuben."

Aaron shook his head slowly. "That had to be so frightening for you."

"*Ya,* it was." Linda took another sip of coffee, ignoring that it was now a bit cold. "It was confusing. I had to move into the *daadi haus* behind my parents' *haus.* My cousin Raymond got the *haus* where I was supposed to grow up with my parents. I found out years later that my *mamm* was going to have a *boppli.*"

She paused to assess her thoughts. "Sometimes I can't help but wonder what life would've been like if that truck hadn't swerved. Would I have had a *bruder* or *schweschder*? Would my parents have had more *kinner* as well? I know I shouldn't think that way, but sometimes my mind wanders. I know it's a sin to question God's plan, and I shouldn't even discuss it. God has the perfect plan for all of us, even if it doesn't make sense to us sometimes. We need to be thankful for what we have."

She realized that she'd never shared those thoughts or feelings aloud before. What was it about Aaron Ebersol that caused her to feel comfortable enough to bare her soul?

"No, I think it's only natural to sometimes wonder 'what if?' " His eyes were full of understanding. "I do the same thing. What if I hadn't left the community? Would I have met someone and been married by now? Would I have my own home and family? I guess it doesn't matter at this point. I made my choices and now I have to live with them."

"That doesn't mean you're stuck," Linda said. "You can always change your life. God gives us the ability to make our own path."

"That's right." He gave her a warm smile. "Thank you for listening to me today," he said. "I was so upset when I left my parents' house that I didn't know what to do. You've been a tremendous help to me."

"I'm *froh* I could help." She stood and took the empty platter and mugs to the counter.

He stood and picked up his coat. "I

125

should let you get back to work. It was really good talking to you. I enjoyed it."

"*Ya.* I did too." She stood at the sink.

"*Danki* for the *kichlin.*" He grinned. "Oh, and my *mamm* loved the flowers. *Danki* for picking them out for me."

"*Gern gschehne.*" She watched him as he walked toward the stairs and her smile deepened.

She'd never had such a warm and meaningful conversation with a man before. She felt as if they truly were friends, but there was a deeper emotion that disturbed her. She was becoming attached to Aaron, and she knew she couldn't allow herself to feel anything for him. He wasn't planning to stay in the community, and he wasn't Amish. She would only set herself up for disappointment if she put too much stock in her feelings for Aaron Ebersol.

Later that afternoon, Linda made her way to Hannah's family suite and knocked on the door. The suite was attached but separated from the main house. It had three bedrooms, one each for Hannah's son and daughter who lived with her and Trey, and a larger master bedroom with two walk-in closets, one big enough for a nursery, and its own bathroom. It also had a sitting room, a second bathroom, and a kitchen. It had originally been a rather large grandparents' suite when the house belonged to an Amish family. But it was expanded even more when the house was converted to an *English* home, complete with electricity and brightly painted walls, before Trey bought it and converted it to a bed-and-breakfast.

"Come in," Hannah called.

Linda stepped into the sitting area and found Hannah sitting in a comfortable chair and reading a Christian novel. Linda recognized it from the cover. Hannah's feet were resting on an ottoman. Although she had left the Amish community to marry Trey, Hannah still dressed conservatively. She was clad in a blue denim maternity jumper and clogs. She wore her long, red hair in a bun, but her prayer covering was gone. The room included a green sofa, two end tables with lamps, a flat-screen television sitting on an entertainment center, and a coffee table. The walls were painted light beige with colorful paintings of landscapes decorating them.

"How are you feeling?" Linda asked.

"I'm doing okay." Hannah patted the arm of the sofa next to her. "Have a seat. How are you doing today?"

"I'm fine." Linda sat beside her. "I wanted

to see if you'd like a snack. I was thinking about baking some more cookies. Aaron finished the ones I made a couple of days ago."

"Oh, I'm not hungry, but thank you. How's Aaron doing?"

"He went to see his parents earlier, and he was really upset when he got back here. We sat in the kitchen and talked for a while." Linda shared some of the conversation she'd had with Aaron, and while she talked, Linda couldn't stop thinking about his warm eyes and handsome face. "I'm hoping Aaron can work things out with his family. I know how much Ruth has missed him, and I can see how desperate Aaron is to have his family back."

"I hope they work things out too." Hannah set her book on an end table and rubbed her abdomen as she spoke. "I know what it's like to miss your *kind*. It's not something I would want anyone else to experience."

"I know you've had a difficult time, Hannah." Linda frowned. "I hope you can have your whole family back soon too. I think things will work out the way you want."

"Thank you." Hannah continued to move her hand in circles. "I can't stop thinking about Lily and how she acted when I saw her today. I have this feeling that maybe I finally got through to her. Maybe she finally understands that I never meant to hurt her and I want her back in my life more than ever."

Linda touched Hannah's hand. "I think you're right. You've told me Lily seemed angry when you've seen her in the past. When I saw her today, she seemed more emotional than angry."

"You think so?" Hannah's eyes brightened with hope, and Linda nodded. "I had the same feeling about our conversation. My most fervent prayers are that this *boppli* will be healthy and I will have Lily back in my life."

"You keep praying for those things, Hannah." Linda squeezed her hand. "Don't give up hope."

"*Danki,* Linda. I appreciate your encouragement." Hannah picked up the book and fingered the cover while considering her thoughts. "Trey wants to find out the sex of the baby, but I think I want to be surprised. I think no matter what we have, it's a miracle and a new beginning for us. But like I told Lillian when I saw her at the grocery store, I want her to be a part of this. I want all of my *kinner* to know each other. I don't want Lillian to be left out of our family. Maybe this *boppli* will be the link we need to bridge the gap between Lillian and me. The baby is a new beginning, yes, but it's also a way to mend old bonds, you know?"

"*Ya,* that makes sense." Linda stood. "Are you sure you don't want anything to eat? I'm going to start cooking supper soon, but I want to be sure you have everything you need."

"I'm fine, *danki.*" Hannah grimaced. "I wish I could do more, but I'm just so tired. That trip to the store took a lot out of me. I feel so useless."

Linda shook her head. "You certainly are not useless, Hannah. You're creating life, and that's an important job. It's much more important than taking care of the *haus* and your business."

"I know you're right. The doctor wants me to take it easy since I'm over forty, and I don't have half the energy I did with my other children. But there's so much to be done around here. I was hoping to rely more on Amanda, but she is so busy lately. She's pursuing her degree in veterinary medicine, and she just started an internship with a vet. She's working long hours along with taking classes.

"You're a tremendous help, Linda. Trey

said he thought he could handle it all, but I
didn't feel right asking him to carry the
entire load. He doesn't like to cook as much
as I do, and he struggles with some of the
recipes. When he suggested we hire someone
part-time, I'm so glad you agreed to come.
Thank you for being here." Hannah reached
to touch Linda's hand.

"You're welcome," Linda said. "I'm *froh*
to be here." Then she smiled and started for
the door. "Call me if you need anything."

As she made her way back to the kitchen,
Linda thought how nice it was for someone
to show appreciation for her, unlike her *onkel*. And she again thought of Aaron. She
hoped to see him again soon, even though
she knew she was risking her heart. For
some reason, she longed to know him better, and she hoped he had enjoyed their talk
as much as she had.

Six

"Are you cold?" Aaron asked his mother while they sat together on the screened porch the following afternoon. He looked up at the gray sky. "Do you want to go inside now?"

"N-no," she said with a lopsided smile. "O-out-s-side." She used her good arm to point toward the window and then pulled her shawl closer to her body.

He smiled. "I understand. I like the outside too. It's refreshing to be outside in the air. I never cared for being inside. I don't like being cooped up and looking out the window at the sunshine. Or even the gray, like we have today."

"Y-you l-liked w-w-working at t-the m-market."

Tears doused Aaron's eyes. *Mamm* had said a full sentence! "That's right. I loved working at the market. I was outside and working with my friends."

Mamm's expression became curious. "D-did y-you kn-know C-Carolyn?" She spoke her garbled words slowly, but he surmised the meaning of the question.

"Are you asking me if I knew Carolyn Lapp?" he asked, and she nodded. "Yes, I knew who she was. I actually ran into her at the Bird-in-Hand Family Restaurant this week. I didn't know her well, but she worked at the market with a group of my friends." He shrugged. "I guess she was an acquaintance. We really didn't talk much."

Mamm still looked curious, as if she didn't think he was telling the truth. "Y-your g-g-girl . . . fr-fri-end?"

"You want to know if Carolyn was my girlfriend?" Aaron was stunned by the question. "No, she wasn't my girlfriend. In fact, I didn't have a girlfriend back then." He took in her curious expression. "Why are you asking me about her?"

She shrugged one shoulder, and then her expression hardened as she closed her eyes. She was struggling to find the words to say something, and Aaron longed to help. If only he could help her find the right words to express her thoughts. He hoped the speech therapist would continue to help his mother make progress. It was painful to watch her struggle with simple sentences.

"W-hy y-you l-leave?" she finally asked.

Aaron knew this question would come up eventually. The sadness in her eyes caused his chest to tighten. He picked at lint on his jeans to avoid his mother's stare. His thoughts moved to Linda's question about why he hadn't come home as soon as he'd heard the news from Saul. Linda was justified to ask him that question. He should have come right home and faced his family instead of being a coward.

"I thought I had caused you and *Dat* enough heartache. My behavior had become so reckless that all *Dat* and I did was argue. And then I had brought shame on the family when the barn burned down. I thought it was better if I left."

Tears sparkled in *Mamm*'s eyes, and he immediately regretted his words. "N-no," she said, her voice weak. "F-for-giv-en."

"I'm sorry, *Mamm.* I wasn't thinking clearly. I was only a kid, and I thought I was doing what was best," he said gently, trying not to upset her further. The emotion in her expression was nearly too much for him to endure. "I thought I didn't belong here. I didn't feel like I fit in."

She squeezed his hand, though weakly, and he knew what she was telling him. She wanted him to know that he did belong in his family.

"Thank you." He looked out toward the barns and spotted a few women getting out of a couple of buggies near the path that would take them to the front door. A few of them waved, and he waved back, afraid of being rude. He appreciated their letting him have this time alone with his family.

"Jocelyn said your friends come every day to help with chores."

"Ya," his *mamm* said.

He shook his head. "That's nice. It's not like that where I live in Missouri. I know my friend Zac would help if I needed him, but I haven't needed anything."

"Haus?" she asked, pointing her finger at him.

"No, I don't have a house," he said, feeling embarrassed. "I rent an apartment. I have two bedrooms, so I use one like an office. And I have a small family room and a tiny kitchen. It's not much, but it's all I need." He looked toward Solomon's house and thought about his brother's family. "So Solomon has four children now."

His mother nodded.

Aaron rubbed his chin. "He has everything he ever wanted. He always talked about having a large family."

"Kin-ner w-want to m-meet you." *Mamm's*

expression brightened. "K-Katie has c-curls." She reached up toward Aaron's hair.

His mother talked haltingly about his brother's children, and a feeling of melancholy overtook him. How he regretted all of the time he'd lost with his family. After he'd heard something about each one, she issued another invitation.

"You st-stay for s-supper. S-see *kin-ner*. Sol-o-mon. Be-Bec-ky."

"I'm sure I'll meet them sometime soon," he said, hoping not to show his emotion. He wasn't sure he was ready to share a meal with everyone.

She beamed. *"G-gut kinner."*

Aaron looked toward his brother's house again and wondered where the older children were. Would he see them working on the farm? What would he say to them?

"C-come h-home?" she asked, her question breaking through his thoughts. She pointed to the floor as if to insinuate he would stay in the community indefinitely. Her eyes were full of so much hope that he couldn't say no. Yet he didn't want to lie to her either.

"I'm not sure."

"Y-you s-stay?"

He didn't know how long he was going to

stay, but he doubted his stay would be permanent. "I'll be here for a while," he promised. "I won't leave right away."

She seemed satisfied with that response for the moment, and he breathed a sigh of relief. He was also glad his *dat* hadn't brought up his staying there at the house again. He still had so much to sort out. And he hadn't seen Solomon or any of his family yet to know how that was going to go.

His mother shivered, clutching the shawl closer to her body, and he again worried she was too cold.

"Do you want me to push your chair back inside?" he asked, and she shook her head. "Well, then you need another blanket." He picked up a blanket from a nearby chair and draped it over her slight shoulders. "Do you want to hear more about Missouri?" he asked.

She nodded.

He told her about his company and more of the projects they had built over the past few years. She listened with interest, and he enjoyed spending time with her. When she began to yawn, he insisted that they move inside. He found Jocelyn waiting in the family room.

"I think it's time *Mamm* takes a rest," Aaron said as he pushed his mother's wheelchair toward the nurse. "She looks pretty worn out."

"That's a good idea." She smiled. "I'll take her to her room."

Aaron leaned down and kissed his mother's cheek. "I'll see you soon."

Mamm touched his arm and smiled.

After they went down the hall to the downstairs bedroom his parents shared, Aaron walked around, taking in the familiar surroundings. The furniture felt like old friends. Memories of the times spent sitting in the family room and visiting with friends and family members flooded his mind. It was as if he'd been a boy only yesterday, and he was still living in the house. He wondered if his old room upstairs was still the same.

He moved to the foyer and looked out the front door. He mentally imagined what kind of ramp he would build if he were to make the house more handicapped accessible for his mother. Then he examined the downstairs bathroom and considered how he would update it if his father would allow him to change it.

"Aaron?"

He turned and found Jocelyn watching him.

"Did you need something?" she asked.

138

"Do you think my mother could use a ramp at the front door?" he asked.

Jocelyn nodded. "Yes, I do. She likes to go outside, so I imagine she'll want to take walks when she's feeling stronger and it's warmer out."

"What else do you think would help her get around?" he asked.

Jocelyn looked toward the kitchen. "I think a ramp out back would be good too. I see you're looking at the bathroom. Were you thinking of making any changes in there?"

"I think a shower would be helpful. All they have in here now is a tub. Maybe a big shower with a seat and also a safety bar."

She nodded. "Definitely. I guess you do home improvement projects?"

"Yeah, I own a construction company in Missouri," he explained as they walked back into the family room. "I was just thinking what I could do here if I had the time."

"I think it would be great," Jocelyn agreed.

"Thanks. I'll discuss it with my parents and hopefully I can get started soon." He pulled on his coat and started toward the back door. "I'll see you later."

He walked through the kitchen and found two middle-aged Amish women talking in *Dietsch* while they cooked. The women wore the traditional dark dresses with black aprons, and they wore prayer coverings. They looked vaguely familiar to him, but he couldn't remember their names. The kitchen was the same as he remembered, including the plain white walls, the plain propane refrigerator and stove, small candles on the windowsill, the long oak table surrounded by six chairs, and a calendar on the wall next to the door.

Once more, he almost felt transported back in time as he crossed toward the mud-room.

The women glanced over at him, and he nodded to them. He stopped on the large, wooden back porch and imagined how he would design a ramp to help his mother safely leave the house that way. He knew she loved being out among the barns and animals. It wouldn't take him long to build the ramps. Enthusiasm surged through him as he mentally designed the structures. His fingers itched to get started. He zipped up his coat and stuffed his hands into his pockets.

He looked toward the pasture and spotted Solomon walking toward the largest barn behind the house. Aaron rushed down the stairs and started toward him.

"Solomon!" he called. "Solomon!"

His brother stopped and faced him. His face transformed to a deep frown.

"Solomon?" Aaron stopped walking a few feet from him. "It's Aaron, your younger brother."

"I know exactly who you are." Solomon moved closer to him, his eyes narrowing to slits. "What are you doing here?"

Aaron was speechless for a moment. He was stunned by the venom that laced his brother's words and the hatred in his eyes. His brother looked older and about twenty pounds heavier than Aaron remembered. His light-brown hair and beard had hints of gray, and lines formed around his blue eyes. Aaron had looked up to Solomon when he was younger, but now he was a few inches taller than his older brother.

"I'm here to see *Mamm,*" Aaron said. "I heard she was sick, so I came."

"Who told you?" Solomon asked.

"Saul Beiler called me." Aaron defensively folded his arms over his chest. "Is it a problem that I came back?"

"*Ya,* it is a problem." Solomon lifted his chin in defiance. "Haven't you caused *Mamm* enough heartache? When you left, she was positively stricken. She cried for months. She was a wreck, and no one could console her. How could coming back here now help when we all know you're simply going to leave again?"

Aaron winced as if Solomon had struck him. His shoulders wilted in response to the hateful words.

"I know I was just a kid, but I thought I was doing the right thing when I left," Aaron said, trying to hold back his growing anger. "I was causing a lot of stress for *Mamm* and *Dat,* so I put an end to it by leaving. I didn't realize then that leaving was a mistake. I'm only fully realizing it now."

"Well, coming back after all these years is an even bigger mistake. You should've stayed gone. We don't need you here. I'm taking care of things now. Go back to Missouri where you belong." Solomon turned and stalked toward the barn.

Aaron stared after him while gritting his teeth. He glanced back toward his parents' house and wondered if he had made another mistake by coming back. Where did he belong? His mother and father seemed to want him here, but his brother had thoroughly rejected him, just as he had feared but even worse than he'd imagined. Confusion and regret rioted within him as he walked to his truck.

■ ■ ■ ■

Aaron parked behind the Heart of Paradise and sat in the truck while considering his options. He could pack up and leave in the morning. But how would his mother feel if he left? He had promised to stay awhile, so he would probably break her heart if he left again. At the same time, his brother had made it clear that he was not welcome.

The brief conversation with Solomon had echoed through his mind as he drove back to the bed-and-breakfast. He had followed Linda's advice and tried again to make things right with his family. Now he didn't know what to do. Should he go back to his lonely life in Missouri or should he stay longer and try to become a part of his family again?

Movement in his peripheral vision drew his eyes toward the house, where he spotted Trey walking down the deck stairs and carrying a wooden shelf. Aaron climbed from the truck and met Trey at the driveway.

"Hi, Aaron." Trey smiled. "How are you?"

"I'm fine. Do you need some help?" Aaron offered.

"Oh, no, thanks. I'm just going to fix this shelf. Hannah has been bugging me about it for about a month, so I figure I better do it. It just needs new hangers." He pointed toward a small barn. "Do you want to walk with me?"

"That would be great." Aaron followed him into the barn, which was clogged with tools, a lawn mower, and other yard equipment. It also had a workbench.

Trey looked through his tools and pulled out a hammer.

Aaron couldn't stop thinking about his painful confrontation with Solomon. He needed someone to talk to, and he needed some good advice. Maybe Trey could offer him some wisdom about how to handle the situation with his brother.

"I went to see my mother again today," Aaron suddenly blurted out.

"Oh?" Trey asked. "How was your visit?"

"Well, it wasn't what I expected." He pointed toward the shelf. "Do you want me to fix it for you?"

Trey cocked an eyebrow. "You don't think I can repair a shelf?"

"I'm sorry." Aaron grinned. "It's just a habit. I've loved to work with wood since I was a little kid. I started helping my *dat* with little projects when I was about four."

"Really?" Trey looked impressed. "That's pretty cool."

144

Aaron shrugged. "I guess it was a way I could relate to my father. That was until I became a teenager and started hanging out with some pretty rowdy kids. That changed everything."

Trey nodded and pushed the shelf toward him. "Go ahead. Thanks."

"You're welcome." Aaron fished through a container filled with nails and hangers, searching for two matching ones to use on the shelf.

"So what happened at your mother's house today?" Trey asked gently.

"I had a nice visit with my *mamm,* but my brother wasn't happy to see me." Aaron started lining up the hangers on the back of the shelf. "It was the first time I'd seen him since I left, and he told me to go back to Missouri where I belong."

"He really said that?" Trey asked, aghast.

"Yes, he did." Once the first hanger was in place, Aaron hammered it onto the shelf. "He said I caused enough heartache when I left, and it will be worse when I leave again." He examined the shelf and then pounded in the second hanger. "How's that?"

"Perfect. Thanks." Trey crossed the barn and returned with two cans of soda. He handed one to Aaron and then sat on a stool. "You've been gone a long time, right?"

"Seventeen years." Aaron opened the can, which popped and fizzed in response. "I left when I was fifteen. Now I'm back, and my brother doesn't want me here. He's my only sibling, and he told me he's taking care of things now and the family doesn't need me."

Trey rubbed his goatee and then sipped the soda. "Is your brother older than you?"

"Yeah, he's eight years older than I am." Aaron shook his head. "Solomon always made all of the right decisions. He has a family, and he's helping run the farm with my *dat.* It will be his someday. I know I messed up, but I never expected him to turn me away. My parents are happy I'm back. I get the feeling Solomon wanted me to stay gone forever."

"That's a shame," Trey said.

Aaron analyzed Trey's tentative expression. "You look like you're holding back your true thoughts. What did you want to say?"

"I was trying to think about this from your brother's point of view," Trey began slowly. "I know it's painful, but maybe Solomon resents that you left him to carry the load — for the farm and for your parents, including their grief over losing you."

Aaron considered this. "I could see how he'd feel that way, but I don't know what to do to prove to him that I'm sorry for leaving. I told him I know now that I made a huge mistake. He said I should go anyway, and I'm wondering if I should."

"Do you really want to leave your parents now?" Trey asked.

Aaron shook his head. "No. My *mamm* is so happy I'm here, and I feel like she needs me right now."

"Could you show your brother that you want to be here?" Trey set the can on the workbench. "Is there a way to show him you want to be a part of the family?"

A spark of hope ignited within Aaron's soul. "Yes, I could do that. I can think of a few ways to do that."

"Good. Maybe showing your brother that you're going to help your parents and him will change his attitude. Just give him time and don't give up on your family."

"That's what Linda said yesterday."

"I think Linda was right." He paused. "Did you know Hannah was Amish?"

"My *mamm* mentioned it to me," Aaron said. "Did she leave the community recently?"

"Yes, she left a couple years ago to marry me." Trey leaned back on the workbench and shared the story of how his wife and daughter had passed away, prompting him to retire and start a new life in Lancaster County. Hannah's husband had also died nearly ten years earlier, and she went to work at the Lancaster Grand Hotel. Hannah met Trey at the hotel, and when they married, they opened the bed-and-breakfast. Aaron was fascinated by the story, and he wondered how Hannah had adapted to life outside the Amish community.

Aaron shook his head. "I noticed your wife dresses a little conservatively, but I had no idea Hannah had been Amish until my mother told me. How did her family handle it?"

Trey blew out a deep breath. "One of her twin daughters refuses to accept her decision to leave. We're hoping our baby will help heal Hannah's relationship with Lillian. Lillian stayed in the community, and she's a schoolteacher. The other two children live with us, and they've adapted well. Andrew is in sixth grade and loves school. Amanda is doing great in college. She wants to be a veterinarian."

"I'm glad two of Hannah's children support her decision. I hope she can work things out with Lillian, and I hope I can fix things with my brother."

"I think you can. Just show him you want to be here." Trey picked up the shelf.

"Thanks for the help. I may need your construction expertise again while you're staying here."

"Just let me know what you need, and I'll give you a hand." Aaron was grateful for a new friend.

Aaron sat at the desk in his room later that evening and pulled out a notepad. He sketched the downstairs of his parents' house and then drew plans for a ramp at the front of the house and one at the back. On separate pieces of paper, he wrote out a more detailed design for the ramps and created a list of supplies and tools he would need. He kept a toolbox locked in the bed of his truck under the camper shell, but he would need a few extra tools. He wondered if his father still had tools in the small shop where he used to tinker with wood when Aaron was a child.

After the ramps were planned out, he considered what he could do in his mother's bathroom to make it more handicapped accessible. He listed some ideas, including a large, walk-in shower, shower seat, and safety bars. He'd have to check, but he thought the doorway to the downstairs bathroom, which was quite large, was already wide enough to accommodate even his mother's wheelchair. Whatever he planned, he would have to discuss drastic changes like that with his father before he started working.

Aaron inspected his lists and construction designs and smiled. Making these changes to the house would be a way to prove to his brother that he wanted to help his parents. But it would also be a way to pay his parents back for the aggravation he caused them when he was a teenager. He still wanted to pay them back the money he cost them by burning down the barn as well.

He had to call Zac and let him know he was staying longer than he'd planned. He pulled his cell phone out of his pocket and checked to see if he had any messages. Finding none, he dialed Zac's number.

"Hey, Aaron," Zac said. "How are things in Pennsylvania?"

"It's going okay," Aaron said while leaning back in the chair. "How are the projects coming along?"

"Pretty well. We ran into one snag at the Anderson house." Zac detailed the project delays at a home addition project. "I think it will all work out, but we'll just be behind schedule a few weeks."

"Yeah, but you know as well as I do that it happens sometimes." Aaron reviewed the ramp drawings again while they talked. "Listen, I wanted to let you know I plan to stay a little longer than I expected."

"Oh?" Zac asked. "What's going on?"

"My mom isn't doing that well, and I feel like I'm needed here."

"Oh no. I'm sorry to hear that."

"Thanks. She's going to be okay, but the recovery is going to take awhile. She has to learn how to walk again, and her speech is slurred. The nurses and therapists are working to get her strength back. I'm going to do a few things at the house to make it easier for her to get around."

"I totally understand," Zac insisted. "You take all the time you need. We've got it under control here."

"Are you sure you're okay with it? I don't want to make life harder on you."

"Aaron, family always comes first. You just worry about doing what you need to for your folks. I can handle anything that happens here."

"Thanks. I really appreciate it."

"Call me in a few days, and let me know how it's going, okay?"

"I will. Thank you," Aaron said before disconnecting the call. He was thankful his friend understood why he wanted to stay. Now he was ready to show Solomon and his parents how much he did care about them. He was going to make things right between his brother and him. He was going to get his family back.

SEVEN

The next morning, Aaron parked his truck in front of his parents' house, hopped out, and fetched his tape measure and a notepad. He began to measure for the ramp near the front steps, and excitement soaked through him as he thought about how much the projects would help his mother. He felt like he was finally doing something thoughtful and positive for his family after causing so much anxiety when he was a teenager. He was going to show his appreciation for his parents for the first time in his life.

The front door opened and his father stared down at him with bewilderment on his face.

"Aaron?" *Dat* asked. "What are you doing?"

"I'm going to make it easier for *Mamm* to get in and out of the house." Aaron held up the notepad, showing the sketch. "I thought I'd build her a ramp for the front and back of the house. I'd also like to make some improvements in the bathroom if you'll let me do it. I know you might think some of them would be a bit too modern, but —"

"Really?" *Dat* stepped out onto the porch and his expression transformed to one of curiosity. "What did you have in mind for the bathroom?"

"I could install a walk-in shower with a bench, and, of course, I would add safety bars on the walls. It's such a large bathroom I think we can keep the tub too."

Dat nodded and rubbed his beard. "Sounds like a *gut* idea. I'm sure the bishop would understand this is for your *mutter*'s safety. How much would the renovations cost?"

Aaron shrugged. "I'm not concerned about that. I want to do it for you, *Dat*. It's my treat. I owe you after what the barn cost you."

"Danki." His father climbed down the steps. "How can I help?"

"You want to help?" Aaron asked with surprise.

"Of course I want to help you," his *daed* said. "Do you think I'm just going to stand by and watch you work on *mei haus*?"

"I'd love to have an assistant. That would be wonderful." Aaron held up the notepad.

"Do you want to write down the measurements while I call them out? Then we can calculate how much lumber we'll need."

"*Ya,* I can do that." His *daed* reached for the notepad and pencil.

Aaron smiled. He felt like a kid again while he and his father planned out the front ramp. He had always cherished the woodworking projects they had completed when he was a child, and now they were working side by side again. It had been much too long since they had talked about creating things out of wood.

After all the measurements were taken and the supply list was complete, his *dat* let Jocelyn know they would be gone for a while, and they went to the home improvement store. They bought lumber, the additional tools they needed, and supplies, then began building the ramp right away.

As Aaron was about to start cutting the wood, he noticed a young man walking toward them. The boy was tall and lean, nearly as tall as Solomon, and he had Solomon's ice-blue eyes and light-brown hair. He was certain it was Manny, his oldest nephew. His eyes widened with a mixture of astonishment and recognition.

"*Daadi,*" the young man said. "What are you working on?"

"Manny?" Aaron placed the saw on the ground. "I'm Aaron, your *dat*'s *bruder.*"

"*Onkel* Aaron." Manny shook his hand with a firm grip. "It's *gut* to meet you. *Mammi* has been so excited that you came back."

"It's great to see you." Aaron was overwhelmed with admiration for his nephew. "The last time I saw you, you were toddling around the farm and learning to talk."

Manny chuckled. "It's been a long time. I'm glad you came back." He pointed toward the pile of lumber. "What are you building?"

"It's a ramp for your *mammi,*" Aaron said.

"May I help?" Manny offered.

"That would great," Aaron said as he picked up the saw. "Do you like to work with wood?"

"Are you kidding?" Manny asked. "I love to."

The three men worked on the ramp for the next hour, and Aaron had the chance to ask Manny and his *dat* questions he had about the farm and hear about what had been happening in the community over the years. After they cut the wood, they began to build the frame. Soon after the frame was assembled, the front door opened and Becky appeared. Time had been gracious to her. Her skin still glowed like a young woman's. A hint of gray teased the light-brown hair that peeked out from under her prayer covering, but to Aaron she didn't look close to forty.

"I've been looking for you two. What are you doing out here? Are you ready for lunch?" Her eyes fell on Aaron and she frowned. "Aaron. I didn't know you were here."

"Hi, Becky." Aaron brushed the back of his hand across his forehead. Although it was mid-January cold, he was sweating from exertion. "It's been a long time."

"We weren't expecting to see you again." Becky continued to scowl. "You left and then we never heard from you. This is a surprise."

"I came when I heard my *mamm* was ill." Aaron stiffened at her accusatory tone and condemning stare. Her demeanor toward him shocked him since his sister-in-law had always been patient and forgiving. He never imagined Becky would reject him, but he assumed Solomon had influenced her. He wondered what his *dat* and Manny were thinking about her tone.

Maybe like Solomon, Becky wants me to leave. Maybe they're both right, and I have no right being here.

157

"Please come in for lunch," she said. The invitation did not soften her cold stare, and she turned and went inside.

Aaron followed his *daed* and nephew into the house, where he found his mother sitting at the kitchen table while two young ladies and Becky prepared lunch. When the girls turned to look at them, he saw that the girls both had Becky's round face, light-brown hair, and dainty features. They also had her brown eyes. They had to be Solomon's daughters, and he was overwhelmed to finally meet the nieces he didn't know existed until this week.

"Aa-ron!" *Mamm* said, his name garbled by her weakness.

"Hi, *Mamm.*" He gently squeezed her hand. "*Dat,* Manny, and I are building you a ramp at the front of the *haus* to help you get in and out."

"A-ach?" Mamm asked. *"D-danki."*

"I'm *froh* to do it, *Mamm.*" He sat down beside her. "I'm going to make it easier for you so you don't have to feel cooped up. Soon you'll be walking around, and you'll want to go outside and enjoy the spring weather. I'm sure you'll be using the walker before you know it."

"Ruthie Joy and Katie," *Dat* said as he made a sweeping gesture toward Aaron.

"This is your *onkel* Aaron."

"Hi!" Ruthie Joy waved at Aaron and then helped bring a platter of lunch meat to the table. "I'm Ruthie. It's nice to meet you."

"It's true!" Katie ran over to Aaron and started to reach for his hair, then stopped, her small hand frozen in mid-air. "I have the same curly hair as you."

"You do?" Aaron asked in awe.

"*Ya,* I do." She pointed toward her prayer covering, even though he couldn't see the curls beneath it. She scowled. "Isn't it terrible in the summer when it's hot and sticky? It's not easy to roll my hair into the bun before I put on my *kapp.* My hair actually stands up when it's humid. I'm one big, frizzy ball of hair. At least, that's what my little *bruder* calls me."

Aaron chuckled. "I can definitely relate. I've been there with the frizzy curls. I considered shaving my head one summer, but I had a friend who wouldn't let me do it. She said she loved my curls, and she would pay money to have hair like mine."

Katie shook her head with a solemn expression. "No, I wouldn't pay *gut* money for this hair. I think I might consider paying money to get rid of it, though. It's too much trouble."

"You just don't appreciate it," Ruthie Joy

chimed in. "My hair is pin straight and has no life at all. You don't know how blessed you two are."

"Let's have lunch," *Dat* said. "I'm so *froh* to have our family together again."

"Where are Solomon and Junior?" Becky asked.

"They went to the hardware store just before I started working with *Daadi* and *Onkel* Aaron," Manny responded as he sat beside Aaron. "They're fixing the fence at the back of the pasture. They'll be back soon."

"I'll be sure they get lunch then," Becky said. "Junior loves to do errands with his *dat* on Saturdays when he doesn't have school."

Aaron's nieces sat across from him, and Katie grinned before bowing her head in prayer. Aaron closed his eyes and thanked God for his family. He thought his heart might burst with the overwhelming admiration he felt for these family members he'd just met. He asked God to soften Becky's and Solomon's feelings toward him. He couldn't bear their rejection and wanted to make things right with them.

After prayers were complete, the kitchen erupted in a chorus of noise as everyone began reaching for food, filling their plates, and talking. Utensils scraped plates, and platters were passed around the long table.

"Tell us about Missouri," Katie said as she dropped a pile of macaroni salad onto her plate.

"*Ya,*" Manny agreed. "What do you do for a living?"

"Where do you live?" Ruthie Joy asked.

"Are you Amish?" Katie asked. "Do the Amish dress like you do in Missouri?"

"Whoa," his *daed* said, raising his voice above the noise. "Slow down and let Aaron answer your questions one at a time."

"I don't mind." Aaron placed two pieces of lunch meat and a piece of cheese on bread. "I co-own a construction company in Missouri. I live in an apartment, and I'm not Amish."

"You're not Amish?" Katie asked. Her eyebrows shot upward with shock.

"What kind of construction do you do?" Manny asked between bites of his sandwich.

Aaron spent the rest of lunch telling his nieces and nephew about his life in Missouri. They peppered him with endless questions about how life in Missouri differed from their lives in Pennsylvania. He looked at his father and found him smiling as he watched Aaron answer the questions. The sentiment in his father's expression touched him deep in his soul. He'd missed his parents for so very long. His mother looked like she was enjoying the conversation too.

Aaron wondered what life would be like if he were to move back to Pennsylvania. Did he truly belong there? Would he fit in? Would he finally be rid of the loneliness that hung over him like a dark storm cloud? The thoughts warmed his soul, and he didn't want the lunch to end.

Becky seemed to avoid his gaze while she ate. As soon as lunch was over, she jumped up and started doing the dishes. She kept her back toward him and faced the sink while she worked. Her silence caused his heart to splinter. He and Becky had always been friends when he was a child. Since Becky and Solomon grew up together, attending the same school and also worshiping in the same church district, Aaron had known Becky his whole life. He'd considered her like an older sister, and now she wouldn't talk to him. Her silence and the resentment he saw in her eyes when she had scowled at him were difficult to accept.

Aaron, his father, and Manny went back outside and worked on the ramp for the remainder of the afternoon. Their conversation flowed easily as they worked.

"I'll come back Monday and stain it," Aaron said as he closed the bed of his truck. "Does that sound good?"

"Ya." His father picked up a hammer. "That sounds perfect. I think we did a great job."

Aaron sat on the bumper and looked at his nephew. "You work well with your hands. You said you loved woodworking. Do you do much of it? Do you do any construction?"

Manny shifted the straw hat covering his light-brown hair. "No, not really. I tinker here and there. *Mei dat* keeps me busy with the farm."

"Daadi!"

"Oh, here comes Junior," his father said, looking past the truck toward Solomon's house. "You'll get to meet the youngest of Solomon's *kinner.* We were so busy, we didn't even notice when Solomon's buggy drove in."

The preteen jogged over to the truck and nodded at Aaron. He looked just like his older brother with his light-brown hair and blue eyes. "You must be my *onkel.*"

"I am." Aaron shook his hand. "And you're Junior."

"Ya." The boy grinned. "Are you staying for supper? *Mei mamm* is making chicken

and noodles with green beans, bread, and potatoes."

"That's a great idea," Manny said as he picked up more tools. "We're eating at our *haus* tonight. You should stay."

Aaron considered the offer, and he was tempted to accept the invitation in order to spend more time with his nieces and nephews. But he rejected the idea when he considered Becky's reaction to him and also the painful conversation he'd shared with his brother. He knew he wasn't welcome in his brother's home, and he didn't want to ruin the perfect memories he'd created today.

"You should stay," Junior echoed. "I was so busy with *Dat* today that I didn't get to spend any time with you. Katie told me you ate lunch with everyone."

"Thank you for the invitation." Aaron stood. "I have to get going, but I'll stay another night, all right?"

Junior frowned, causing guilt to rain down on Aaron.

"I'm coming back Monday to stain the ramp," Aaron began. "Maybe I'll eat lunch with you then."

"I have school." Junior kicked a rock with the toe of his boot. "I won't get to see you."

"I might still be here when you get home,"

Aaron added.

Manny placed his hand on his brother's arm. "Maybe after your chores, *Dat* will let you help us stain the ramp."

"*Ya?*" Junior grinned up at his brother.

"*Ya,*" Aaron's *daed* said. "I'll make sure you can help."

"Great!" Junior nodded. "I want to help."

"I'll let you help if your *dat* says it's okay." Aaron fished his keys from his pocket. "I better head out now, but I'll see you all Monday."

After going into the house and saying good-bye to his mother, Aaron climbed into his truck and drove back to the bed-and-breakfast. His mind was racing with excitement after spending the day with his family. His lips were turned up in a permanent smile. He hoped his relationship with his parents and his brother's children would continue. Maybe, just maybe, with God's divine help, Aaron could finally get his family back.

Linda was making hash browns Monday morning when she heard footsteps on the stairs. Her pulse skittered when she thought about seeing Aaron again. Even though she knew it was silly to get attached to him, she'd been looking forward to seeing him after their conversation over coffee and cookies last week.

"Gude mariye."

She looked over her shoulder and found Aaron grinning at her from the doorway. *"Gude mariye,"* she repeated as heat radiated from the tips of her ears. "You're up early. Breakfast won't be ready for another thirty minutes."

"I have to head out early." Aaron tapped the woodwork. "I just wanted to say good morning before I leave."

"Oh no." Linda shook her head as she pushed the hash browns around in the pan. "I can't send you out hungry. I have strict instructions to feed the guests breakfast when I'm here. Let me make you a plate."

"I'm sure I'll grab something to eat while I —"

"No," she said the word more forcefully than she meant to, and he lifted his eyebrows. "I will get you a roll. Or I can make you a quick egg sandwich you can eat while you're driving."

"Well, I certainly don't want to be responsible for your getting into trouble with your employer." His lips twitched as he eyed her. "Fine. You win. I'll take the time to eat something before I leave."

"Gut." She pointed to the table. "Have a

seat. I'll bring you some coffee."

"I can get my own coffee. You don't need to wait on me." He made his way to the cabinet and brought out a mug.

"So would you like eggs?" she offered.

"Yes, please." His grin was wide. He seemed to be smiling more than usual this morning, which astonished her.

"Coming right up. Why are you so chipper this morning?" Linda glanced at him over her shoulder while she beat two eggs in a bowl.

"It's a *schee* day." He filled a mug, and the aroma of fresh coffee filled her senses. "The sun is shining, and there isn't any snow in the forecast all week."

Linda took in his expression and couldn't stop herself from smiling along with him. "You seem different. You're much happier than you were last week. What happened?"

"I had a fantastic visit with my family. Well, actually, it was with my parents and my brother's *kinner.*" He stirred sweetener into the mug. "I'm going back this morning."

"Really?" Linda moved the eggs around in the pan. "That's *wunderbaar*! Tell me what happened." She dumped the hash browns onto a platter and set them on the table.

He leaned against the counter beside her. "I decided to make the *haus* more handicapped accessible for *mei mamm,* and I started building a ramp for the front of the *haus* on Saturday. My *dat* and my nephew Manny helped me. I also had lunch with them and met my two nieces, and later my other nephew. It was truly *wunderbaar.*"

"*Ach,* that is fantastic news!" Linda exclaimed. "I'm so glad you didn't give up on them."

He held up his mug as if to toast her. "*Danki* for your encouragement."

"Ruth will appreciate the ramp too." Linda slipped the eggs onto a plate. "Would you like *brot* also?"

"Yes, please."

She put two pieces of freshly baked bread on the plate and then handed it to him. "I'm going to start the bacon now. I'm sorry it's not ready yet."

"You don't need to apologize. This is perfect." He sat at the head of the table. "Why don't you sit with me?"

"Oh, I can't." She waved off the suggestion and pulled the bacon out of the refrigerator.

"Please?" he asked. "Just give me a couple of minutes to tell you more about my visit with my family."

Linda glanced over her shoulder and found him looking at her rather intensely. She couldn't bring herself to say no to his hopeful expression. "Okay."

"Great." His smile was back.

She sat down, and Aaron told her all about the day he'd spent at his parents' house, detailing how wonderful his nieces and nephews were and how at home he felt.

"I'm so *froh* for you." Linda placed her elbow on the table and rested her chin on her hand. "The Lord is healing your family."

He slathered peanut butter spread onto a piece of bread. "I was thinking that yesterday. I'm so grateful I finally feel like a part of the family." He stopped speaking and handed her the bread. "I feel rude eating in front of you. Please, have this."

"Danki." She accepted his offering and took a bite of the bread. "What inspired you to build the ramp?"

"I felt like I needed to do something to show my family I still care about them," he said.

"They already know you do." She noticed his smile had faded. "Something is on your mind. What is it?" She asked the question and then immediately felt she was the one being rude. Who was she to ask him to share

169

his private thoughts?

"I talked to my *bruder* last week, and he told me I shouldn't have come back." Aaron looked at his plate while he spoke. "He said I had caused enough heartache when I left years ago, and that I will hurt my *mamm* again when I return home. He told me to leave and go back to Missouri where I belong."

Linda gasped with shock. "Solomon said that to you?"

"Yes, he did," Aaron said. "Becky had a similar reaction to me on Saturday. She took one look at me and glared. It was obvious that she didn't want me there. She didn't ask me to leave, but she wasn't thrilled to have me there either. She invited us in for lunch, but she never spoke to me. She averted her eyes all during lunch and then quickly started washing the dishes when we were done eating. That isn't the Becky I remember from my childhood. She and I used to talk and laugh. She's obviously disgusted with me, just like Solomon is, only she didn't tell me to leave."

"I'm so sorry, Aaron," Linda said. She longed to take away the sadness in his eyes. "I was hoping everyone in your family would be *froh* to see you. Ruth asked for you for so long that they should see how

170

much having you back means to her."

"Danki." Aaron met her gaze and studied her eyes. "I thought about leaving and going back to Missouri, but Trey talked me out of it. He said I should think about this from Solomon's point of view, that Solomon may resent me because after I left he had to shoulder all the responsibility of taking care of our parents. He said I should do something to show how I want to be a part of the family and help."

"And that's one reason you're building a ramp for your *mamm.*" She finished his thought, and he nodded. "That's a *wunderbaar* idea. The whole family will appreciate the ramp."

"I'm going to build a ramp for the back of the house, too, and do some work in the downstairs bathroom near my parents' bedroom."

"I think that's a great idea." Linda smiled. "Solomon will see how much you care for your parents, and he'll welcome you back into the family. Trey is absolutely right."

Aaron searched her eyes as if he were seeking answers to impossible questions. "You've been through so much heartache in your life, Linda. How do you stay so positive?"

She was baffled by the question and

struggled to answer it. The truth was that she often struggled to stay positive, especially on the rough days when her uncle was particularly cold and hurtful toward her. She gave him a halfhearted shrug instead of responding to him.

Aaron went on. "You've faced a lot of difficult situations. Losing your parents, having to move out of the only home you'd ever known. But you still find the good in people. That's pretty amazing to me."

The compliments mystified her, and she looked down at the table to avoid his intense expression. "I sometimes struggle to stay positive, but I always try to remember that God will carry us through the difficult times. We have to hold on to our faith. Your family will accept you. Just keep doing what you're doing, and give them time."

"Do you think Solomon and Becky will truly forgive me? Solomon looked at me with pure hatred in his eyes. He nearly spat when he said my name." The hurt in Aaron's expression tugged at her heart. "And Becky doesn't want to have anything to do with me."

"Like I said, you have to trust God to mend your broken relationship with your *bruder* and Becky," she said gently. "With God, all things are possible. I truly believe

172

that." She ate the last bite of bread and then glanced at the clock above the sink. "*Ach,* I need to get that bacon started. The other guests should be coming downstairs soon." She stood and reached out a hand. "Do you want more coffee?"

He placed his hand over the top of his mug. "I told you, you don't have to wait on me. I can get my own coffee. You worry about that bacon. I want a piece before I leave."

She chuckled. "All right."

"Danki."

Linda grabbed another frying pan and soon the bacon sizzled and popped as she moved it around in the pan. She fished out the fully cooked pieces with metal tongs and placed them on a platter beside the stovetop.

"You haven't said anything about my *Dietsch* today." His voice was soft in her ear.

She nearly jumped. Aaron was standing directly behind her. He seemed to be awaiting her response, but she couldn't speak for a moment as she processed how close he was to her.

"Haven't you noticed how many *Dietsch* words I'm using now?" He placed his mug in the sink, seemingly unaware of how his close proximity affected her.

"*Ya,* I have noticed," she finally said before smoothing her hands over her apron. "You're an expert."

"I told you I was." He winked at her as he swiped two pieces of bacon. "I have to run, but I'll see you later. *Danki* again for your encouragement. It's working."

"Have a great day." As she watched him leave, she knew she was in trouble. They'd shared another meaningful conversation, and she could feel her attachment to him blossoming.

She truly had feelings for Aaron Ebersol, and she'd be left nursing a broken heart when he went back to Missouri and left Pennsylvania behind.

EIGHT

"Why did you leave the community?" Manny asked Aaron as they stained the ramp.

Aaron set his brush down and adjusted the ball cap perched on his head. He looked toward Solomon's house and wondered what his brother had told his children about him. Had they learned anything about their uncle at all over the years?

"What has your *dat* told you about me?" Aaron asked

Manny shrugged as he dipped his brush into the stain. "Nothing really. I once asked him about you, and he only said that you'd left. He wouldn't discuss it other than to say you had gone."

Aaron nodded. He hadn't expected to hear anything different, but it still hurt knowing that his brother had written him off with one simple sentence. They were brothers, not acquaintances who barely knew each other.

"It was more than that. I didn't just wake up one morning and decide to run off to see the world." Aaron picked up his brush again, put more stain on it, and moved it across the wood. "I got in with a wild group of *buwe*. They weren't all *buwe,* really. Some of them were young men. We were constantly in trouble. We drank alcohol, smoked cigarettes, and snuck out at night."

Manny grimaced. "*Mei dat* wouldn't tolerate that."

"*Mei dat* didn't either, but I didn't listen to him or obey." Aaron blew out a deep sigh. "I'm not proud of what I did. I caused my parents a lot of stress and constant headaches. The last straw was when I burned down the bishop's barn."

Manny gasped. "Did you do it on purpose?"

"No, but it was my fault." Aaron explained how the fire happened. "It was terrible. My parents had to pay for replacing the barn, which was a real burden since the farm wasn't doing well that year. One of my friends suggested we leave because they were all tired of constant restrictions. We went off to Missouri and started a new life there."

"And you were only fifteen?" Manny

looked astonished.

"*Ya,* I was. It wasn't smart at all, and I know now that I hurt my parents much more by leaving than if I had stayed and worked through my problems with them." Aaron paused long enough to compel Manny to look at him. "Staying and facing my problems would've been the best way to handle the situation. You can't run away from your problems. It only makes things worse because your problems will follow you wherever you go."

Manny seemed to be listening, but Aaron wondered what his nephew was thinking.

"My advice to you is to stay on the straight and narrow path," Aaron continued. "Don't get involved with the wrong crowd."

"I won't." Manny pushed his hat up and brushed back his hair. "I haven't had the opportunity to get into trouble, and I really haven't been interested in doing anything bad. *Mei dat* is strict, but I don't mind it, really."

"That's *gut.*" Aaron wasn't surprised to hear this since his brother had always been so serious. Aaron didn't recall any times when Solomon was in trouble or when he disobeyed their parents. He always made the right choices, and he never caused their parents any stress.

"You sound like the opposite of *mei dat,*" Manny said. "I don't think *mei dat* knows how to break rules."

"That's not a bad quality to have." Aaron stared at his nephew and wondered about his life. "Are you baptized?"

"*Ya.*" Manny went back to running his brush over the ramp. "I was baptized last year. Most of my *freinden* joined the church then too."

"*Gut.*" Aaron couldn't help but feel happy to hear this. "I'm sure your parents and grandparents were happy to see you baptized."

Manny nodded. "I really didn't think twice about it. I'm happy with my life. I guess you weren't baptized since you left the Amish so young."

"No," Aaron said. "And I didn't know if I was ever going to be. I wasn't sure what I wanted back then."

"Do you know what you want now?" Manny asked.

Aaron was stumped. "I'm not sure how to answer that. I have everything I need back in Missouri. I have a good job and a growing business. I have a place to live. At the same time, I miss my family."

"Do you miss the church?"

Aaron considered the question. "In some

ways I do miss the church. I miss the community more than anything. You don't realize how wonderful the community is until you leave. I have some friends in Missouri, mostly people I work with, but that's not the same as being a member of a community that pulls together when one of the members is in need."

They continued their work in silence for a few minutes, and Aaron realized he wanted to know more about Manny. Perhaps he hoped Manny had all the things he wished he could've had if he'd stayed in the community.

"Do you have a *maedel*?" Aaron asked.

Manny looked up at him and grinned. "*Ya,* I do."

"What's her name?" Aaron asked with a smile.

"Nancy," Manny said. "Her parents own Fisher's Deli. I've known her since we were *kinner.* She's *schee,* intelligent, and sweet. I'm so grateful the Lord brought us together."

"That's great." Aaron was honored that Manny was sharing so much personal information with him.

"How about you?" Manny asked. "Do you have a *maedel*?"

"No." Aaron stood and stretched his back.

"I don't."

"Why not?" Manny asked, incredulous.

"I haven't found the right one, I guess."

"Have you dated at all?" Manny stood and stretched his back too. "Oh, I'm going to be sore tomorrow."

"I'm going to be sore too. I always seem to forget to stand and stretch periodically during a project like this, and then I suffer for a few days." Aaron examined the ramp, taking in the planks that weren't quite straight, unhappy the ramp wasn't perfect. *I should've done a better job.*

"You're avoiding the question." Manny waved his brush toward Aaron.

"What?" Aaron pretended not to understand the statement, but it was true — he was avoiding the question. He didn't want to discuss his lonely life with his nineteen-year-old nephew.

"Why won't you tell me about your love life?"

"My love life?" Aaron laughed. He might as well answer the question. "Okay. There's nothing to tell you — except that I don't have one. Dating is not a part of my life."

"So you've never dated at all?" Manny looked stunned. "How can that be? Aren't you in your thirties?"

Aaron sank onto a pile of lumber beside

the ramp. "I guess I dated a couple of women in Missouri, but it wasn't really dating."

"What do you mean?" Manny took a drink from his bottle of water.

"I took them out for coffee once or twice. One woman went out to dinner with me a few times, but that was it. Nothing came of it. We talked on the phone for a while, but we were really only friends. I wouldn't say she was my girlfriend because we were never really a couple."

"Why not?" Manny looked confused. "Doesn't taking a woman out a few times make her your girlfriend?"

"Not really. I didn't feel a connection with her. We really didn't have much in common. She was sweet, but she didn't really understand me. I guess she wasn't the right one for me." He paused and thought not just about his dating history, but his life. "I can't seem to find where I belong, I suppose." He was bemused to hear himself open his heart to a teenager, even though Manny was his nephew. Although it felt strange, it also was cathartic.

"Maybe you've been looking in the wrong places," Manny said.

Aaron chuckled and tossed a work glove at Manny, hitting him in the chest.

"What was that for?" Manny demanded.

"You're way too young to be so profound."
Aaron stood. "Let's finish this ramp."

Manny grinned, and Aaron shook his
head. He was thankful to have gotten to
know his nephew. In fact, he was overflow-
ing with admiration for the young man.

Aaron climbed into his truck that afternoon
and looked at the completed front ramp.
He was grateful for his two nephews' assistance finishing it up today. Although the
ramp wasn't perfect, it looked decent. And,
most importantly, it was functional. He
started the engine and steered down the
road toward the bed-and-breakfast. His
mind wandered, and he found himself
thinking about Linda.

She'd been on his mind all day long. He
contemplated her suggestion to visit Elmer
Smucker. He knew facing the bishop and
apologizing again for the barn fire would
help clear his mind and his conscience. He
needed to find a way to forgive himself, and
facing the transgression straight on would
help him do that.

Making up his mind, Aaron turned right
at the next intersection and drove toward
the bishop's farm. He'd already learned
Elmer was not only still the district bishop

but lived in the same place. His stomach clenched as he pulled into the driveway and eased his pickup to a stop. As he climbed out of the cab and walked up the rock path toward the white, two-story house, he scanned the pasture behind the house and spotted the large barn that replaced the one he'd burned down. It was nearly identical to the one he remembered — red with a black roof. He sighed. He should've stayed in town and helped rebuild that barn, but he couldn't change the past. Instead, he could only try to make amends for the future.

Standing on the bishop's porch, Aaron took a deep breath. Then he knocked on the door before folding his arms over his coat and shivering in the cold breeze.

A moment after the door opened, Elmer Smucker stood in front of him with a baffled expression on his face. Now in his late-seventies, the bishop looked even shorter than Aaron remembered. He was a stocky man, and he had a long, silver beard. "Hello. May I help you?"

"Hi, Elmer." Aaron stuck his hand out. "I'm Aaron Ebersol. Jonas and Ruth are my parents."

"Aaron!" The older man shook his hand. "I heard you were in town. It's so *gut* to see you." He opened the door wide. "Please come in."

"Danki." Aaron followed him into a large family room. "I won't take much of your time." He sat down on a sofa and placed his coat beside him as Elmer sat down across from him in a wing chair.

"Don't be *gegisch.*" Elmer rested his hands in his lap. "What can I do for you?"

"I want to apologize for all the trouble and heartache I caused you years ago. I don't think I ever gave you a proper apology." Aaron could already feel the anxiety lifting from his shoulders.

Elmer waved off Aaron's words. "There's no need to apologize again. That has long been forgotten. You were always forgiven, and you should've known that."

"I feel like I need to discuss this with you and set things straight. It's time I take responsibility for my actions."

"I heard you went to Missouri. Is that true?"

"*Ya,* that's true." Aaron shared his story, including how he co-owned a construction company with his friend. "We also hire former Amish workers and help them adjust to the *English* life."

"Is that so?" Elmer fingered his beard and frowned. "I'm not sure that's the best

184

practice for the Amish community. We want our lost members to make their way back home, not find their way in the outside world."

Aaron longed to take back his words and ease Elmer's mind. He didn't want to upset the bishop. "We don't encourage them to forget the community. We help them find work. We're all trying to find our way, so we offer them a way to start a new life."

"I see." The older man nodded. "What brought you back home after all this time? Was it your mother's illness?"

"Yes. Saul Beiler called and told me about *mei mamm*'s stroke. He managed to locate me on a hunch with some help from a friend, using the Internet." Aaron paused and rubbed his hands together. "I thought my family had forgotten me, but I realize now that they didn't, and I caused more pain by leaving than I would've if I'd stayed and faced all the problems I'd created."

"*Ya,* that's true." The bishop nodded slowly. "You didn't have to leave. There's nothing so bad that it can't be solved with some prayer and your family's support."

"I know. I've missed out on so much," Aaron continued. "*Mei bruder* has a nice family, and I'm enjoying getting to know them. My nephew Manny and I are build-

185

ing handicapped ramps for *mei mamm* so she can get in and out of the house when she's able to walk again. Manny and I are enjoying spending time together."

"That's *wunderbaar.* Do you think you might stay now?" the bishop asked.

Aaron shook his head. "I don't know if I can. I have my business in Missouri, and I don't know how I can come back here to stay after all this time. It would be a huge adjustment. I mean, I'm not Amish anymore." He surprised himself by deciding to confess to the bishop how confused he was feeling. "I don't know if I'm supposed to be Amish or if I'm supposed to remain *English.* I drive a truck, own a cell phone, and use a computer. I haven't been to an Amish church service since I was fifteen."

Elmer watched Aaron while again fingering his beard. He seemed to be deep in thought before responding. "I would imagine the Lord led you back here for a reason, *ya*?"

"I have a feeling you're right." Aaron couldn't help but agree. He was starting to think there was a deeper meaning for his visit beyond seeing his mother.

"Supper!" A woman's voice called. "It's ready."

"Would you like to join *mei fraa* and me

186

for supper?" Elmer asked. "She made her *wunderbaar* stew. You will really enjoy it. It's the perfect meal for a cold winter's evening."

"Oh, I don't want to impose." Aaron shook his head. "I only wanted to apologize to you."

"You're not imposing." Elmer stood and motioned for Aaron to follow. "Come on, now. You don't want to insult Fannie. She won't stand for people leaving here hungry."

Aaron followed Elmer into the kitchen, which resembled his parents' kitchen, including the plain white walls, the plain propane refrigerator and stove, and a long kitchen table with six chairs. The only decorations were candles on the windowsills and shelves, a clock, and a calendar decorated with flowers on the wall.

After welcoming Aaron, Fannie served her stew with bread, and then they had chocolate pie for dessert. During the meal, they discussed Aaron's life in Missouri, as well as how much the surrounding tourist community had grown since he'd left.

"*Danki* for the meal," Aaron told Fannie when his plate was clean. "It was positively *appeditlich.*"

"*Gern gschehne,*" Fannie said as she stood to take his plate to the counter. "You're welcome here anytime. We're so *froh* you came by to see us."

Elmer stood. "Let me grab my coat on the way to the front door and walk you out."

The two men stood on the porch together as Aaron pulled on his own coat, zipping it up in an attempt to stop the frigid air from seeping beneath his shirt.

"Do you need any work done to your barn or home?" Aaron asked.

"No." The older man lifted a gray eyebrow with confusion. "Why do you ask?"

"I feel like I need to do something for you to make up for the stress I caused you when I was a kid." Aaron motioned toward the large barn. "I can replace rotten boards or do any repair work you need."

Elmer chuckled. "You don't need to do anything for me, Aaron. The barn was rebuilt, and we're thankful. It's over."

Aaron nodded, and he thought of what Linda had said. Perhaps he needed to forgive himself.

"Do you attend church services in Missouri?" Elmer asked.

Aaron nodded. "I would be lying if I told you that I went regularly, but I have attended church. I've gone to the community church periodically, but it's not the same. I miss the Amish services I grew up with."

"Really?" Elmer folded his arms across

his wide middle. "You should come to church with us while you're here."

Aaron's lips formed a frown. "I don't know how that would be received."

Elmer's eyes widened. "What do you mean? You would be welcomed back. You know that already. You know we are always *froh* to see former members of the community return."

"I know," Aaron said with a sigh. "I'll think about it." He knew he was welcome, but he wondered how comfortable he'd feel. Would he feel out of place sitting with the congregation?

"The members of the community would enjoy seeing you again." The bishop's expression darkened. "You should remind your workers who were formerly Amish that they would be welcome back to the fold as well. You should encourage them to go back to their communities. They shouldn't hide on your construction crews. Their communities miss them."

"I'll do that," Aaron said. He didn't want to argue with the bishop, but he knew the men who worked for them had their own reasons for leaving.

"Think about coming back to church, and also think about what I said earlier," Elmer continued. "The Lord may be leading you home for a reason. Open your heart and listen to what he has to say."

"I will. *Danki.*" Aaron shook the bishop's hand. *"Gut nacht."*

By the time he stepped into his room at the bed-and-breakfast, he was deep in thought. He couldn't help but wonder if the Lord was leading him back to the community. But if God was calling him back to his hometown, why did Solomon and Becky want him to go back to Missouri?

Thursday evening Linda pulled the second loaf of bread out of the oven and set it on the counter. She smiled as she breathed in the warm, delicious aroma. The bread had turned out perfectly, not too brown but not underdone either.

"What are you doing?"

Linda started. She hadn't heard her *onkel* Reuben come in from working out in the barn. "Why are you still cooking? Do you know what time it is?" he demanded.

"*Ya,* I know." Linda smiled at him despite his permanent frown. The evening was still young. Her *onkel* just didn't like anything outside their regular routine. "I made these loaves of bread for Ruth Ebersol. I'm going to take them to her tomorrow when I get off work at the hotel."

"Tomorrow is Friday," Reuben barked. "Why are you working at the hotel tomorrow?"

"I'm going to help Madeleine because our new coworker needs to take the day off. Madeleine and I are going to take some food to the Ebersol family when we leave the hotel." She pointed toward the bread. "Isn't it perfect? There's nothing like fresh *brot.*"

He nodded. "Smells *gut.*"

"*Danki.*" Her smiled deepened. He'd actually complimented her!

"You need to head to bed soon," he said. "It's getting late."

"I will. *Gut nacht.*" She wrapped up the bread as he disappeared toward the bedrooms. Her thoughts turned to Aaron as she began mixing macaroni and cheese for Ruth and her family. She had seen Aaron briefly on Wednesday, but they hadn't had a chance to talk. He had walked through the sitting room while she was checking in guests. He'd given her a wide smile that caused her heart to thump, and she longed to talk to him and see how he was doing.

Earlier in the week, Linda and Madeleine had discussed visiting Ruth and helping her family. Linda was not only eager to see Ruth, but she also hoped Aaron would be there. Maybe she could sneak in some time to visit with him as well.

She pushed the thought away as she slipped the macaroni and cheese into the oven. She knew she should be focused on helping the Ebersol family, not talking to Aaron. Yet she also knew she was developing feelings for him. She thought about him more often than she cared to admit. She knew she had to guard her heart. After all, Aaron wasn't baptized, and he never gave her any indication that he wanted to be a member of the Amish church. He also didn't live in Pennsylvania anymore. He was *English;* therefore, having a relationship with him was strictly forbidden.

And Linda was sure she'd never want to leave the church like Hannah had.

Aside from all those reasons, she knew Aaron would never be romantically interested in her. If he knew she had a disabling limp and scars on her legs, the result of the buggy accident that killed her parents, he would surely reject her. How could he possibly love a woman with those glaring flaws, the ones she worked so hard to keep hidden from the world? She was destined to be alone and take care of her uncle. That was God's plan for her, and she had to be satisfied with that. Wishing or hoping for anything more would not only set her up for heartache, but it would also be a sin.

As Linda cleaned up the kitchen counters, she let her thoughts wander to her conversations with Aaron. She hoped he could work things out with his *bruder;* she knew how much he wanted his family back. Yet she hoped he would gain even more — a new *freind.*

Linda relished the thought of being Aaron's *freind.* She knew she would be blessed if they were more than *freinds,* but she would be satisfied with friendship — even if he joined the church and married someone else.

Then she frowned. Linda knew she was lying to herself. She didn't like the idea of seeing Aaron marry someone else. And she knew one thing for certain — she didn't want him to go back to Missouri.

Lillian parked her scooter outside her grandparents' home. She climbed the steps and entered the house through the mudroom, and after kicking off her shoes and hanging up her coat, she made her way into the kitchen.

"Hi, *Mammi,*" she greeted her grandmother, who was setting the table for supper. "How was your day?"

"*Gut,* Lily." *Mammi* smiled at her and then grabbed an oven mitt from a nearby drawer. "How was yours?" She opened the oven and pulled out a baking tray with breaded pork chops.

"*Gut.* The *kinner* were very well behaved today, even on the playground. They were attentive during their lessons and did well on the schoolwork. I'm glad I stayed late to grade all their papers. Now I'm ahead for tomorrow." Lillian moved to a cabinet and brought out a stack of dishes. "I'll finish setting the table. Dinner smells *appeditlich.*"

"*Danki.* I have a surprise for you," *Mammi* said as she placed the pork chops on a platter. "I made your favorite dessert — carrot cake!"

Lillian placed the third plate at the head of the table, where her *grossdaadi* sat, and then turned toward her *grossmammi. Mammi* proudly held up the cake, which was iced with Lillian's favorite cream cheese frosting. A lump swelled in her throat as she remembered the conversation she'd had with her mother in the grocery store only a few days ago. *Mamm* had invited her over to visit the bed-and-breakfast and promised to make her a carrot cake. The memory of her *mutter*'s words overtook her mind, and her lip quivered.

Lillian had tried to put the conversation out of her mind, but she couldn't stop contemplating the desperation in her *mutter*'s eyes when she'd asked Lillian to visit her. After nearly two years, Lillian felt her determination to push her *mutter* away cracking.

"Lillian?" *Mammi*'s smile faded. *"Was iss letz?"*

"Nothing." Lillian cleared her throat while trying in vain to stop her threatening tears.

"I thought you loved carrot cake." *Mammi* looked at her.

"I do. *Danki* for making it." Lillian busied herself with folding napkins and placing them by the three dinner plates. An errant tear escaped her eye, and she quickly brushed it away with the back of her hand.

"Lily?" *Mammi* sidled up beside her and placed a hand on her shoulder. "Please talk to me."

Lillian sighed and sank into a chair as *Mammi* sat down beside her.

"Please tell me what's wrong," *Mammi* said as worry enveloped her expression.

"I didn't tell you that I saw *mei mamm* at the grocery store the other day," she said. "She was so *froh* to see me. She asked me again to visit her and see the bed-and-breakfast. Her *boppli* is due in the spring, and she told me she really wants me to be a part of the *boppli*'s life." Her voice was thin. "She seemed so genuine, and I felt different this time." She sniffed as her eyes filled with fresh tears.

"How did you feel different?" *Mammi* touched her hand.

"I didn't feel angry, like I normally do when I see her." She examined the blue tablecloth, afraid of disappointing her *mammi.* "Instead, I felt like I was tired of arguing. I actually wanted to talk to her. I wanted to listen to her, but I thought it would be best if I left." She held her breath in anticipation of her *grossmammi*'s angry words. *Mammi* had made it clear that she would never forgive Lillian's *mutter* for leaving the community and taking Lillian's siblings with her. *Mammi* had been heartbroken that two of her *grossdochdern* had left the Amish church.

"Lily," *Mammi* began, her voice calm. "Lily, please look at me."

Lillian lifted her gaze and was astonished by her *grossmammi*'s sympathetic expression.

"Lily, there's something I've wanted to tell you as soon as we had a *gut* chance to talk. I think now's the time. I know you'll be surprised by this, and it's not what most

196

people in our community would expect from Barbie Glick, but I'm not angry with your *mamm* anymore. The Lord has been changing my heart toward her and the decision she made. And I'm sorry I have encouraged you to be angry with her.

"It's okay if you want to forgive your *mamm.* I know she misses you, and she wants you to be a part of her life. I know you miss her, too, even though you've told me you don't need her. She's your *mamm,* and she'll always have a special place in your heart. If you want to visit her, then you should."

"*Danki.*" Lillian smiled as a weight lifted from her shoulders. "I'm so *froh* you understand how I feel and have changed how you feel about *mei mamm* too. I was afraid to tell you."

"*Ach, mei liewe,*" Mammi said. "I'm sorry you felt that way. But you don't need to be afraid to talk to me, even about your *mamm.* You can always tell me how you feel."

"*Danki.*" Lillian fingered the hem of her black apron and considered her *mutter.* "I don't think I'm ready to go see her yet, but in my heart, I know I will be ready soon."

"That's *gut.*" Mammi touched her cheek. "Don't rush your heart, but don't give up."

Lillian swiped away another tear and

smiled at her *grossmammi.* "I won't."

"Now why don't you finish setting the table while I put the boiled potatoes in a bowl?" *Mammi* stood and crossed to the counter. "*Daadi* will be in here soon and you know he likes to have supper on time."

Lillian considered her grandparents as she gathered utensils for their meal. She was so grateful they had taken her in when her *mutter* left the community to start a new life with Trey at the bed-and-breakfast. Lillian knew in her heart that she belonged in the Amish community. For the first time since moving into this house, however, she realized that she could be Amish but still make a place in her life for her *mutter.*

NINE

The following afternoon, Aaron looked up from cutting a piece of wood. He'd heard the van pulling into the driveway on the opposite side of his parents' house. Two Amish women climbed from the back, one carrying a covered dish and the other balancing both a covered dish and a basket. Their arrival made him smile about how thoughtful and generous the community had been to his parents.

Aaron also wondered what delicious food was tucked away in the serving platters and basket the women carried toward the house. He hoped he'd have the opportunity to sample some of it. He'd enjoyed eating authentic Amish dishes since he'd returned to Pennsylvania. The home-cooked meals certainly beat the frozen pizza and fast food he'd grown accustomed to eating in Missouri.

As the women walked to the front porch,

the shorter of the two glanced up, and his breath caught when he recognized Linda. He and Manny were working where the two women couldn't readily see them, so Aaron took his time staring. Linda looked beautiful in her black winter coat, talking and laughing with the other woman, who was several inches taller than Linda.

When Becky met them at the door, the three women stood outside a moment and greeted one another. Though she still didn't see him, Linda was facing his way, and Aaron was captivated by her smile. Even from a distance, he could tell her eyes were sparkling and she was glowing like an angel.

How had he not noticed her when they were teenagers?

"What are you looking at?" Manny's question yanked Aaron back from his thoughts.

"Huh?" Embarrassed, Aaron cleared his throat and rounded the sawhorse so his back was to the front porch. "Nothing, nothing." He pointed toward the wood. "Let's finish cutting this wood."

"Oh, no." Manny grinned. "You were staring at those *maed*." He pointed toward the porch. "Which one do you like?"

"Stop pointing." Aaron gritted his teeth. "They'll see us talking about them."

"So who is it?" Manny asked, wagging his

200

eyebrows. "You like Linda Zook? Or is it Madeleine Miller?"

"I don't know Madeleine." Aaron glanced over his shoulder and saw Linda and Madeleine walking into the house. He turned his attention back to the stack of wood he'd purchased to repair the screened-in back porch. He'd decided he might as well take care of everything needed out there, especially before any snowfall. His *dat* and Solomon had been too busy to get to it, and that wouldn't change anytime soon.

"So it's Linda." Manny's voice was full of amusement.

"I don't really know her." Aaron began marking a piece of wood. "I just talk to her at the bed-and-breakfast. She works there part-time. We grew up together."

"Were you *freinden* with her when you were *kinner*?"

Aaron shrugged. "I already said that I didn't really know her."

"Does that mean you two reconnected?"

Aaron analyzed his nephew's smile. "Why are you enjoying this so much?"

"I don't know." Manny picked up a container of screws. "I just think it's neat that you reconnected with an old *freind.* It's like a reunion, right?"

"We weren't exactly friends. I just knew

who she was." *But I didn't notice her because I was an immature and out-of-control teen.* "All right. Let's get started replacing those rotten rails." He carried the lumber around to the back porch while Manny brought the hammer and nails.

"Did you go to singings and youth group when you were a teenager?" Manny asked as he removed the first of the old posts.

"*Ya,* I did." Aaron took down the railing at the far end of the porch. "I was more focused on getting into mischief than participating with the group. I don't recommend you do that. Enjoy your time with your friends. You're only young once."

"*Ya,* I know. *Mei dat* has told me that more than once."

"Really?" Aaron's eyebrows soared toward his hairline. "Your *dat* told you to enjoy being young?"

"He said he doesn't regret getting married young, but he had no idea how many responsibilities he'd have until they moved into their *haus.*" Manny tossed another rotting post onto the pile. "He warned me not to jump into marriage too quickly."

"Are you thinking of proposing to Nancy?"

Manny shrugged and kept his eyes on the post in front of him. "I've thought about it,

202

but I don't think I'm ready. I think we should be at least twenty."

"That's a *gut* plan."

"Do you want to get married someday?" Manny asked.

"Sure I do. When the time is right, I suppose." Aaron shrugged off the question even though the answer was truly a resounding yes. He just didn't know when or how it could happen for him. He again wondered why Linda wasn't married. Had she ever been in love? He knew he hadn't, but he longed for a home and a family with whom to share his life.

"I'll have enough money saved up to ask Nancy next year," Manny said. "I guess we'll see what the Lord has in store for us. It's best to rely on him."

"*Ya,* that's very true." Aaron wondered what the Lord had in store for him as well.

"I'm so *froh* you came by today," Becky said as Linda and Madeleine followed her into the kitchen. "I know Ruth will be thrilled to see you."

"How's she doing?" Linda asked as she placed the basket and covered dish on the table.

"She's doing better." Becky's smile faded. "Jonas thinks having Aaron back here has helped Ruth. He says she isn't as agitated, and I have noticed a change in her too. She hasn't been quite as frustrated when she talks, and she's even talking more. But at the same time, I'm not certain it's a *gut* thing Aaron is back."

When she heard Aaron's name, Linda's heart turned over in her chest and the tips of her ears heated.

"What do you mean?" Madeleine asked as she placed her covered dish beside Linda's. "Ruth talked about him constantly even before she had the stroke. She always worried about him and wondered if he was safe and healthy. She was heartsick over missing him. After the stroke, she was adamant about seeing him again. I think it's a blessing that he returned. How could it be a bad thing?"

Becky shook her head and crossed her arms over her black apron. "Solomon and I have talked about this, and we both agree that Aaron is getting Ruth's hopes up that he's going to stay. He's not going to stay. Instead, he'll visit just long enough to make her *froh* and then go back to his life in Missouri and not return for another seventeen years."

Linda fiddled with her apron. "I hope that's not true," she said softly while studying her hands. "I know he's been excited about meeting his nieces and nephews. I think he may consider staying. He told me he's *froh* that he's connected with his family again."

"You've spoken to him?" Becky asked.

Linda met her questioning gaze and nodded. "*Ya,* I've talked to him quite a bit. He's staying at Hannah's bed-and-breakfast, and I'm working there part-time to help her out. She has to rest more since her *boppli* is due in the spring."

"If his family meant so much to him, then why did he stay away all these years?" Becky asked. "He left and never looked back. He claims he wrote letters to Ruth, but she never got any."

"But he's back now when his *mamm* needs him," Linda said. Maybe it wasn't a good idea to get into a debate about the letters.

Becky shook her head. "Solomon is very upset. Aaron caused a lot of pain when he left. Ruth cried for months, and she never got over that pain of losing him. Now he's back, and she's *froh.* But her heart will break when he leaves again, and she's in such a fragile state that we're afraid she may not be able to survive another heartache. Solomon thinks it may have been better if

Aaron never returned. If he'd stayed away, it would have saved Ruth the heartache and disappointment she's going to feel from losing him again."

"I don't think Solomon's right," Madeleine said, shaking her head as she looked out one of the kitchen windows. "I think God sent him home when Ruth needed him."

"Ya," Linda chimed in. "There's a reason he came back now. If he didn't love his parents, then he wouldn't have come back at all."

"I agree with you, Linda. He came when Ruth needed him, which proves he loves his family." Madeleine gestured toward the window she'd been looking through. "Is that Aaron working outside with Manny?"

"Ya, he's been working on the *haus."* Becky motioned toward the front of the house. "I'm sure you noticed the ramp. He built that last week and finished it up on Monday. He and Manny are working on the back porch now. They're replacing the posts and railing and then they're going to build another ramp."

"That's wonderful." Madeleine turned toward Linda. "Ruth will appreciate that."

"Ya, she will," Linda agreed. "I think it's fantastic that he's using his talents to help

his family."

"I do too. It's nice that he's spending time with Manny and teaching him construction," Madeleine said. "I'm sure Manny is enjoying getting to know his *onkel.*"

Becky grimaced. "They have been working together quite a bit. In fact, Manny has been working with Aaron every day since they started these projects. I can tell he's getting attached to his *onkel.* That's another reason it would be terrible if Aaron left again. I know Ruth and Jonas are enjoying having their family all together again after so long. But Aaron won't stay. He built a business in Missouri that he'll go back to. He's going to hurt his parents and my *kinner.*"

Linda's hands trembled as she contemplated Becky's negative words. *I pray you're wrong about Aaron!*

"He could open a construction business here," Madeleine said. "I can tell he has talent. That's a nice ramp out front."

"Ya." Linda moved to the doorway to the mudroom and looked through the windowed door to the back porch. She could see Aaron and Manny taking down the old posts and rails. "Look at them working together."

It warmed Linda's heart to see Manny

learning so much from his *onkel.* She knew it meant a lot to Aaron too. As she watched Aaron, she found herself drawn to his confidence and skill. She couldn't look away, taking in his beautiful blond curls as they swayed in the breeze. She intently watched how he moved his tall, muscular body with grace. He turned toward Manny and said something that caused them both to laugh. She imagined the sound of the warm laugh she already knew as Aaron's as she observed him enjoy the moment with his nephew.

"What did you bring, Linda?"

"What?" Linda spun and found Becky looking at her. "I'm sorry. I didn't hear what you said."

"I saw the dish and the basket, and I was wondering what you brought," Becky said.

"Oh, I made bread and baked macaroni and cheese. I hope Ruth likes it."

"She will. *Danki.*" Becky carried one of the two covered dishes to the refrigerator, and placed it on the bottom shelf. "We appreciate the community's help so much."

"That's what I love most about the Amish," Madeleine said as she handed Becky the second dish. "I love how we all pitch in together and help each other. I'm so eager to start baptism classes in the spring."

"Are you enjoying living like an Amish person?" Linda asked.

"*Ya,* I am. I sold my pickup truck and turned off my cell phone, and I don't miss them. It's so refreshing to be immersed in the community and the culture." Madeleine pushed the ties to her prayer covering over her shoulders. "I know I made the right decision. I feel so at home here."

"How is Saul?" Linda asked.

"He's doing well." Madeleine's smile was wide. "We're enjoying getting to know each other better. He's such a *wunderbaar* man. I'm so thankful our paths crossed. I've never been this *froh* before."

"That's *gut,*" Linda said. "I know you enjoy spending time with Emma too."

"*Ya,* I do. She's such a sweet *maedel.*" Madeleine looked at Becky. "What can we do for you?" Madeleine asked. "We've brought most of what you'll need for supper, so there's not a lot of cooking to do. Can we help you clean or do laundry?"

"Oh, you can just visit with Ruth," Becky said. "I don't expect you to work."

"We came to help," Linda insisted. "Let us do something for you."

Madeleine glanced around the kitchen.

"How about we clean?"

Becky laughed. "Are you saying the kitchen is dirty?"

"No." Madeleine chuckled. "It's not dirty, but we can always clean the floor, right?"

"That's a *gut* idea," Linda chimed in. "Let's go visit with Ruth, and then I can sweep and dust and you can clean the kitchen. Sound *gut*?"

"Ya" Madeleine nodded.

"Fine, fine. It's true that some of the women who've been coming to help couldn't make it this week, and the girls and I had to do some cleaning at our house. If you want to clean, then I'm not going to tell you that you can't." Becky started toward the family room and motioned for them to follow. "Let's go see Ruth. I think I heard her nurse take her in there from the bedroom while we were talking."

They found Ruth sitting in a chair in the family room. She was moving her left leg up and down while wearing ankle weights. When she saw them in the doorway, she smiled.

"You have visitors, *Mamm,*" Becky said. "Look who came to see you. And they brought supper too."

"Ma-d . . ." Ruth tried to pronounce Madeleine's name, but the word wasn't clear. "L-linda! *K-k-kumm!*"

Anguish consumed Linda as Ruth struggled to say their names. She'd hoped Ruth would have been further along in her recovery.

"If it's okay with your nurse, Ruth, we'll let you three visit." The nurse readily agreed and Becky headed back into the kitchen. The nurse excused herself while Linda and Madeleine pulled their chairs up beside Ruth's.

"How are you?" Linda asked as she touched Ruth's hand.

"G-gut." Ruth gave her a lopsided smile. "A-a-aron h-here."

"I know." Linda's smile widened. "That is a blessing."

"We miss you at the hotel," Madeleine began. "I have some funny stories to share."

"Oh?" Ruth asked with a lopsided smile.

Madeleine and Linda shared stories about the hotel, laughing until the nurse returned and asked Ruth to continue her therapy.

Linda and Madeleine gathered cleaning supplies from Becky and, as Linda worked, she lost herself in thoughts of Ruth and her recovery. She hoped Ruth would be able to walk soon. She hated to think she could be restricted to a wheelchair for the rest of her life.

■ ■ ■ ■

Aaron stepped back from the porch and admired their work. All the rails and posts had been replaced. "Looks *gut.* We can stain it all tomorrow." He smiled at his nephew. "You make a *gut* assistant."

"Just *gut*?" Manny's expression feigned irritation. "You mean to tell me you have a better assistant than me?"

"Maybe I do." Aaron chuckled. "Are you hungry?" He glanced at his watch. "It's not suppertime yet, but I'm starved after all that effort."

"I'm starved too." Manny picked up a hammer.

"We can go get a snack and then clean up these tools and supplies." Aaron started for the mudroom door. Although he was hungry, he had an ulterior motive for wanting to go into the house — he longed to see Linda before she left. He'd been listening, but he hadn't heard any outside doors opening or closing or anyone calling good-bye. He hoped she was planning to stay for supper so they could possibly eat together. They hadn't had a chance to talk much lately at the bed-and-breakfast.

Aaron stepped into the mudroom and

heard women talking in the kitchen. He pulled off his work boots, set them under the bench, then shucked his coat and hung it on a peg.

He stood in the wide doorway for a moment and watched Linda as she wiped a counter and talked to Becky and Madeleine. He couldn't pull his gaze away from her. He'd thought she looked lovely when he'd seen her outside with her coat on, but she was stunningly beautiful in her deep-purple dress. The color complemented her fair skin, dark hair, and chocolate-brown eyes. He knew he had to walk into the room, but he felt stuck there, enjoying the view.

Linda suddenly looked his way and met his gaze. Her rosy lips turned up in a tentative smile, and he saw a pink blush spreading across her high cheekbones. He smiled back at her and wished he could pull her into the family room and talk to her alone. He missed their conversations. He hadn't had a nice, long talk with her in nearly a week, and he was craving some time alone to tell her . . . everything.

Linda watched him, and she tilted her head in question. He wondered what she was thinking while she stared back at him.

Manny moved past Aaron and into the kitchen. "Hi," he said to the women. "Is there anything to eat?"

"We're going to start preparing supper now," Becky said while pulling some bowls out of the cabinets. "You can have a small snack, but I don't want you to ruin your appetites."

"Did you see how hard we worked, *Mamm*?" Manny gestured toward the back of the house. "*Onkel* Aaron and I replaced all the posts and rails on back porch. We worked up an appetite, right, *Onkel* Aaron?"

"I can wait." Aaron stepped into the kitchen, still looking at Linda. "I'm sure it won't be long before supper is ready since Linda and Madeleine brought food." He forced himself to look at Madeleine. "We, uh, saw you when you arrived. Manny told me who you are. I'm Aaron."

"Nice to meet you, Aaron," Madeline said.

Manny frowned. "Outside you said you were starved."

Aaron smiled at Becky. "I don't want to cause your *mamm* any trouble."

Before Becky could answer, Linda turned to her. "I have an idea for a little snack. Can they have some *brot*? I brought two loaves. I'll pull one out for Manny and Aaron."

Becky paused, then started pulling utensils out of a drawer. "*Ya,* that would be fine."

"Let me help you set the table." Madeleine crossed the kitchen and pulled glasses out of the cabinet.

Linda removed the bread from the basket and found a container of butter. "I made this last night, but it should still be fresh."

"I'll help you." Aaron grabbed a knife from the drain board by the sink and handed it to Linda. He stood so close to her that he could smell the scent of lilac from beneath her prayer covering.

"Danki." Linda nearly whispered her response, and he wondered if she was enjoying being close to him as much as he enjoyed being close to her.

Only the eyes of everyone else in the room made him take a step back.

Linda cut four slices of bread and buttered them before handing two to Aaron and two to Manny.

"Danki." As soon as Aaron swallowed his first bite, he nodded. "It's almost as *gut* as your *kichlin.*"

Linda smiled. "I'm glad you like it. I also made baked macaroni and cheese, and Madeleine brought a tuna casserole."

"That sounds fantastic," Aaron said as he took another bite.

"Linda, you and Madeleine need to stay

for supper," Becky said. "We have plenty of food."

"Oh, I can't stay," Linda said. "I have to cook for my *onkel.* I don't want him to be upset. He expects supper promptly at six."

"And I'm making supper for Saul and Emma tonight, so I have to get going too. What time is it?" Madeleine asked.

"It's four forty-five," Manny said when he glanced at the kitchen clock. "This *brot* is amazing. *Danki,* Linda."

"You're welcome."

"Our ride will be here soon then," Madeleine said. "I asked him to be back by five."

Aaron was still looking at Linda, thinking about what she had just revealed. "Really? Your *onkel* gets upset if you're late?" he said, nearly whispering.

Linda nodded but didn't explain. Then she seemed to be avoiding his gaze. Did the subject upset her? He felt the need to find out why she didn't want to talk about her uncle. If he drove her home, he'd have time to talk to her alone. Maybe then he could find out what was going on with her uncle.

"I'll take you home," Aaron said.

Linda shook her head. "You don't need to do that. Madeleine's driver is coming back to get us soon enough for me to get home on time. I don't want you to go out of your way."

"No, I insist." He slid his cell phone from his pocket. "You can call and cancel your ride. There's no need for you to spend that money when I can take you for free."

"Are you sure?" Linda's eyes seemed to search his.

"Of course I am. You spent the afternoon helping *mei mamm.* You don't need to spend money paying a driver." He held out the phone. "Cancel your ride. I'll take you both home."

"That would be nice. Thank you." Madeleine took the phone from him and made the call.

"Danki," Linda said.

She continued to study him, and he wished he could read her thoughts. Was she uncomfortable with his offer? Or did she feel something deeper for him, the same feelings that had been growing inside him? He hoped the latter was the case.

"Thank you, Aaron." Madeleine handed him the phone after she was finished talking to the driver.

"Maybe we'd better get going now." Linda hugged Becky. "It was so *gut* seeing you. We'll come again soon."

"Next time you'll stay for supper," Becky

said. "I won't take no for an answer. In fact, you can bring Reuben with you, and he can join us too."

"*Danki.*" Linda turned to Aaron. "I'm going to go say good-bye to your *mamm.* She's in the family room doing some more exercises."

"I will too," Madeleine said. "We'll be ready to go in a few minutes."

"Take your time." Aaron watched them disappear into the family room.

"I'm going to call the girls over here. They've been doing their chores." Becky stepped into the mudroom and pulled on her coat.

Once Becky was gone, Manny sidled up to Aaron. "I think she likes you too."

"What?" Aaron asked with bewilderment.

"Linda," Manny said with assurance in his voice. "I think she likes you too. She stares at you the same way you stare at her."

"You think so?" Aaron hated how desperate and needy he sounded, but he couldn't help it. Did she care for him the same way he cared for her?

Manny nodded. "*Ya,* I think so. But you're not baptized, so she can't —"

"Okay," Madeleine announced as she stepped into the kitchen. "We're ready to go."

"You can head out to the truck." Aaron made a sweeping gesture toward the back door. "It's unlocked. I'll be right there."

Madeleine and Linda walked past him, grabbed their coats from the pegs on the wall in the mudroom, and left.

Madeleine had interrupted Manny, but Aaron knew what he was going to say. Aaron couldn't even consider dating Linda since he wasn't a baptized member of the church. He didn't live in Pennsylvania anymore, either. Why was his heart jumping to conclusions that didn't make logical sense? Is that what love did to a man? Did love give men crazy notions, such as dreaming about dating an Amish woman when the guy wasn't even Amish anymore?

"I'll come back after I drop them off, and I'll help you clean up the mess outside," Aaron told Manny as he pulled on his coat.

"Don't worry about that. Just enjoy your ride." Manny winked at him, and Aaron resisted the urge to scold his nephew. He was grateful Madeleine and Linda hadn't seen Manny's obvious gesture.

"No, I'll be back," Aaron said. "I don't feel right leaving this mess for you." He smiled. "Besides, I know you can't clean it all up alone. You can't handle it without me."

Manny crossed his arms over his chest. "Is that so? That sounds like a challenge. I'm sure I can handle it just fine."

Aaron shrugged. "I guess we'll see about that. See you soon." He grinned at his nephew and sauntered out the door.

Ten

Linda climbed into the front passenger seat of Aaron's big, fancy pickup truck. She'd never been in a truck that had four doors. She settled in and buckled her seatbelt as Madeleine climbed into the seat behind her.

"I think Ruth's color was better this time," Madeleine said as she snapped her seatbelt together. "Her complexion was brighter, and she actually looked *froh.* I think having Aaron home has made her happier."

"Ya." Linda smoothed her hands down her coat and touched her prayer covering. She had never before worried about her appearance, but she was suddenly self-conscious. Did that have something to do with Aaron's presence?

"I don't understand why Solomon and Becky aren't happy that Aaron is home," Madeleine continued. "I think it's a blessing for their family that he came back."

"I agree," Linda said. *And it's a blessing*

for me also. The thought rocked her to her core. She had to suppress her feelings for Aaron or he would destroy her heart when he went back to his life in Missouri. She couldn't let her feelings for him overshadow her judgment. He wasn't Amish. She would be shunned if she let their relationship progress from friendship.

Linda heard the screened-in porch door slam and saw Aaron walking toward the truck. Her stomach flip-flopped as he climbed into the driver's seat beside her.

"All right," he said as he jammed the key in the ignition and turned it. The truck's loud engine roared to life. "Where am I headed?"

Linda gnawed her lower lip. She'd hoped he would drop Madeleine off first, but she didn't know how to suggest it without sounding overly eager to spend time with him.

"I think I live the closest," Madeleine said from the backseat. "Just go down this road and turn left." She explained how to get to her house, and Linda inwardly breathed a sigh of relief.

"Oh, you live by Saul Beiler," Aaron said while looking in the rearview mirror at Madeleine.

"That's right. My grandparents owned all

that land years ago and sold most of it to Saul. I moved into their house, which is at the front of the property."

While Aaron drove to Madeleine's house, she explained that her grandparents were Amish and she inherited their house when they died. She also shared how excited she was to join the baptism class in the spring and be baptized in the fall.

"So your grandparents were Amish, but your mother left the community?" Aaron asked with interest.

"Yes, that's right," Madeleine said. "I was looking for a place to make a new start, and I felt like God led me here. I always enjoyed visiting my grandparents when I was a child, so it made sense to come back here again."

"That's interesting," Aaron said slowly, as if he were contemplating her words. "God sure knows what we need before we do, doesn't he?"

"Oh, yes," Madeleine said. "I agree. I just felt something special when I came back, you know?"

As Madeleine continued to discuss her love for the community, Linda was thankful Madeleine was talkative. She found herself wondering what she would say to Aaron once they were alone, even though she had been looking forward to being alone with him. Suddenly, Linda began doubting her ability to hold a conversation with him. All her insecurities rained down on her, and she felt inadequate sitting next to Aaron in his fancy truck while he talked easily to Madeleine. Perhaps, she thought, she should've asked if Aaron could take her home first so she could avoid any awkward silence when they were alone.

Aaron steered the truck into Madeleine's driveway and stopped.

"Thank you for the ride," she said as she pushed open her door. "It was nice meeting you, Aaron."

"Thank you for helping my parents," Aaron said.

"You're welcome. Your *mamm* is a dear friend to me," Madeleine said.

"I'll see you at work," Linda said.

"Okay. Good-bye!" Madeleine waved before turning for her back porch.

"Madeleine has had an interesting life," Aaron said as he backed the truck out of her driveway.

"*Ya,* she has," Linda agreed as she smoothed her hands over her coat again.

"She went from serving in the military to wanting to be Amish," he said. "That's a real change."

"*Ya,* it is." Linda kept her eyes focused on

the road ahead of them, but she was aware of Aaron's glances toward her whenever he spoke. "She said she felt a connection to the community when she came here. She's also very close to Saul and his *dochder,* Emma."

"That's nice." Aaron turned right onto the main road. "I know Saul has been through a lot."

"That's true. I have a feeling he is going to ask Madeleine to marry him after she joins the church. They get along very well."

"I'm glad to hear that. I'm sure Saul is happy to find love after what happened with Annie." Aaron drummed the steering wheel. "So how do I get to your place from here?"

Linda gave him directions and then tried to think of something else to say. "The ramp you built is very nice. And you did a fantastic job repairing the back porch."

"Thanks." He gave her another sideways glance. "I'm really having a good time with Manny. He's a real character. We've had some good talks about life."

"That's *wunderbaar.*" She turned toward him and smiled. "I'm so *froh* to hear that. I told you your family would be thrilled to get to know you."

He nodded. "You were right. It's been a lot of fun."

225

"I heard you're going to put a ramp at the back of the *haus* too," she said. "Are you planning to do more projects for Ruth?"

"I'm also going to work on the downstairs bathroom," he explained as he turned onto another street. "I want to put up a couple of safety bars and install a walk-in shower. That way she's less likely to slip in the bathroom. I was afraid *mei dat* would think it was too modern, but he agreed. I think he appreciates the work I'm doing. He sees that *mei mamm*'s safety is the most important issue, not how modern the changes are. He insisted the bishop would be fine with it since the work is for safety purposes. *Dat* says he's just really grateful for my help."

"I'm certain he is," Linda said. "Your *mamm* is so *froh* that you're here. The first thing she said to me today was that you were back. She had tears in her eyes."

"Danki," he said quietly.

"Gern gschehne," Linda said. "You're a blessing to your family." She felt her cheeks burn as she voiced the compliment, but she couldn't stop it from jumping from her lips. She realized that even though she'd been worried about talking to him, the conversation was flowing between them like a babbling brook.

He looked over at her, and his eyes

sparkled with warmth and affection. "That means a lot."

She nodded and turned toward the passenger window. Her body prickled with insecurity. Why couldn't she be comfortable in her own skin?

"I went to see the bishop just as you suggested." He steered the truck onto the road leading to her cousin's farm.

"You did?" She faced him, forgetting her self-doubt. "What happened?"

"It went really well. I apologized, and he told me I didn't need to apologize because I'd already been forgiven." He kept his eyes trained on the road but slowed when they reached the driveway leading to the larger house. "We had a really nice conversation, and I even stayed for supper."

"That's fantastic!" Linda clapped her hands together. "I'm so *froh* for you. I told you it would go well. Does it make you feel better knowing that Elmer never resented you?"

He nodded. "*Ya*, it does. I actually felt a weight lift off my shoulders right away. You were right, Linda. You've been right about a lot of things."

She quickly let him know that she and her *onkel* lived in the smaller house in back, and Aaron brought the truck to a stop there.

Then he turned in his seat and faced her. The intensity in his eyes caused her pulse to accelerate and beat erratically. She'd never felt such an attraction to anyone before, and it both excited and terrified her all at once. Was she ready for this? Was she prepared to give her heart away to this man?

He wasn't even Amish!

"I was thinking about you the other day while I was working on the ramp," he said. "I realized that, though we grew up together, I never got to know you. Why didn't I ever see you at singings when we were young?"

Linda's mouth dried and her hands trembled. She wasn't sure how to handle this sudden and intense emotion she felt sparking between them. "I never went to singings."

He turned the ignition key, and the engine went dead, filling the truck with silence. She wondered if he could hear her heart thumping.

"Why didn't you go to singings?" he asked.

She shrugged and looked out at the cottage. "I guess I never felt like I belonged there. I wasn't like the other *kinner.*"

"What do you mean?"

"I didn't have parents or a family like the other *kinner.* I just kept to myself a lot, I

228

guess." She inspected the hem of her coat to avoid his kind eyes. "I've realized that, after I lost my parents, I retreated inwardly to protect myself from more heartache. My shyness was like a crutch and it kept me from being hurt again."

"I understand."

She looked up at him and was in awe of the gentleness in his expression. "You do?"

"I guess I've done the same thing since I left the community," he explained. "I've stayed by myself all these years. I haven't really dated anyone in Missouri, and I haven't even joined a church. I guess I subconsciously thought that if I stayed alone I wouldn't get hurt. But at the same time, I'm hurting myself by staying alone. It's a paradox."

"I've never dated anyone," she said the words softly, embarrassed by the revelation.

"You've never dated anyone?" His words were kind, not insulting.

She shook her head.

"I'm surprised," he said, resting his elbow on the steering wheel.

"Why are you surprised?"

"You're so kind and *schee.*"

"You think I'm *schee*?" She had to be dreaming or she'd heard him wrong. No one had ever called her pretty before.

"Of course I do." Aaron looked startled. "Why wouldn't I think that?"

She was dumbfounded, unable to speak for a moment.

"I thought you were married when I first met you."

"No, I've never . . ." She motioned toward the small house. "I just live with *mei onkel.*" She pointed toward the large farmhouse behind the truck. "I lived there with my parents until they died. My cousin got the *haus* after my parents were gone, and I moved into the *daadi haus* with *mei onkel* and *aenti.* I'm convinced this is God's plan for me. I'm called to take care of *mei onkel,* and I'm satisfied with that."

"You say you're satisfied, but are you really *froh*?" His eyes searched hers for the truth.

She hesitated. *"Ya,"* she finally said.

"No, you're not. You hesitated before you responded." His expression challenged her. "Tell me the truth, Linda. Do you dream of something more?"

"I don't know." She picked at a piece of lint on her coat. "I suppose every *maedel* dreams of having a family, but I'm satisfied with my life. I have everything I need, so why would I even think of asking for more? I don't want to be ungrateful and say that I want more."

Aaron shook his head and grimaced. "Don't say that. God wants for you to be *froh*. Tell me the truth now — are you *froh* with your *onkel*?"

She was astonished by his concern for her. "I suppose I am."

"You deserve happiness. You lost your parents, but you don't have to be alone."

She swallowed as a lump appeared in her throat. "And you're worthy of your family, Aaron."

"Thank you." He reached over and placed his hand on hers. "*Danki* for helping *mei mamm* today. It means a lot to me."

Aaron's touch was warm and comforting, and the gesture touched her deep in her soul. Linda suddenly felt the urge to flee. She had to exit the truck before she lost her heart to this wonderful man.

"I should go," she said. "As I said, *mei on-kel* isn't patient when it comes to his supper. *Gut nacht.*"

Aaron hesitated, as if he wanted to say more. But he only said, "I'll see you at the bed-and-breakfast."

"*Danki* for the ride." She hopped out of the truck, shut the door, and hurried up the porch steps. She turned and watched him back out of the driveway, wondering what had just happened. Something deep and meaningful had passed between them. What did it mean?

Am I in love with Aaron Ebersol?

She gasped at the question. What did she know about love? And how could she develop feelings for this man who wasn't even a member of her community? This was certainly a sin! She could be shunned if anyone found out what she was feeling. She had to find a way to guard her heart before it was too late.

Aaron waved and the horn beeped as the truck rumbled down the street.

Onkel Reuben opened the front door. "Linda? Where have you been? I'm starving. Are you going to make supper?"

"Ya, ya." She stepped into the house and hung up her coat. "I'll start it right now."

As she moved into the kitchen, her shoulders hunched and her left leg favored her right one, giving her the familiar slight limp. Aaron's words echoed through her mind. He thought she was pretty and he believed she deserved a family of her own. Was he right? Did she deserve those things? The questions swirled through her mind as she pulled out a pot and filled it with water for noodles.

She wasn't sure if she believed she deserved them, but she did know one thing for certain — she liked how Aaron made her feel when they were together. She felt attractive and valuable as a person when he was around. But she couldn't figure out why he had that effect on her. What did it mean?

She didn't know what it meant, but she felt something change inside her. For the first time in her life, she began to wonder if she was worthy of love. And the thought made her smile.

Aaron grinned as he parked his truck in his parents' driveway. He was consumed with thoughts of Linda. And he was happy, truly happy, for the first time in a long time. He was not only thrilled with the strides he was making reconnecting with his family, but he was also enjoying getting to know Linda. He wondered why she was so stunned when he told her he had assumed she was married when he'd first seen her.

Did she truly believe she wasn't attractive or deserving of a family? He was stuck on this detail. The Amish women he'd known were never prideful, but Linda seemed to be unusually humble, well beyond mere shyness, almost self-effacing. Why was she so meek? He longed to know her better and find out what had broken down her spirit and self-worth.

And he still wondered about her uncle being upset with her if she was late with his supper. Linda said it was her calling to care for him, but she was, after all, a grown woman.

He climbed from the truck and found his father on the back porch.

"Aaron," *Dat* said. "I was hoping Manny was correct that you planned to come back. Join us for supper. I think they've started without us. I told Manny to tell them I was held up with one of the cows."

"Thank you," Aaron said as he climbed up the porch steps. He glanced around their workspace and saw that it was clean. "I was going to help Manny clean up the mess, but I see he took care of it."

"I helped him clean it up." *Dat* patted Aaron's shoulder. "You and Manny did a great job on the porch. *Danki* for fixing it. I'd wanted to do that for years but never seemed to have the time."

"I'm happy to help."

In the house they found his mother and brother's family already seated around the kitchen table. They hung up their coats on pegs in the mudroom and stepped into the kitchen.

Manny greeted Aaron with a smile. "*Daadi*

and I finished picking up outside, so you don't need to worry about that. I told you I didn't need your help."

"Thank you. I appreciate that." Aaron turned to Becky. "And thank you, Becky, for supper." She nodded in return, but with a frown. Aaron slipped into an empty seat next to Katie and bowed his head in silent prayer. He covered his plate with baked macaroni and cheese, tuna casserole, and a piece of bread before digging in.

Conversations swirled around him. The women were discussing sewing projects and their plans for the next day. Aaron glanced across the table, and his brother glowered in response. Obviously, neither Solomon nor Becky had softened. Aaron's stomach clenched as he remembered last week's conversation with his brother. He wondered how he could possibly repair their broken relationship, and Linda's positive words echoed through his mind. She had said he was a blessing to his family, and he had to believe that God would help him win his brother's friendship again. He was so thankful for Linda and her support.

"Aaron," his father began from the far end of the table, "Manny was telling me more about your plans. As I said earlier, the work on the ramp and back porch turned out well. You both did a *gut* job. Of course, Junior and I helped a little, right, Junior?"

"Right!" Junior said, as soon as he swallowed.

"Danki." Aaron buttered another piece of bread. "Manny has been a fantastic main helper."

"Helper?" Manny scowled. "I'm more than a helper."

Aaron grinned. "You'll work your way up. Everyone has to start at the bottom."

Dat chuckled. "You know he's only teasing you, Manny. I know Aaron appreciates your help."

"Of course I do. In fact, I appreciate you so much that I'll let you help me stain the porch starting tomorrow." Aaron bit into the bread as his father chuckled again. He glanced over at Solomon and found him frowning at his plate.

"Are we going to start on the bathroom after we finish the back porch?" Manny asked while scooping macaroni onto his spoon. "I can't wait to start on that. I've never done that kind of work."

"Ya, that's the plan." Aaron turned to his father. "As long as that's okay with your *daadi."* He looked at Solomon. "And your *dat,* of course. I know he depends on your help around the farm."

Solomon kept his eyes trained on his plate.

"It sounds *gut* to me." *Dat* looked at Solomon. "How about you, Solomon?"

Solomon responded with a curt nod. "As long as your other work gets done too."

Aaron scowled. He looked over at Becky, who apparently had been listening. She was frowning as well and slightly shaking her head. He wondered if she had witnessed Solomon's reaction to him. She seemed to share Solomon's aversion toward him. How could he prove to them that his feelings for the family were genuine?

"Have you worked on a lot of bathrooms?" Manny asked between bites of tuna casserole. "I've always wanted to learn more about plumbing."

"Yes, I have." Aaron helped himself to another piece of bread from the loaf. "I once worked on a home that had six bathrooms."

"Six?" Katie gasped from the chair beside him. "Why would anyone have six bathrooms?"

"That's *gegisch,*" Junior chimed in. "It sounds so wasteful."

"It would be nice, wouldn't it?" Ruthie Joy asked. "We would all have our own bathroom, and no one would ever have to wait."

"Unless you had company over," Katie countered. "Then you'd have to share a bathroom."

"But it would be nice to have six bathrooms when we had church at our *haus*. The line to wait would be much shorter," *Dat* said.

Everyone laughed, except for Solomon. He lifted his glass and sipped his water while keeping his eyes focused on his mostly uneaten food. Aaron tried to ignore the hurt that coursed through him when his brother wouldn't even look at him. Aaron hated feeling invisible in his brother's presence.

"Tell us more about that *haus*, *Onkel* Aaron," Katie said. "If it had six bathrooms, then how many bedrooms did it have?"

"This *haus* was so big that it had ten bedrooms," Aaron told her.

All the children gasped this time, and he enjoyed having his nieces' and nephews' attention and interest. He shared more interesting details about the house and other construction projects for the remainder of the meal.

After dessert, Becky and the girls began to clean up and Aaron's father moved to his mother's wheelchair.

"Are you ready to get your bath? I think I heard your evening aide slip in the front

238

door," *Dat* said to his *mamm.*

"*Ya.*" *Mamm* held her hand out to Aaron. "*K-kumm* b-back."

"I will." Aaron kissed her cheek. "*Danki* for supper."

"*Gut nacht,*" his father said before shaking his hand. "See you tomorrow."

"I'm going out to check on the animals." Solomon stood. "Manny and Junior, are you coming?"

"*Ya, Dat.*" Junior hopped up from his seat. "See you tomorrow, *Onkel!*" He rushed toward the mudroom and pulled on his coat.

"Get plenty of rest, *Onkel.*" Manny stood. "We're going to work hard tomorrow."

"*Ya,* we are." Aaron smiled. "I look forward to it." He smiled at Solomon, but only received a cold stare from him before he followed his sons to the mudroom, closing the door to the mudroom with a loud slam.

Aaron looked over at Becky and found her still frowning. "Well, *danki* again for supper. *Gut nacht.*"

Becky gave him a curt nod and his nieces said good-bye. He made his way to the mudroom and he pulled on his coat.

"*Mamm,* I'll be right back," he heard one of his nieces say. "I need to go tell *Dat* something."

Aaron stepped out onto the porch.

"*Onkel* Aaron. Wait." Ruthie Joy rushed after him, a shawl hastily thrown across her shoulders, grasping a dish towel in her hand. "I want to say something, but you can't tell my parents I'm discussing this with you." She lowered her voice and motioned for him to move farther away from the house.

"Ruthie Joy," Aaron began, "I don't want to get you in trouble." Ruthie Joy may be sixteen and out of school, but she still lived under her parents' roof.

"No, I have to say this to you. It's weighing heavily on me. I feel like I need to say something."

He nodded. "All right." He stuck his hands in the pockets of his coat.

"I saw how *mei dat* was behaving during supper." Ruthie Joy took a deep breath. "He's having a hard time accepting you, and it's wrong for him to treat you this way. I heard my parents talking about you the other night, and they're afraid you're going to leave and hurt *Mammi* again. They're still upset that you left the community for so long. But my siblings and I are grateful that you came back."

"*Danki.*" Aaron nodded. "I appreciate that."

"Please promise me that you won't give

240

up on my parents." Her eyes pleaded with him. "I'm hoping they'll realize how wrong they are about you. I see how much you enjoy being here, and *Mammi* is delighted that you're back. *Mei dat* is stubborn and set in his ways. Just give my parents time. Don't let them drive you away."

"Your parents have made it clear they don't want me here," Aaron said while zipping his coat. "I don't think they're going to change their mind. Your *dat* told me I caused enough heartache when I left and that it would've been better if I'd stayed away."

Ruthie Joy shook her head. "That's so wrong. *Mammi* is thrilled that you're back. I heard the nurse say you've already made a huge impact on her recovery." She paused and fingered the dish towel in her hands. "You're part of our family. Promise me you won't go home to Missouri just yet. We need you here. *Mammi* and *Daadi* need you."

"I promise I won't leave. Not yet." He sighed. Her sweet words touched his heart. "Thank you for talking to me."

"Gern gschehne," she said. *"Gut nacht."*

Ruthie Joy went back inside and Aaron stood on the porch for a few minutes thinking about his promise. When he made his way down the porch steps to his truck, he

241

was shocked to see Solomon walking out of the shadows. Aaron pulled the keys from his pocket as he stood in front of his brother.

"After seeing the hateful expressions you were sending my way during supper, I have a feeling this isn't a friendly visit," Aaron said.

"I was glad to see your truck still here when I came out of the barn just now. I told the boys to stay out there and finish their chores. I want to talk to you alone." Solomon crossed his arms over his wide chest.

"I will allow Manny to help you with the projects you're doing for *Mamm* and *Dat*. I only approve of it because you're helping our parents."

"That's good to know." Aaron held up his truck key and hit the Unlock button. *"Gut nacht."*

"Just a minute." He held up a finger. "I'm not done with what I have to say to you. While I will permit Manny to help you, I will not allow you to get close to my son."

Aaron rubbed his chin while holding back the words of frustration running through his mind, giving Solomon time to go on.

"I don't need you influencing *mei kinner* to leave the community and run off to do other things like you did." His eyes were full of anger, possibly even hatred. "It's one thing for *mei* son to help you work on our parents' *haus,* but it's another to have you filling his head with ideas about the outside world."

"I'm not a bad influence," Aaron said, seething, his blood boiling. "I've already told Manny I made bad choices, and I've warned him not to follow in my footsteps. Why can't you give me a chance to prove to you that I've learned from my mistakes? I want to be a part of this family."

"You're not even close to making up for what you've done." Solomon turned and started for the barn.

"What about forgiveness?" Aaron called after him. "We've all sinned and fallen short of the glory of God."

Solomon spun and quickly stepped back to face Aaron. "You have no idea the heartache you caused when you left." He jammed a finger into Aaron's chest. "I was the one here picking up the pieces while you were making your money working on *Englishers'* homes. You have no right to show up here and act as if nothing happened. I still remember how much it hurt to watch *Mamm* crumble after you ran away."

Then Solomon turned again and stalked toward the barn.

Aaron stared after him, wondering again

how he could show his brother that he wasn't the same person he had been seventeen years ago.

Later that evening, Ruthie Joy knocked lightly on her parents' bedroom door. She took a deep breath and silently asked God to give her the words that would convince her parents to welcome her uncle back into the family.

"Come in," her mother called from the other side of the door.

Ruthie Joy opened the door and found her father propped up in bed. He'd been reading the Bible and her mother had been reading a Christian novel Ruthie had also read.

Ruthie Joy stood in the doorway and took another deep breath. She'd spent all evening considering how to broach the subject of her uncle since she knew her parents would most likely not want to discuss it with her.

Her mother stared at her. "*Was iss letz*, Ruthie Joy?"

"Dinner was nice this evening, *ya*?" she asked as she absently fingered her robe.

"*Ya*," her mother said while giving her a confused expression.

"It was nice that Madeleine and Linda brought the food to share with us," Ruthie Joy said.

"*Ya,* it was," *Mamm* said while placing her book on the nightstand next to the bed. "We're blessed that the community has been reaching out to your grandparents."

"And it was nice to have the family together," Ruthie Joy continued. "Right, *Dat*? Wasn't it nice?"

He grunted and turned his eyes back to his Bible.

"*Daadi* and *Mammi* enjoyed having *Onkel* Aaron with us," Ruthie Joy prodded. "Have you noticed how *froh* they are, *Dat*?"

Solomon looked up and watched her over his half-glasses. "What are you getting at, Ruthie Joy?"

"When are you going to accept your *bruder* back into the family?" Her hands shook as she watched her father's eyes flare with irritation. She knew she was being disrespectful, but she wanted her family to heal. She couldn't stand the tension when Aaron was around her parents.

Dat glowered. "You're out of line, Ruthie Joy. It's not your place to question your parents. You need to remember that you are the child, not the adult."

"Please talk to me about it, *Dat*. I want to know why you're so angry."

"I have my reasons." He turned his gaze back to the Bible. "You don't need to be concerned with adult issues. Your mother and I will handle this. You're too young to understand."

Her mother gave her a warning glance. "You need to get back to bed, Ruthie Joy. We get up early in the morning."

"Please don't dismiss me," Ruthie Joy said, her voice thick with emotion. "I want to discuss this and work it out for our family's sake. Jesus told us to love our neighbors. He's your only *bruder,* and we need him in our family."

Dat slammed his hand on the nightstand and Ruthie Joy jumped. "He's been gone for seventeen years, and then he just shows up one day. It's going to take me awhile to forget the pain he caused when he left. You don't know anything about it."

"I'm sure you remember the pain, *Dat.* But why can't you forgive him? You know that's not our way." Ruthie Joy felt a surge of confidence despite her father's booming voice and scowl. She took a step toward her parents' bed. "*Dat,* please talk to me."

"There's nothing to say." He sat up straighter in the bed and placed the Bible on the nightstand. "I can't help how I feel."

"*Ya,* you can." Ruthie Joy insisted as she moved toward the bed. "You can give your *bruder* a chance. Katie, Manny, Junior, and

I want to get to know him better. *Mammi* and *Daadi* are so *froh* he's back. How can you not see the positive effect he's having on the family?"

"Ruthie Joy," her mother began, "you need to go to bed. This isn't something you should be discussing with your *dat.* This is a subject he and I need to discuss. You're still a *kind.* It's not your place to talk about how we feel about Aaron."

Her father removed his reading glasses, and Ruthie Joy felt the sting of frost in his blue eyes. "I don't want him influencing you or your siblings."

Ruthie Joy couldn't let her parents dismiss her when she knew in her heart that she was right about her uncle. "I don't see how *Onkel* Aaron is a negative influence. He left years ago, but he's *froh* to be back. He's said he wants to be here and he wants to be a part of the family."

"Ruthie Joy." Her father glared at her. "I will not discuss this with you any further. It's time for you to go to bed and leave this alone."

Tears trickled down Ruthie's cheeks. *"Dat —"*

"Ruthie Joy," *Mamm* chimed in. "You need to stop."

"Fine." Ruthie Joy brushed her hand

across her cheeks. "But you both need to think about what I said. You know I'm right. *Gut nacht.*"

Ruthie Joy closed the door quietly and walked slowly down the hallway to her room. She snuggled under the quilt on her bed and sniffed. She'd hoped to make her parents realize they were wrong to hold a grudge against her uncle. She wanted her family to heal and come together to support *Mammi.* She believed her grandmother needed all of them to heal from her horrible stroke.

As she fell asleep, Ruthie Joy begged God to melt her parents' hearts.

ELEVEN

Linda hummed to herself while moving the vacuum cleaner back and forth in one of the second-floor guest rooms at the bed-and-breakfast. When she thought she saw movement in her peripheral vision, she glanced over her shoulder. Finding Aaron in the doorway, she cupped her hand to her mouth and gasped with a start.

He flung his head backward and let out a bark of laughter.

Linda blushed as she clicked off the vacuum cleaner. "You got me again."

Aaron rested his back against the door frame while gasping for breath as his laughter subsided. "I am so sorry." He folded his arm over his middle. "I didn't know how to get your attention without scaring you, so I was going to wait until you stopped vacuuming. I guess I scared you anyway."

"There's no use in lying, Aaron." She felt her lips twitch as a smile overtook her face.

"You like to scare me."

"No, I don't, but you are awfully cute when you're startled." His eyes sparkled with playfulness.

She was stunned by the compliment and instantly touched her prayer covering to make sure it was straight. *He thinks I'm pretty* and *cute*? She could get used to the constant compliments he gave her.

"I wanted to see how you're doing," he said, continuing to smile. "I missed you on Monday. I checked the kitchen, but Trey said you had to run to the store with Amanda early in the morning to pick up a few things you needed for breakfast."

"Oh, *ya.*" Linda leaned on the vacuum cleaner. "Amanda had to go to the store before her first class, and I offered to go with her. How is your week going?"

"It's going well. Manny and I finished the back porch for now, so we've started on the bathroom. It's a big project, but we're having fun. Manny is really getting a kick out of learning how to make home renovations."

"That's *wunderbaar!*" Linda exclaimed. "I know you're enjoying every opportunity to become good friends with your nephew."

"*Ya,* I had a nice dinner with the whole family Friday night after I took you home. My nieces and nephews wanted to hear more about my life in Missouri. It's a shame you couldn't have stayed to eat with us."

"*Danki.* I couldn't disappoint *mei onkel.* He likes things a particular way, and I have to respect that. After all, he did take me in when I lost my parents."

Aaron nodded. "I understand. What did you make for him?"

She smiled while trying to remember Friday night. "I think I made baked chicken and egg noodles."

"I bet that was *gut.*" He stood up straight. "We enjoyed all the food you and Madeleine brought over."

"I'm so glad to hear that." She paused before going on. "Things are definitely coming together for you and your family. I told you they would."

His smile faded. "Solomon is still angry with me. He warned me not to get too close to Manny or to be a bad influence over him or the rest of the *kinner.* I tried to tell him that I'm not going to be a bad influence, and I explained that I've told Manny not to make the same bad decisions I did. Solomon wasn't convinced, and Becky also thinks I'm going to hurt my *mamm* when I leave. Ruthie Joy told me she heard her parents discussing me and how they think it would've been best if I hadn't come. She asked me not to give up on her parents, and I said I'd try. But I don't know what to do."

"Just keep doing what you're doing. God will work on them. I promise you."

Aaron looked unconvinced.

"God answers prayers, Aaron. I know he does."

"*Danki.* I know you're right." He glanced at his watch. "I better get going." He lingered for a moment and studied her. "I'd like to see you again."

"Oh." She didn't know what to say in response. Was he asking her out on a date or was he saying he wanted to talk again? She was confused but also delighted by his interest in her.

"We'll have to catch up again soon," he added.

"Ya." She nodded. "Have a *gut* day."

"You too." Aaron gave her another warm smile and then disappeared down the hallway, leaving Linda to wonder why he'd suggested they catch up. What more was there to know?

Solomon pushed the shopping cart toward the cashier at the hardware store. He stopped when he spotted a display of shovels on sale. He'd been meaning to replace the old shovels in the barn. They dated back to his childhood, and they were starting to show their age.

"Solomon."

He looked up to see Saul Beiler walking over to him. Frustration boiled inside of him as he glared at the man who had contacted Aaron and suggested he come back home. This was the man who had caused the problems with his brother to resurface in his family.

"*Wie geht's?*" Saul asked as he shook Solomon's hand. "I thought that was you. How are you?"

"Fine." Solomon frowned. "How are you and Emma doing?"

"We're doing *gut.*" Saul pointed to Solomon's full cart. "I see you've found some supplies."

"*Ya,* there are some *gut* sale prices today." Solomon looked at the shovels. "I'm thinking about getting a couple of these shovels. Mine seem to be falling apart. I can't complain since *mei dat* bought most of them years ago, possibly before I was even born."

"*Ya, ya.* I know what you mean. I have some tools my parents may have bought before I was born," Saul said. "Sometimes they do last a long time." He paused before going on. "Your *bruder* is back."

Solomon leaned his elbow on the cart. "I

heard I have you to thank for his sudden visit."

"*Ya,* that's true. I tracked him down and called him." Saul tilted his head with confusion. "You don't sound *froh* that he came back."

"If I had wanted him back, I would've contacted him myself." He paused, afraid if he wasn't more careful he'd give away his secret, the truth about the letters. "Of course, how would I know where he was? Frankly, I didn't care."

"I thought I was doing something *gut* for your family," Saul said, his explanation changing rapidly. "Maddie told me your *mamm* was desperate to see him after she had her stroke, so we did some research and found him."

"He didn't need to be found," Solomon said, his voice laced with anger. "Our family was better off with him in Missouri. He left a long time ago, and he should've stayed gone."

Saul gaped. "I'm sorry. I guess I should've minded my own business. But —"

"What's done is done, but now I have to deal with the issues it's caused. I need to get going. Good-bye." Solomon fetched two shovels off the display and stalked toward the cashier.

Aaron decided he needed a break from working on his father's house Friday afternoon. Instead of going to his family's farm, he drove through Paradise, taking in the familiar landmarks and wondering what life could've been like if he'd stayed.

As he was driving past a farm, he spotted a sign for homemade Lancaster County souvenirs, and he slowed the truck to a stop by the side of the road. He'd wanted to pick up something special for Zac and his family as a thank-you for all he'd done to keep the business going while he was gone. Not only was Zac running the business in his absence, but he was also forwarding Aaron's mail so he could keep up with his bills while he was out of town.

A small building beside the house on the property had a sign that read "Homemade Country Gifts."

Aaron stepped into the store and looked around at the candles, dolls, quilts, knick-knacks, and wood carvings. He picked up a small quilt and wondered if Zac's wife would like something like that to put in her guest bedroom.

"May I help you?"

Aaron turned and found an Amish man around his age smiling at him. Aaron's eyes widened when he recognized the face of one of his good friends from youth group. "Peter?"

"Ya?" Peter Lantz's eyes narrowed in question, and then he laughed. "Aaron Ebersol? Is that you?"

"Yes, it is." Aaron put the quilt back on the stand and shook his friend's hand. "It's been a long time."

"Too long!" Peter smacked Aaron's arm. "How have you been?"

"I've been doing all right. I just got back in town a few weeks ago. Saul Beiler called to tell me my *mamm* had suffered a stroke, so I came home to see her."

Peter's expression transformed to one of sympathy. "I was so sorry to hear about your *mamm.* How is she?"

"She's doing better, *danki.* She's working with both a physical and a speech therapist and getting stronger, but the progress has been slow." Aaron gestured around the store. "This is amazing. How long have you had it?"

"Three years," Peter said. "This was my *fraa*'s dream. I told her we'd give it a try, and it's been really successful." He pointed toward a back room. "Come and sit, and

256

we'll get caught up. I have some sodas back there. I want to hear about your life."

Aaron followed Peter into a small office, and they sat down on stools. Peter gave him a can of soda, and Aaron told him about his business.

"So do you have *kinner*?" Aaron asked.

"*Ya*, I do." Peter placed his can on the desk behind him. "I have two and one on the way."

"Wow. Three *kinner*. Did you marry someone from our youth group?" Aaron took a long drink.

Peter's smile was back. "*Ya*, I did actually. Do you remember Susannah Dienner? She's a couple of years younger than we are."

"Let me think. Susannah." Aaron let the name roll around in his mind while he thought back to their youth group friends. "She was blonde, right? Her father owned a shoe business."

"That's right." Peter folded his hands in his lap. "We got to talking one night when I was about eighteen, and we've been together ever since." He gestured toward Aaron with his hand. "So how about you? Do you have a family in Missouri?"

"No, I don't have a family." Aaron shook his head, still holding the cool soda can. "I stay busy with our company."

"I always wondered what happened to you and the rest of the guys who left," Peter said. "I wondered if you would ever come back."

"I thought I was making the right decision leaving the community after I burned down the bishop's barn. Everything seemed to be falling apart, so when a few of the guys planned to leave, I followed them."

"You went because of the barn?" Peter looked incredulous as Aaron nodded. "You didn't need to go. Elmer forgave all of us for what happened that night. You weren't the only one who came forward."

"What do you mean?" Aaron asked.

"Merv and I went to see the bishop and gave him all our names. We all apologized, and we told him everything. We told him how we'd been sneaking around and drinking in whatever barns we could get into. The bishop and everyone forgave us. But you had already gone. We all cleaned up our acts after that. We stopped drinking and started working and putting money away for our futures. We all helped rebuild the barn too. The whole community came together, and other church districts pitched in to help us."

Peter chuckled. "We were just stupid kids back then, but you didn't have to run away. Nothing was that bad."

Aaron nodded slowly. "I'm beginning to see that."

"After I joined the church, I started dating Susannah. Our parents helped us buy this place." Peter stood. "Let me show you around."

Aaron followed Peter out of the store and into the large farmhouse. They found Susannah in the kitchen, where a boy and a girl toddled around.

"Susannah," Peter began, "do you remember Aaron Ebersol? He's visiting from Missouri."

"Aaron." Susannah smiled as she walked over from the stove. He noticed she had a little belly protruding from underneath her black apron and blue dress. "It's *gut* to see you again."

"*Danki.* It's nice to see you too." He shook her hand and then looked down at the children as they shyly held on to her apron. "Hi there."

"This is Levina and Peter Junior," Susannah said with a smile. "They're four and two."

Aaron looked down at them. "It's nice to meet you."

"Are you back for good?" Susannah asked.

"No, I'm only visiting. *Mei mamm* had a stroke, so I came back to see her and do what I can to help out the family," Aaron explained.

"Oh, I'm sorry about your *mamm.* I hope you decide to stay for a while," Susannah said. "I know everyone will be *froh* to see you again."

"I appreciate that. It's great visiting everyone. It's like taking a trip down memory lane." Aaron nodded toward the children. "You have a lovely family."

"Danki." Peter motioned toward the back door. "I didn't mean to hold you up. Did you want to look around the store?"

"That would be great." Aaron nodded at Susannah. "It was nice seeing you."

Aaron and Peter walked back outside, and Aaron looked toward the row of barns. "You have a large piece of land here."

"Ya, Susannah's family owned all of it, and they gave us twenty acres. I grow corn, beans, and a few other crops too." He pointed beyond the barn. "Susannah's parents live back there. She also has a few other relatives around us. It's nice to have family so close."

Aaron considered again how lonely his life had been for the past seventeen years. "I imagine it is nice to have family nearby."

They walked into the store.

"What are you looking for today?" Peter asked.

"I was hoping to find some gifts for my business partner. He's keeping the company running while I'm here, and I thought I'd do something nice for him." Aaron browsed a display with wood signs and plaques. "What are your biggest sellers?"

"Most tourists are looking for dolls and quilts. Does your friend have a family?" Peter asked.

"*Ya,* he does. His wife would probably love a quilt." Aaron walked over to look at them again.

Thirty minutes later, Aaron left the store with two bags containing a quilt, a doll, two wooden garden signs, and a few knick-knacks. He climbed into his truck and looked at the house. He contemplated everything his friend Peter had — a loving wife, adorable children, a beautiful farm, and a successful store. He thought about what Peter said, about how it hadn't been necessary for Aaron to run away after the barn burned down.

Aaron couldn't help but wonder over and over what would've happened if he'd stayed. Would he have gotten his life together and then met and married someone special? Would he have built a home and a business

261

here in Paradise?

When he started thinking about the bed-and-breakfast, he decided to go there.

He parked behind the house and went in through the kitchen, hoping Linda was there. Finding the kitchen empty, he climbed the stairs up to his room. His phone was sitting on the dresser where he'd left it the night before. When he found no waiting voice mail messages or texts, he stuck the phone into his pocket and looked out the window, past the barn. He was surprised to see a pasture with a pond beyond it. He'd never noticed the pond at the back of the property.

Aaron went back to the kitchen and found Linda carrying a mop from the laundry room. His heart warmed as he enjoyed the view of her pretty face. "Hi."

"Hi." Linda leaned the mop against the wall and smoothed her hands over her apron. "I thought you'd be working at your parents' *haus* today."

"I decided to take the afternoon off. Why are you still here this late?"

"Two couples are arriving tomorrow, so I thought I would do a few extra chores before I left. I don't want to leave all the work for Trey or tempt Hannah to do too much."

An idea popped into his mind. "Do you have your coat?"

Her brow furrowed in question. "*Ya.* Why?"

"Will you put it on?" he asked.

"I have to mop."

"The mopping can wait. Get your coat."

Linda hesitated and then smiled. "Okay." She disappeared into the laundry room and returned with her coat on. "Where are we going?"

"You'll see," he said with a smile.

Linda followed Aaron out the back door and down the deck stairs. The cold air caused her bad leg to stiffen, and she felt herself limp slightly as they walked side by side.

"Are we going for a ride? I can't leave the bed-and-breakfast without telling Hannah where I'm going. She thinks I'm going to finish the cleaning I planned to do."

"We're not leaving the property."

Linda realized now that they were heading toward the barn. She gazed up at his smile and wondered what he had up his sleeve. The afternoon sun gave his curls a deeper, golden hue and caused his eyes to twinkle. He looked even more handsome than usual as they walked right past the barn. He stood close to her, and their hands brushed, sending her heart thudding against her rib cage.

"Did you know there's a pond back here?" he asked as they rounded the fence by the pasture.

The grass was a dull brown, and the trees were bare. Winter was still in full swing, and the farmland beyond the bed-and-breakfast looked sad and lonely without the colors and life that spring would bring in a couple of months. Though it had snowed a couple of times since Aaron arrived, the daytime temperatures had stayed warm enough for the snow to melt rather quickly.

"*Ya,* Hannah told me about the pond. She likes to go back there and sit in the spring."

"It's February," Aaron said with a smile. "Spring is coming soon."

"Not soon enough." She shivered in the cool breeze and hugged her coat closer to her body. Her leg continued to feel stiff, and it made her self-conscious. She hoped he didn't notice her limp.

"Oh, this was a bad idea." His smile faded as he stopped walking. "We should go back in the house before you get too cold."

"No, no." She shook her head. "This is an adventure, and I need more adventure in my life."

He laughed, and the sound was music to

her ears. "This isn't much of an adventure. I just want to see the pond."

"So let's go see the pond." They reached the end of the pasture and came to the icy pond, sparkling in the bright sunlight like stars in a dark night sky.

Aaron pointed toward the bench. "Want to sit for a minute? I promise we won't be out here long enough to freeze."

"*Ya,* let's sit." She moved to the bench, and they sat beside each other. The wooden seat was cold under her bottom, but she didn't mind. His leg brushed hers, and she again felt her pulse skip with delight. "It's *schee* out here."

"It is." He smiled at her. "Do you like to ice skate?"

"I've never tried."

"What?" He turned to face her, his expression held disbelief. "You've never been ice skating?"

She shook her head and gnawed her lower lip as embarrassment overtook her. She'd never had the opportunity to ice skate, but she also never thought she would be able to because of her leg injury. She'd watched her cousin Raymond and his family skate once, but she'd never even attempted to join them.

"We have to go." He snapped his fingers.

"There was a rink in Lancaster. If it's still there, I'll take you sometime."

"No, no." She shook her head. "I don't think —"

"Yes, we have to. I'll teach you how." His eyes were hopeful, and she didn't want to extinguish their radiance.

"Okay," she said softly, hoping he'd forget the promise and not make her tell him that she couldn't skate. She didn't want him to know she had a disability. She knew she could never be more than his friend, but she didn't want to risk losing his precious friendship. Sometimes pity chased people away.

"Great." He turned back toward the pond. "I saw Peter Lantz today. I just happened to stop by his farm when I saw the sign for a gift shop. I was surprised when I found him running the store."

"Oh, *ya*," she said. "Susannah opened that store a few years ago. It does a *gut* business. I bet he was excited to see you."

"*Ya*, he was. We talked for a while. I saw Susannah and met his *kinner*."

While Aaron shared the details about seeing his friend again, Linda enjoyed watching him and listening to his cheerful, comforting voice. Despite the cold breeze and the even colder bench, she wanted the moment to last forever so she could imagine what it would be like to be married to a kind, handsome man like Aaron Ebersol.

TWELVE

Linda filled one side of the sink with hot, soapy water for washing and the other side with plain hot water for rinsing. She placed the breakfast dishes into the frothy water and began to scrub them before rinsing them in the plain water. She heard a knock.

"Someone's at the door!" *Onkel* Reuben yelled from his bedroom.

"I'll get it." Linda grabbed a dish towel and wiped her hands as she limped toward the door. She swung it open and found Aaron standing on the porch, holding up a red heart-shaped box. "Aaron?" she asked, and her posture immediately straightened at the sight of him.

"Happy Valentine's Day!" He held out the box.

Linda stared at the box with her eyes wide in surprise.

"Take it." He grinned at her. "It's candy. For you."

"Aaron, I-I . . ." She stammered while staring up at him. She had to be dreaming. She took the box of candy and looked up at his adorable grin. *"Danki."*

"Gern gschehne, but that's not all." He jammed his thumb toward the truck. "We want to take you ice skating today for Valentine's."

"We?" She craned her neck to see the truck behind him, humming in the driveway.

"My *bruderskinner* are coming with us."

"Oh." She wasn't sure what to do.

"Who's at the door?" Reuben appeared behind her and scowled at Aaron.

"Onkel Reuben, this is my friend Aaron Ebersol," Linda said, introducing them. "You remember. I told you he was visiting from Missouri."

"Hi, Reuben." Aaron held out his hand.

"You're Jonas and Ruth's son." Reuben peered at Aaron over his half-glasses and gave his hand a halfhearted shake. "You left a long time ago. Why are you back now?"

"I told you he came back to see his *mutter.* She had a stroke," Linda said as her cheeks heated with embarrassment and frustration. Why didn't her uncle ever listen to her?

"That's right. I want to take Linda ice skating," Aaron said. "My nieces and nephews are coming with us too."

Reuben looked at Linda. "Don't you have chores to do today?"

"I can do them when I get home." Linda held her breath with anticipation, hoping Reuben would let her go without a fuss. She suddenly realized she wanted to go with Aaron, even if she couldn't skate. She wasn't worried about her disability humiliating her or holding her back. In fact, she would go anywhere with him.

"I promise I'll have her back at a decent time," Aaron said, his expression pleading with Reuben to say yes. "You name the hour, and I will have her home on time." Linda could tell that, even though she was a grown woman, Aaron knew her uncle expected to grant his permission.

Reuben gave him a curt nod. "Fine. No later than two."

"Danki." Linda smiled at her uncle despite his sour expression, and he disappeared back into the house.

She turned to Aaron, who was beaming. "I just need to grab my coat and purse."

"You don't need your purse," Aaron said.

Linda looked down at the dish towel in her hand. "Well, I would like to get rid of this."

Aaron chuckled. "That's a good idea. We'll

be waiting in the truck."

Linda hurried into the house and tossed the dish towel and pretty box of chocolates onto the kitchen counter. She then rushed to the bathroom, where she checked her appearance. She examined her face and then pinched her cheeks, hoping to give herself a little more color. She knew it was vain to worry about her appearance, but she wanted to look her best for this outing.

Is this a date?

She quickly pushed that thought away. Of course, it wasn't a date. She lived in the community, and he kept his permanent residence in Missouri. Why was she torturing herself with such wild notions of any romance blooming between them? They were from two different worlds. She hurried out to the front of the house, where Reuben now sat in his favorite chair, reading the paper.

"I'll see you later." She grabbed her coat and pulled it on.

"Be careful," Reuben said without looking up.

She paused for a moment, wondering why he would caution her to be careful. Then she rushed out the door to Aaron's pickup truck, still purring in the driveway. As she approached the passenger side, she saw his niece Katie sitting in the middle of the front seat.

Katie leaned over and pushed the door open. "Hi, Linda! Come on up. You can sit next to me."

Linda climbed up into the seat and said hello to Manny, Ruthie Joy, and Junior in the backseat before she buckled her seat belt. As Aaron drove toward the main road, Katie asked a question.

"Do you like to skate?"

"I've never skated," Linda said.

"You've never skated?" Ruthie Joy sounded amazed.

"That's okay," Aaron chimed in. "We'll teach her how to skate, right?"

"Oh, *ya.*" Katie waved off the question. "It's easy as pie."

"It depends on the pie. Some pies aren't so easy to make," Ruthie Joy joked, and everyone laughed.

"That's true." Linda felt her stomach lurch at the thought of putting on skates in front of her friends. What if Aaron noticed her limp? What if she fell? What if she simply couldn't skate? Would he still like her if he knew she wasn't athletic? She hoped she would be able to at least make one lap around the rink. Then she could tell Aaron she was tired and preferred to watch from the sidelines, which is what she'd done her whole life. She believed she belonged on the sidelines, not in the midst of the flurry of activity happening around her. She was more comfortable watching from afar and enjoying everyone else's joy and accomplishments.

Aaron's nieces and nephews chattered with excitement about going to the rink and skating. When they arrived, they all rushed through the parking lot to the front door before Aaron and Linda had even left the truck.

"You seem *naerfich,*" Aaron said as he held the door open for Linda. "You don't need to be nervous. It will be fun."

Linda forced a smile as worry drenched her. They joined the children at the front desk inside, where Aaron paid the entry fee and rented the skates. Linda marveled at how quickly the children laced up their skates and hurried out onto the ice. The four of them were skating as if they were walking across the floor in their shoes. They raced around, chasing each other and laughing as they moved among the other skaters in the rink.

Linda turned her attention to her own skates and slowly began to remove her shoes. She loosened the laces on the first skate and then eased her right foot into it.

"Do you need help?" Aaron offered from beside her.

"Oh, no, *danki.*" Leaning down, she began to lace the skate, trying to get used to the feel of the blade under the boot.

"How is it?" He turned toward her. "Too tight? Too loose?"

"It's okay." She shrugged, not having any idea if it was too tight or too loose. She'd never been on skates before, so she didn't know how it was supposed to feel.

"You sure?" His eyes were full of concern.

"*Ya,* I'm sure." She tied the excess length of the laces in a bow and then slipped her left foot into the other boot. "Just promise me you won't laugh at me when I fall."

"I would never laugh at you." The serious expression in his face caused her skin to prickle with delight.

Linda finished tying the second skate and then looked up at him. "I guess this is it."

"You say that so unenthusiastically." Aaron stood and held out his hand. "I'll be by your side every step of the way."

Linda gnawed her bottom lip and stared at his hand.

"I promise I won't let you fall, Linda. You have my word." His eyes were encouraging.

"Okay." Her stomach clenched as she took

his hand. His skin was warm, and his grip was strong and reassuring. At first she felt unbalanced, as if one of her legs were longer than the other. She steadied herself and held tight to his hand.

"Are you okay?" he asked.

She nodded.

"Do you want to try the ice?" he asked. "I won't pressure you. You can sit on the bench by the ice and watch us if you're not comfortable."

Confidence surged through her and she felt herself stand a little taller. "I'm tired of sitting on the sidelines. I want to go on the ice."

Aaron grinned. "Fantastic. Let's go."

Aaron loved the feel of Linda's small hand clamped to his as he led her to the ice. He could feel her body shaking, and he worried that this had been a bad idea. Yet her statement about not wanting to be on the sidelines any longer had confirmed what he was thinking — that she wanted to try something new. He'd been contemplating her confession that she'd never dated, and it sounded as if she'd never had much of a social life beyond her job at the hotel. She just might have felt as lonely as he'd felt during the past seventeen years.

"All right," he began as they stood by the rink, "I'm going to step onto the ice. You take your time coming out, okay? I'll hold you up."

Linda's eyebrows drew down as she concentrated. She looked adorable. She moved one foot slowly onto the ice and then started to slip. She grabbed his arm with both hands and gasped.

"I've got you," he said softly. "You're not going to fall. I promise. Just trust me, okay?"

She blew out a sigh and smiled. "That was close."

"No, it wasn't." Aaron shook his head. "I told you, I won't let you go."

"Linda!" Katie skated over and slowed to a stop. "You're doing great. Want me to show you how to skate?"

Ruthie Joy appeared next to her. "I'll help too."

Linda hesitated and looked up at Aaron, as if pleading for him to encourage her again.

"You'll be fine," he insisted.

"All right." Linda gave his nieces a tentative smile.

"Just move your feet like this." Katie moved in long, slow strides as she slipped away. She looked back over her shoulder. "Just go easy. You'll glide."

"*Ya,* that's right. Do what she did." Ruthie Joy moved to the other side of Linda and took her free hand. "*Onkel* Aaron and I will hold you up."

Linda moved her feet slowly, and her body teetered. Aaron held on to her hand and looked over at Ruthie Joy, who smiled. Together, he and his niece guided Linda slowly around the rink once. Each time she started to teeter and slip, he and Ruthie steadied her.

Soon, they were laughing as Linda became more and more comfortable on the ice. After nearly two hours, she skated one whole lap by herself and then moved to the wall.

"I think I'm ready to sit." She steadied herself on the wall with her hands. "My feet and legs are sore."

"Wait until tomorrow," Katie said as she stopped beside Linda. "You're not going to be able to move when you wake up in the morning."

"Oh no." Linda scrunched her nose as if she smelled something bad, and Aaron laughed. She eyed him. "What's so funny?"

"Your expression is priceless." He stepped off the ice and held out his hand. "Let me help you."

Linda took his hand and he supported her

as she stepped onto the carpet. "Wow." She beamed up at him. "I didn't think I could do it. I actually skated!"

He studied her. "Why didn't you think you could do it?"

She shrugged as she sank onto the bench. "I just didn't think I could."

"You can do anything you set your mind to." He sat down beside her. "Don't limit yourself."

She stared into his eyes as if searching for something and then turned her attention to her shoes.

Junior walked over to them. "I'm hungry. Can we have lunch?"

"Sure." He glanced at Linda. "Are you hungry?"

"Ya." Linda nodded while pulling off a skate. "I am hungry. I think I worked up an appetite."

Aaron turned back to Junior. "Would you go get your siblings? We can eat at the snack bar if you want."

"Can we have pizza?" Junior's expression was hopeful.

Aaron shrugged. "Why not?"

"Great!" Junior clapped his hands together and then hurried back onto the ice.

"Kinner love pizza, *ya?"* Linda asked.

"They do love pizza. *Englisher kinner* love

it too." He unlaced his skates.

"Do you miss Missouri?" Linda asked.

"No." He gave her the answer without hesitation. At that very moment, he didn't want to go back to Missouri. Instead, he wanted to spend more time getting to know Linda and his brother's children.

"You don't miss it at all?" She looked surprised as she unlaced the second skate.

"No, I don't." Aaron removed his skates and pulled on his shoes. He knew she was watching him, and he longed to read her thoughts. Was she enjoying their time together as much as he was?

The children returned from the rink and put on their shoes. After taking back their skates, they all made their way to the snack bar for pizza and sodas. Aaron sat across from Linda and enjoyed watching her while she talked to his nieces and nephews. He couldn't help but think this had been the best Valentine's Day he'd ever had.

Disappointment surged through Linda as Aaron steered the truck into her cousin's driveway later that afternoon. The hours had flown by too fast. As soon as the truck came to a stop, Aaron's nieces and nephews said good-bye to her.

"I'll walk you to the door," Aaron offered.

Linda climbed out of the truck and met Aaron at the front bumper. "I had a lovely time," she said as they walked to the porch together.

"I did too." He stuffed his hands in the pockets of his jeans as they walked to the front door.

"This was the best Valentine's Day I've ever had." She smiled up at him. "Actually, it's the only one I've ever celebrated, other than the parties we had in school when we were kids."

"I'm glad you enjoyed it. I had a fantastic time." His eyes probed hers, and she felt the air around them spark with intensity.

"Linda!" Reuben's voice boomed from inside the house. "It's ten minutes after two!"

Linda felt her shoulders hunch at the sound of his voice. "I have to go."

"I understand." Aaron touched her arm. "I'll see you at the bed-and-breakfast."

"I look forward to it." She watched him lope down the steps and hop into the truck.

The truck's horn tooted as Aaron backed out of the driveway. Linda waved and then stepped into the house, where she found her uncle in his chair, reading a newspaper. She wondered if he'd moved from the spot even once the whole time she was gone.

"You're late," he barked as she hung up her coat.

"I'm only ten minutes late, *Onkel,*" she muttered. "I don't think that's unreasonable."

"You have chores to do and supper to make."

"I know." Linda stood in the doorway to the kitchen and found the breakfast dishes still sitting in the now brown water. A new pile, including a dirty dish, a dirty glass, and utensils, sat on the counter, which she presumed was from her uncle's lunch. Most days she felt like his servant instead of his niece since he never acknowledged how hard she worked to take care of their home. Reuben never treated her the way Aaron treated his nieces and nephews. Aaron smiled at them with more love in his eyes today than she'd ever seen her uncle bestow upon her. She wondered what it would feel like to be loved that way.

"What are you doing with that man?" His question broke through her thoughts.

She turned and faced him. "What do you mean?"

Reuben closed the newspaper and folded it in his lap. "You spent most of the day with a man who isn't Amish. What are you thinking?"

"He's my *freind.*" She enunciated the word. "And I wasn't alone with him. His two nephews and two nieces were with us. We went ice skating in a public place. After we finished skating, we had pizza in the snack bar and then went out for ice cream before they brought me home. That's it. It was just a friendly outing for Valentine's Day."

Her uncle shot her a piercing glare over his half-glasses. "You need to be careful. He's not a baptized member of the church. Not only is the perception people of our community could have of you risky, but you're also risking your heart."

"It was nothing serious. We only went ice skating. That's it."

"It's not a *gut* idea for you to see him," he barked, his voice growing louder. "I think you should stop working at that bed-and-breakfast and only keep your job at the hotel. You spend too much time away from the *haus,* and you haven't been keeping up with your chores. I need you at home more, and you need to stay away from that young man. He's a bad influence. People will talk if they see you with him, and I will not allow you to dishonor the family that way. You are to stay away from him and that bed-and-breakfast. If you want to earn extra

282

money, you can take on more hours at the hotel."

Linda's face burned with frustration. "No, I will not quit the bed-and-breakfast."

Her uncle's eyes widened. "Are you deliberately defying me?"

"No, I'm not defying you. I'm allowed to make decisions when it comes to where I work, and I refuse to quit working at the bed-and-breakfast. Hannah needs me, and I won't let her down." She had to stand her ground. Working for Hannah meant too much to her.

Onkel Reuben regarded her with disgust. "I've never seen you be so disrespectful, Linda. That Aaron has changed you."

"This has nothing to do with Aaron. I like working with Hannah, and she depends on me. I can't give that up." She turned toward the kitchen. "I have work to do."

Her hands shook as she limped into the kitchen. Linda had never stood up to her uncle before, and she felt a mixture of guilt and relief. She felt guilty for talking back to him, but she felt a sense of relief at finally standing up for something she truly believed in. She enjoyed her job at the bed-and-breakfast and didn't want to let it go so easily. Not only did she want to help Hannah, but she also couldn't let go of her opportunity to see Aaron.

She walked over to the counter, picked up the heart-shaped box of chocolates, and smiled as she ran her fingers over the embossed lid. She knew her uncle was right when he said she should stay away from Aaron, but she couldn't stop that twinge of excitement deep in her soul every time she thought of his gorgeous smile.

Linda unpacked her lunch bag as she sat in the hotel break room with Madeleine on Tuesday afternoon. Her thoughts had been stuck on Aaron since their skating outing. She'd seen him briefly on Monday during breakfast, and he was just as friendly and sweet to her as he had been on Saturday. While she was thrilled that their friendship was blossoming, her uncle's warning still echoed in her mind.

"Did you have a nice weekend, Linda?" Madeleine asked while unwrapping her sandwich.

"*Ya.*" Linda picked up an apple. "I actually did something really fun on Saturday."

"Oh?" Madeleine asked. "What did you do?"

"Aaron Ebersol surprised me." Linda smiled. "He came to my *haus* unexpectedly and took me ice skating with his nieces and

284

nephews. I'd never been ice skating before. It was *wunderbaar.*"

Madeleine's eyebrows shot up with surprise. "Aaron Ebersol took you ice skating?" She smiled. "That's so nice."

Linda examined her apple. "He gave me a box of chocolates for Valentine's Day, and he was so nice and kind to me. He even held my hand to teach me how to skate. It was *wunderbaar.*" She paused. "But I'm worried."

"You like him," Madeleine said slowly.

Linda nodded. "I don't know what to do. I'm so confused. I've never dated, and he's not Amish. It's just a mess." She set down her apple and hid her face in her hands.

"You've never dated?" Madeleine asked gently.

"No, I haven't." Linda looked at her friend through her splayed fingers. "I never went to a youth group meeting, and I never knew how to even talk to *buwe.* I was usually by myself or with my *aenti* and *onkel.*" She shook her head and unwrapped her own sandwich. "But that doesn't even matter. Aaron isn't a member of the church, and he hasn't said that he's going to stay here. He may go back to Missouri, and I'll never see him again. I don't know how I'll get over it if he leaves. I know I'm going to have a broken heart."

"Don't give up on him," Madeleine said. "I saw how happy he was at his mother's house. He seemed really pleased to be working on the porch with his nephew. And we both know how overjoyed he has made Ruth by coming home. Maybe he'll decide to stay here and join the church."

"I don't know. He's been away from the church for so long. Why would he want to come back?"

"Just think about it." Madeleine nodded. "Family and community are so important to us all. He may realize how much he wants to be with his family again. And maybe you'll show him that."

Linda shook her head. "I don't know. I have a bad feeling this won't end well. But, at the same time, I'm enjoying every minute with him."

"Pray for him," Madeleine said. "Ask God to guide his heart."

Linda nodded. "I will." She hoped Madeleine was right and Aaron would decide to stay. She'd waited so long to find someone like Aaron — even as a friend. The notion of losing his friendship forever caused her heart to ache. She couldn't face the thought of losing him, not when he meant so much to her.

THIRTEEN

Linda walked into the house after working at the hotel. Once she'd hung up her coat and dropped her tote bag on the bench by the front door, she limped into the kitchen. She pulled out her cookbook and found her favorite chicken noodle soup recipe. She reviewed the recipe and then began pulling together the ingredients.

"What are you doing?" *Onkel* Reuben asked from the doorway. Why was he always asking her that? Wasn't it obvious what she was doing when she was in the kitchen?

"I'm going to make chicken noodle soup and cookies for Ruth Ebersol," she said as she retrieved a pot from the cabinet. "I have leftover chicken from the other night, and I thought Ruth might enjoy the soup. I plan to visit her today and see if I can help Becky with anything."

"I'll go too," Reuben said. "I need to go to the pharmacy for my medicines."

"Oh." She looked at him over her shoulder. "You want to see Ruth?"

"*Ya.*" He shrugged. "Why not?"

"Okay. I'll let you know when I'm ready."

"Fine."

Linda frowned. She'd wanted to spend time with Ruth, but she also wanted to see Aaron. Her uncle had made it apparent that he didn't approve of her friendship with Aaron, so she would certainly feel self-conscious when he was there with her. She knew she shouldn't be disappointed that Reuben wanted to go with her. After all, it was thoughtful of him to want to visit Ruth. She only hoped she'd get a chance to at least talk to Aaron without her uncle hovering around them.

When the cookies and soup were ready, Linda packed up the food and climbed into the buggy with her uncle. She set the container of soup on the floor between her feet and held the box of cookies on her lap. She spent the ride thinking of Aaron and hoping he'd be there working in his mother's house. She couldn't wait to see him.

"We don't have much time to visit," Reuben said while guiding the horse down the road. "I have to get to the pharmacy to get my medication."

"I wanted to help Becky do some chores

288

around the *haus*," Linda said. "I know even with help from some of the other women in the community, she and her daughters still have too much to do with Ruth not well."

"You'll have to go back another day to help with chores," Reuben said, keeping his face focused on the road. "Today isn't a *gut* day for you to stay. We have things to do, and Becky will understand. We all have households to run. The floor hasn't been mopped in the kitchen this week. It's in desperate need of attention."

Linda couldn't mask her disappointment. She felt her body wilt as she stared at the box of cookies in her hands. She had been looking forward to helping Becky and possibly spending time with Aaron. Now her plans were ruined. *Onkel* Reuben wanted to keep her chained to the house. Was he afraid of losing her? Didn't he know how unhappy and lonely she was? She'd told Aaron she was satisfied with her life, but that wasn't true.

"Don't look so forlorn," Reuben snapped. "I told you about the sticky spot in the kitchen earlier this week, and you still haven't taken care of it. Chores need to be done, Linda. That's just how life is. We all have things we must do, whether we like it or not."

"Ya, Onkel," she said softly. "I understand."

While they rode the rest of the way to Ruth's house, Linda wondered if she should've had her driver take her straight to Ruth's house after work. Bypassing her uncle altogether would've prevented him from ruining her afternoon. She could've stopped at the store or the bakery for something to take to Ruth.

Reuben guided the horse into the driveway, and Linda immediately spotted Aaron's pickup truck. Her heart turned over in her chest, but she knew she wouldn't be able to spend any time with him. Most likely, Reuben would allow her to say hello to Ruth and then they would have to leave. It would be sweet torture to only be able to look at Aaron from afar and not enjoy his company.

Linda breathed a deep sigh as Reuben halted the horse. She should be happy that she would even get the pleasure of saying hello to Aaron today. Seeing his attractive face and tender smile would bring her joy, and it would have to be enough for now.

"So, we'll put the shower here." Aaron pointed to the corner of the bathroom. "I found a unit I liked with the features we need at the bathroom supply store. I want to take my *dat* down there before supper and see what he thinks. I'd like you to come too."

Manny nodded. "*Ya,* I'd love to come."

"Once we agree on a shower unit, I can find a plumber, and we'll get started installing it."

"*Gut, gut,*" Manny said.

"Great." Aaron took a couple more measurements and then heard a familiar voice coming from the kitchen. Was that Linda's voice or was he imagining it? He'd been thinking of her nonstop since their ice-skating outing. He longed to spend more time with her beyond saying hello at the bed-and-breakfast.

"That was so nice of you to make soup and *kichlin.*" Becky's voice sounded from the kitchen. "And it's so *gut* to see you, Reuben. How have you been?"

"Reuben?" Aaron stood.

"*Was iss letz?*" Manny asked.

"Nothing." Aaron handed him the measuring tape. "Would you finish measuring this for me?"

"*Ya.*"

Aaron stepped to the doorway leading to the kitchen and saw Linda standing with her uncle. They must have come in the back way. Reuben was detailing his aches and pains for Becky. Instead of seeing Linda's beautiful smile and sparkling eyes, Aaron was shocked to find her frowning without any light in her eyes at all. Her shoulders were slightly hunched, and she fiddled with her coat while her uncle spoke. The change in her demeanor worried him. Was she okay? Was she ill? What had happened to the carefree woman who had giggled while ice skating with him last week?

"Ruth will be delighted to see you both," Becky continued. "Let's go see her."

Reuben and Linda followed Becky toward the hallway. When they passed him, Reuben gave Aaron a stiff nod. Linda kept her gaze trained on the floor, and her left leg seemed to favor the right one, giving her a slight limp he'd never noticed before. Had she been injured in the last few days? Surely she wasn't still sore from ice skating.

"Linda?" he said her name, and her gaze snapped up to him.

Reuben stopped walking and looked at Aaron, giving him a scowl.

Linda looked at her uncle and then at Aaron, and her expression was tentative and almost nervous.

"Hi, Aaron," she said, her voice soft and meek, reminding him of a mouse.

"Are you okay?" He reached for her arm and then stopped, realizing it would be inappropriate to touch her, especially in front of her uncle.

"*Ya.*" She gave him a forced smile that resembled a grimace. "We're going to visit your *mamm.*"

"*Kumm,* Linda," Reuben grumbled. "I need to get to the pharmacy to get my pills." He started toward the family room again, his footsteps heavy and loud.

"Linda." Aaron moved into the kitchen. "Wait."

She looked up at him and whispered. "I can't talk now."

"But Linda —" he began.

"I need to go," she said, interrupting him. "I'll talk to you soon." She pointed toward her uncle.

He watched her follow him to the family room, and his heart sank. Why was Linda behaving so differently? Did her uncle cause this change in her demeanor? He'd never seen Reuben smile, not today and not last week when he picked her up to go ice skating. Was it his influence that transformed her from a sweet, affable friend to a nervous, awkward person who seemed more like a stranger to him?

The thought caused irritation to boil within him. Linda was a beautiful, thoughtful woman, and she deserved to be happy.

He couldn't stand the thought of Reuben suffocating Linda's sweet spirit.

Linda sat on the sofa beside her uncle while they visited with Ruth. *Onkel* Reuben didn't even want her to take off her coat. Although she was happy to see Ruth, she longed to run back and talk to Aaron. She could tell by the expression on his face that he was confused, maybe even hurt, when she said she couldn't talk. But she knew *Onkel* Reuben would be annoyed if she talked to Aaron. He had made it clear they would not stay long, but she wanted to defy him. She wanted to tell him she was staying at Ruth's house and Aaron would take her home later. Yet she knew she couldn't go against his wishes. She had to be obedient and behave like a proper lady or he would berate her even more than usual.

Linda looked toward the doorway to the kitchen while Reuben complained to Ruth about how much his back had been hurting him lately — as if his ailments were worse than what Ruth was going through. She wondered if Aaron would come out too. Maybe he would sit down and visit with the three of them.

"Well, it was *gut* seeing you, Ruth." Reuben stood. "We need to go to the pharmacy.

I can't go without my medications."

Ruth gave him a lopsided smile. *"D-danki."*

Reuben gestured toward Linda. "Linda made you some soup and *kichlin.*"

"D-danki," Ruth repeated.

"I hope you like them," Linda said while fiddling with the edges of her coat. "I used my favorite recipe for the soup. And Aaron really likes the *kichlin.* I made them at the bed-and-breakfast, and he finished them."

Ruth chuckled. "Aaron al-always l-loved *k-kichlin.* Oat-m-meal r-raisin?"

"Ya," Linda said with a smile. "They were." She knew her uncle was watching her, and her smile faded. "I hope you're feeling better soon. You look better."

Ruth nodded and pointed toward a nearby walker. "I w-walk-ed y-yes-ter-d-day."

"Oh, *gut!*" Linda clapped her hands together. "That is *wunderbaar.*"

"We better go." Reuben tapped Linda's arm. "Take care, Ruth." He started for the front door. Obviously, he wanted to avoid seeing Aaron again.

Linda squeezed Ruth's hand. "I'll visit again soon. I promise."

Ruth smiled. *"D-danki."*

Linda deliberately lagged behind her uncle and walked slowly toward the foyer. Reuben made his way out and stopped on the front porch talking to Jonas. She slowed her steps even more and hoped Aaron was still in the house.

"Linda." Aaron came up behind her. "Are you all right?"

"*Ya.*" She turned and looked into his eyes, wishing she could stay and visit longer. "I made those *kichlin* in the kitchen for you."

"Thank you." He seemed confused as he studied her.

She glanced toward the front door and saw her uncle shaking Jonas's hand. "I have to go."

"I want to talk to you." Aaron's expression pleaded with her.

"I can't talk now. I'm sorry, but I have to go. Good-bye." She rushed out the door, hoping she'd see him again soon.

Aaron watched Linda climb into the buggy. He wanted to run after her and bring her back into the house. He couldn't stand seeing her leave in such a rush. He longed to ask Reuben why he treated her so badly. There seemed to be something amiss there.

Once the buggy was gone from his sight, Aaron let Manny know he could knock off for the day and made his way into the kitchen. He filled a plate with cookies and went to the back porch, where Becky said she'd just taken his mother.

"Did you have a nice visit with Linda and Reuben?" Aaron asked as he held out a cookie to her.

"*Ya.*" *Mamm* took the cookie and bit into it. "*Gut.* I see why th-these are y-your f-favorites."

Aaron tilted his head. "How did you know these were my favorites?"

"L-Linda s-said." *Mamm* smiled.

"She told you that?" Aaron broke a cookie in half.

"*Ya.*" *Mamm* ate another piece.

He was impressed and also touched that Linda remembered his favorite cookies.

"*Dat* and I are going to look at shower stalls for you before supper," Aaron explained between bites. "Then I'm going to find a plumber. We'll have your bathroom all set up for you in no time. I think you're going to like it."

"*D-danki.*" *Mamm* placed her hand on his. "Will y-you g-go to ch-church with m-me? First t-time f-for me s-since stroke." Her eyes were full of hope.

Aaron took another bite of the cookie while his mother continued to gaze at him. He didn't know what to say. A part of him longed to return to the Amish way of worshiping. Yet he also battled with his fear of rejection. Did the community truly want him back?

"I'll think about it," he finally told her, and she nodded, seemingly satisfied with that response. "So let me tell you what else we're going to do around here. You're going to love it." He took her hand in his and shared all his plans to make the house easier for her to navigate.

Becky found Solomon reading his Bible in their family room later that evening. She sat in a chair across from him while thinking about all the wonderful things his brother had been doing since he'd returned. She couldn't stop thinking about what Ruthie Joy had said about Aaron. Becky was beginning to feel her heart soften toward her brother-in-law, and she couldn't stop thinking that her daughter had been right about him. Maybe God had sent Aaron here to help Ruth heal and also to bring their family back together. Ruthie Joy was right; they needed to forgive Aaron for the hurt he'd caused in the past. All that mattered was their family and getting Ruth well.

She longed to find a way to help Solomon accept Aaron back into the family. She'd spent all afternoon wondering what she could do to encourage Solomon to help

Aaron with his home projects, thinking that was one way to bring them together. She'd decided to hit the subject head-on, even if it upset Solomon. She couldn't stand his silence any longer. She felt in her heart that she had to help him accept his brother back into the family for her in-laws' sake.

"Your *mamm* is doing well," Becky said, hoping to pull him into a conversation by starting with the improvement in his mother's condition. "She seemed very upbeat today, and Jocelyn said she's doing well with her physical therapy. She even walked a little bit with the help of a walker, which is a tremendous improvement."

Solomon looked up from the Bible and nodded. "*Ya*, I noticed she looked well this afternoon. She reminded me of how strong she used to be."

"*Ya*, I thought so too." Becky ran her fingers over the chair arm. "I think having Aaron here has really helped with your mother's recovery."

Solomon's eyes widened with surprise. "You think so?"

"*Ya*, I do." Becky nodded, encouraged that he was listening. "I've been thinking about what Ruthie Joy said to us about Aaron, and I think she's right. Your *mamm* is so *froh* to have him back. She told me that she invited him to church today. She's hoping he'll go and even consider staying and joining the church."

She continued speaking despite the frown that had appeared on her husband's face. "She was so excited when she told me about it. He said he'd think about going to church, which sounds positive."

"Becky, are you listening to yourself? You know he's going to break her heart again."

"Why are you so convinced that will happen?" Becky challenged him.

"Because I've seen it before. Don't you remember how *Mamm* sobbed for months when Aaron left?" Solomon placed the Bible on the end table and pointed his finger at her. "You even said to me that Aaron had shattered her heart and should come back and apologize to her. But he never did either of those things."

"He's back *now*," Becky said, raising her chin. "And Ruthie Joy was right when she said we need to welcome him back into the family."

Solomon's scowl deepened. "This is between *mei bruder* and me."

"Have you seen what Aaron and Manny are doing in your parents' *haus*?" she asked, ignoring his statement. "They went with your *dat* to pick out a shower stall today.

They showed me a picture of it, and it's *schee.* You should really ask to see it. I think your *dat* has the picture. Maybe you could help them work on the bathroom. Manny is enjoying helping Aaron, and I would imagine they would appreciate your help too."

Solomon ran his hands down his face, and his cheeks turned bright red.

"I think Ruthie Joy was right when she said it's a miracle from God that he came back," Becky continued. "You should embrace this. This is *gut* for our family, Solomon. It's especially *gut* for your *mamm.* And our *kinner* love him. Katie keeps talking about how much Aaron's hair is like hers. Manny is thrilled with all he's learning about construction and renovation. You must see how *gut* this is."

Solomon stood and started for the stairs. "I'm going to bed."

Irritation surged through her as she stared after him. "Why are you dismissing me, Solomon? You know what I'm saying is true, but you're too stubborn to admit it. Look at me, Solomon. Why won't you talk about this?"

He turned to face her, and his eyes were narrow with frustration. "I'm tired of hearing how *wunderbaar* it is that my long-lost *bruder* came back!" His voice boomed through the downstairs of their house.

"Solomon! Don't raise your voice like that," she warned him. "The *kinner* are sleeping."

"No, you started this," he seethed. "Now you're going to hear what I have to say." He pointed to his chest. "Everyone is so *froh* that Aaron came back, but they forget that I'm the one who stayed. I'm the one who helped *mei dat* run the farm and helped my parents. I was the one who had to give up my dreams to take care of the mess Aaron left behind. You know I never wanted to run this farm with *Dat.* All they see is that Aaron came back, but they don't see the work I had to do in his absence."

Becky gasped. "Solomon, how could you say that? We have a good life here. You're still holding on to the past. That's not what Jesus teaches us in the Bible."

"It's the truth. Aaron came back, but he hasn't fixed any of the problems he caused when he left."

Becky shook her head. "That's not true. Your family is back together. You should be thankful. You should be praising God for bringing your *bruder* back to you safely."

Solomon started up the stairs. "I'm going to bed," he said again.

Becky folded her arms over her middle.

302

She'd hoped she could convince Solomon to welcome his brother back to the family. She couldn't do this on her own. She needed God to show her the way.

Fourteen

Aaron stood in the lobby of the Lancaster Grand Hotel Tuesday morning. The large and ornate lobby boasted a sparkling chandelier, elaborate woodworking on the fireplace, and impressive paintings on the walls.

He hoped Linda was working today. He'd been thinking about her ever since he saw her last week, but he hadn't run into her at the bed-and-breakfast. Once he'd asked where she was, and Trey said she'd gone to the market with Hannah. He wondered if Linda had been avoiding him. He couldn't stop worrying that he had said something wrong that caused her not to speak to him at his parents' house and then avoid him at the bed-and-breakfast. He couldn't stand the worry any longer, so he drove to the hotel that morning in the hopes of asking her if she was upset with him.

"May I help you?" a young lady at the desk asked.

"I was wondering if I could speak to Linda Zook," Aaron said. "She works here."

"Sure." She smiled. "I'll get her for you. I think I saw her go toward the supply closets." She walked around the front desk and started down a hallway.

Aaron rested his elbow on the counter while he waited for her to return with Linda. A few minutes later, Linda came in, standing tall as the two women made their way to the front desk. The limp he'd spotted last week was gone, and she was smiling. His Linda, the one who had gone skating with him, was back. The tension released from his shoulders.

Her eyes met his, and her pink lips formed a smile as she approached him. "Aaron. I wondered if it was you when Stacey described you."

He looked at the blonde, who was back behind the desk. "Thank you."

"Thank you, Stacey," Linda repeated.

"Can we go somewhere and talk?" Aaron asked Linda.

"*Ya.*" She turned to Stacey again. "If Gregg asks for me, tell him I'm taking a quick break."

"Okay." Stacey smiled.

Linda looked up at Aaron. "We can sit over there." She pointed toward a sitting area. "We also have fresh coffee. Would you like to have a cup?"

"That would be perfect." Linda walked him to the canisters in a corner of the lobby, where he poured two cups of coffee. Then he followed Linda to a table at the far end of the sitting area.

"How's your day going?" he asked as they sat down.

"Fine." She sipped her coffee and then gave him a curious expression. "I never expected you to come to the hotel. What brought you out here today?"

"We haven't talked in a while." Aaron was enjoying the sight of her beautiful face.

"*Ya,* I know." She placed her cup on the table. "I think we've both been busy. Trey said I missed you yesterday too. I was hoping you'd still be at the bed-and-breakfast when I got back. Hannah was eager to get out of the *haus,* and she asked me to go to the market with her. I'm sorry we missed each other."

"I'm sorry too," he admitted, grateful that she wasn't avoiding him. "I've been worried about you."

"You were worried about me?" She tilted her head in question. "Why would you worry about me?"

"You were different when I saw you at my

mamm's *haus* a week ago."

"I know I couldn't stop to talk because *mei onkel* was in a hurry, but what do you mean I was different?"

"You weren't yourself." Aaron fingered his cup while he spoke. "You held yourself differently and you seemed to be limping. You didn't stand up straight, and you looked unsure of yourself. You weren't the same *maedel* who ice skated with confidence the week before."

Linda hesitated and then looked down at her coffee.

"Linda." He leaned forward in an attempt to encourage her to meet his gaze. "Look at me."

She raised her eyes to meet his, and her expression was cautious.

"Are you afraid of your *onkel*?" he asked gently.

Her eyes widened. "Why would you ask me that?"

"You just seemed uncomfortable around him. I'd noticed it a little bit when I picked you up to go skating, but it was much more pronounced last week." He hoped he wasn't crossing a line by asking her such personal questions, but he had to know the truth.

Linda blew out a sigh and looked down at her cup again.

"You can trust me," he pressed on. "I'm only asking because I care about you."

She met his gaze, and her eyes were full of such affection that his heart felt like it turned over.

"You know *mei onkel* and *aenti* took me in when my parents died," she began. "*Mei onkel* has always treated me as if I were unlovable, and it's only become worse since *mei aenti* died. He's made it clear that all I'm good for is cleaning house, washing dishes, and taking care of laundry because of my disability. So after my aunt died, I took the job at the hotel to try to show him I could do other things besides take care of him."

"Wait. Your disability?" He shook his head with bewilderment. "What disability are you talking about?"

"I told you I was hurt in the accident that killed my parents. I had surgery on my legs. I have a limp." She paused and looked embarrassed. "My left leg favors my right leg because my right leg was mangled in the accident."

"You don't have a limp," he insisted.

"*Ya,* I do." Her eyes glinted with tears, and she sniffed. "Especially when I get tired. That's why I had never ice skated before. *Onkel* Reuben made me believe I couldn't do what other children could do. He said I'd never be able to do anything like sports because of my legs. That's why I never played softball at school or went to youth group and played volleyball with the other *kinner.* He said my limp would always hold me back in life." A tear escaped her eye, and she quickly brushed it away with the back of her hand. "He even said the same thing about the scars on my legs. I overheard him tell *mei aenti* that no man would ever want me because of my scars."

He was stunned by her words. Anger boiled inside him as he thought of her uncle. How could he have convinced her she was disabled? Why would anyone want to break someone's spirit — especially someone like Linda, who was beautiful both inside and out? "I don't understand your *onkel.* I only saw your limp once, and that was last week when you were with him at *mei mamm*'s house."

Linda sniffed again and then sipped her coffee.

"Linda, your *onkel* is wrong about everything. You're not disabled, and you're not ugly because of scars on your legs, and you're not unworthy of love." Aaron reached across the table, took her cup from her, and set it down before taking one of her hands in his. "You're *schee,* and you're confident both at the bed-and-breakfast and here. I never thought of you as disabled."

Another thought came to him.

"Linda, do you limp mostly when you're at home?"

"Well, yes. But that's because I'm tired —"

"Are you sure? Why would you have been tired when you and your *onkel* visited *mei mamm* last week?"

"I . . . I don't know."

"I don't doubt that the effects of your injury are real, but maybe how pronounced your limp is, how pronounced you think it is, could have something to do with discouragement, not just fatigue. Think about it, won't you?"

"Okay. I will."

Linda looked down at their hands. He enjoyed the soft, warm touch of her skin. "So, your *onkel* is the reason you never participated in singings?"

She nodded. "I thought I belonged at home."

He leaned forward and fixed his gaze on her deep-brown orbs. "He's wrong about you, Linda. Don't let him hold you back. He can't keep you locked up forever. You need to live your life."

She nodded slowly, her eyes wide. "Okay."

"I don't think anyone has ever told you how special and wonderful you are. You can't let him keep you from the life you deserve." He ran his thumb over the palm of her hand.

"Danki." She wiped her eyes as a few tears trickled down her cheek. "How are things with your family?"

"They're okay." He unclasped her hand and leaned back in the chair. "Manny and I are making progress on the bathroom. The new shower is going to be installed later this week." He sipped his coffee. "*Mei mamm* invited me to come to church."

"Really?" Linda's expression brightened. "Are you going to come?"

"I'm not sure." He ran his fingers over the table. "I don't know how the community would react to seeing me at church again."

"What do you mean? We're all *froh* that you're back."

"Not everyone is *froh* I'm back." He grimaced.

"Solomon and Becky." Her smile faded, and he nodded. "They're still cold to you."

"Becky seems to be coming around. She hasn't been as aloof as she was when I first arrived. Solomon is the same, though." Aaron held up the coffee cup. "It's obvious that he doesn't want me here. In fact, he's eager for me to leave."

"Aaron, I have faith that Solomon will come around," she said. "You need to be patient." Her expression became hopeful. "Please come to church. The congregation will be delighted to see you."

He couldn't say no to her hopeful expression and her captivating eyes. "All right."

Linda grinned. "*Wunderbaar!* I'm going to hold you to that promise." She glanced toward the clock on the wall and her eyes widened. "*Ach,* no. I went past my break time. I have to get back to work."

He picked up their empty cups and stood. "I didn't mean to keep you so long. I just had to see you."

She stood and pushed her chair in. "It was a nice surprise. I enjoyed the break."

"I'll see you at the bed-and-breakfast," he said as they walked to a trash can.

"And at church." She smiled up at him. "You promised me you'll come."

"Yes, I did promise." He touched her hand again. "Have a *gut* day."

"You too." Her smiled widened. "You're doing well with your *Dietsch.*"

He chuckled at her expression. "I'm trying."

"You'd better brush up on the language

before church. I don't want you to get lost during the sermon. See you later." She started walking toward the hallway — with no limp at all. She turned once to give him a little wave and was gone.

He waved back at her, and at that moment he knew he was losing his heart to Linda Zook.

Linda felt as if she were walking on air as she made her way back to the supply closets. She couldn't stop her smile while she filled her cart with towels and toiletries. She'd never expected Aaron to visit her, and she'd never dreamed of sharing her deepest secrets with him. She'd never told anyone about how unkind her uncle had been or the scars on her legs. Not even her limp. Aaron had listened with sympathy, and he'd told her that her uncle was wrong. Aaron thought she was worthy of love! She'd felt as if she were dreaming when he'd said that.

Could he possibly love her?

The notion sent excitement skittering through her. But she had to suppress these feelings. Aaron wasn't a member of the community, but he had promised to go to church. Perhaps he'd be inspired to join the church after attending a service and realizing how much he'd missed worshiping in the Amish church.

She'd hold on to that hope.

Aaron parked his truck in the driveway at Saul Beiler's farm a few weeks later. He was determined to keep his promise to Linda and also make his mother happy; however, he was apprehensive. What if the congregation rejected him? What if his friends weren't happy to see him after all? All his worries swirled through his mind as he walked up to the barn where the male members of the congregation were gathered before the service.

Saul spotted him and walked over. "Aaron! It's so *gut* to see you."

"*Danki.*" Aaron shook his hand. "My *mamm* asked me to come to a service. I thought I'd come today."

"I'm *froh* that you could join us." Saul patted Aaron's arm. "Come see everyone."

Aaron walked over to the group.

"Look who came to visit," Saul announced. "Remember Aaron Ebersol?"

"Aaron!" A familiar face emerged from the crowd. "I heard you were back."

"It's great to see you." Another friend approached with his hand ready to shake his. "*Willkumm!*"

"Where have you been?" a third asked.

Aaron was overwhelmed by the encouraging welcome. His old friends shook his hands and told him they were happy to see him. All of them had beards, evidence that they were married. They stood and talked for several minutes, assuring him they were interested in hearing about his life in Missouri.

"Aaron!" His father sidled up to him. "It's great to see you here. Your *mamm* mentioned she invited you to church. I'm so thankful you made it."

"Danki, Dat." Aaron looked past his father to Solomon, who scowled at him and then walked away. "I'm glad to be here." He meant the words, despite his brother's cold stare.

"Your *mamm* will be delighted." His father's expression was full of gratitude. "You've made us so *froh. Danki* for coming home."

Tears stung Aaron's eyes as a lump swelled in his throat. For a moment he couldn't speak. He only nodded in response to his father's emotional words.

"Aaron." Becky appeared behind them, pushing his mother in a wheelchair. "It's *gut* to see you. I'm glad you decided to come to church with us today. And look who else is here! One of the reasons your *mamm* can come to services is that new ramp you built."

"*Danki,* Becky." Aaron was grateful that Becky smiled at him. The gesture helped to heal his battered heart.

His mother's eyes sparkled with tears. "Y-you c-came."

"Mamm." Aaron leaned down and kissed her cheek. "I'm sorry it took me a few weeks, but I'm finally here."

Mamm reached up and touched his cheek. "Y-you're h-here. I'm *f-froh.*"

"It's time." His father pointed toward the barn. "Let's head inside."

Aaron walked with his father toward the barn, which was set up with rows of benches. While his father went to sit with the other married Amish men, Aaron found a place in the back where the other non-Amish guests sat. He folded his hands on his lap while members of the church made their way into the barn.

Although it had been many years since he'd participated in an Amish service, he quickly felt comfortable. Glancing across the barn, his father met his eyes and smiled at him. Solomon sat beside their father and kept his gaze trained on the hymnal in his hands.

The women filed in and sat in the rows in

316

front of him. He searched for Linda, and his pulse accelerated when he saw her making her way to her seat. Without looking back toward him, she sank onto a bench beside Madeleine. He longed for her to turn around and see him. After all, it had been three weeks since he'd promised her he'd go to church. She'd mentioned it a few times at the bed-and-breakfast. He told her he would keep his promise and attend a service, but he didn't promise when he would go. Now that he'd kept that promise, he wanted her to see him. He watched her, hoping she'd feel his stare and turn to face him.

Madeleine looked over her shoulder, and she smiled when she saw him. He nodded in response. She leaned close to Linda and whispered in her ear. Linda's eyes widened as she looked over her shoulder at him. Her face lit up with a beautiful smile as she raised her hand in a slight wave. He returned the smile as he waved in response.

He knew at that moment he'd made the right choice in coming to church.

Linda turned toward the front again, and his eyes moved toward the married men across the barn with his father and Solomon. He found Reuben in the sea of faces, and he grimaced. He wondered why the older man didn't see the beauty Aaron found in Linda. How could Reuben treat Linda so badly?

The service began with a hymn, and Aaron redirected his thoughts to the present. He joined in as the congregation slowly sang the opening hymn. A young man sitting across the barn served as the song leader. He began the first syllable of each line and then the rest of the congregation joined in to finish the verse.

While the ministers met in another room for thirty minutes to choose who would preach that day, the congregation continued to sing. Aaron saw the ministers return during the last verse of the second hymn. They hung their hats on the pegs on the wall, indicating that the service was about to begin.

The minister began the first sermon, and his message droned on like background noise to the thoughts echoing in Aaron's head. Although he tried to concentrate on the preacher's holy words, he couldn't stop looking at Linda. He studied her back, taking in her slight frame and the dark hair peeking out from under her prayer covering.

While the minister continued to talk in German, Aaron lost himself in memories of

318

the past, of sitting with the young men in the congregation and thinking of what mischief they could get into when the service was over. He redirected his thoughts to the sermon, taking in the message and concentrating on God. He wondered what God had in store for him. Did he want him to rejoin the community? Was Aaron supposed to become a member of the Amish church just as his friends who were sitting in the barn had done?

The first sermon ended, and Aaron knelt in silent prayer along with the rest of the congregation. He closed his eyes and thanked God for bringing him back to the community and for blessing his mother during her recovery. He also prayed for Linda, asking God to help her find confidence to believe in herself. After the prayers, the deacon read from the Scriptures, and then the hour-long main sermon began. Aaron willed himself to concentrate on the sermon, listening to the deacon discuss the book of John.

Relief flooded Aaron when the fifteen-minute kneeling prayer was over. The congregation stood for the benediction and sang the closing hymn. While he sang, Aaron's eyes moved again to Linda. He wondered if she could feel his eyes studying her. He hoped they would have a moment to talk after the service was over. Would she feel confident to be herself despite her uncle's presence?

"Aaron!" Peter approached him and shook his hand. "It's so *gut* to see you. Welcome to church again."

"*Danki,*" Aaron said. "May I help convert the benches into tables?"

"*Ya, ya.*" Peter leaned down and they started setting up the tables. "How did you like the service? Did it seem odd to you?"

"Not at all," Aaron said as they slipped the benches into the stands so that the benches converted into tables for the noon meal. "It all came back to me."

"That's great." Peter grinned. "You'll have to eat with the guys and me. We can get caught up."

"That sounds *gut,*" Aaron agreed.

Linda stepped into Saul's kitchen and found Madeleine and Emma placing peanut butter spread and bread on trays. Several other women were helping to serve the meal as well. "Let me help you deliver the food."

"*Danki.*" Madeleine moved closer to her. "Are you going to talk to Aaron?"

Linda felt her cheeks heat. "I can't really talk to him now. *Mei onkel* is here and

320

everyone will see me talking to a man who isn't baptized."

"He's your friend." Madeleine looked at her. "I'm not baptized, and I'm friends with Saul. We can't date until I'm baptized, but we can still talk."

"But you're going to take classes and everyone knows it. It's different for me," Linda whispered as the other women moved about the kitchen. "Aaron hasn't decided to be baptized. And *mei onkel* has made it clear he doesn't approve of our friendship."

Madeleine gave her a skeptical look. "You're thirty-one, right?"

Linda nodded.

"You're not a child, Linda," Madeleine whispered with emphasis. "You're allowed to have friends, even friends who are *English.*" She handed Linda a coffeepot. "Go fill coffee cups and make a point of talking to Aaron."

Linda hesitated, and her hands shook as she nodded. "I will." She carried the coffeepot into the barn and started filling the men's cups. Her pulse fluttered when she realized she was serving the table where Aaron sat surrounded by a group of young men and his father. Aaron looked up at her and smiled, and butterflies swirled in her stomach.

"How are you?" he asked.

"I'm fine." She held up the pot. "Coffee?"

He nodded, and her hands were shaking slightly as she filled his cup.

"I told you I'd keep my promise." His voice was soft and warm.

"You certainly did." She gave him a tentative smile and then filled the other cups nearby.

When she finished at that first long table, the coffeepot was empty. She was walking toward the house for more when she heard someone call her name. Turning, she found Aaron approaching her with an anxious expression on his face.

"Aaron," she said. "What's wrong?"

He hurried over to her. "You didn't seem to want to talk to me in the barn."

She frowned. "I don't want to give *mei onkel* the wrong impression. You're not baptized, and he doesn't approve of my friendship with you."

Aaron's expression was wounded, and her heart twisted. "I thought you agreed with me when I said you shouldn't let him hold you back," he said.

"I appreciate what you said, and I do agree. But I also have to follow the rules of the community. People talk." She motioned toward the house. "I need to get more coffee. I'll see you at the bed-and-breakfast."

She started to turn, then smiled. "I'm glad you came. I can tell your friends are *froh* to see you. I told you the community would welcome you back."

He smiled, and her heart fluttered. *"Danki."*

"Did you understand the sermons?"

He laughed, and she delighted at the sound. *"Ya,* I did."

"Gut." She smiled at him and then walked back to the house, her pulse skittering with every step. She hoped she'd see him at church again soon. Maybe God did intend for Aaron to return to his Amish roots.

Fifteen

"The weather is nice, *ya*?" Linda asked her uncle in the buggy as they traveled home after the church service. "It's getting warmer."

"It should be warmer since it's finally March," Reuben muttered while guiding the horse down the road.

Linda tried to think of something to say that would brighten her uncle's permanent bad mood. Her thoughts turned to her conversation with Aaron in the hotel a few days earlier. She wondered if Aaron was right, that she did behave differently around her grumpy, old uncle — that even when her limp was more pronounced, it was when she especially felt his harsh words and indifference to her happiness.

Did she truly allow him to beat down her spirit? If so, then what could she do about that? What could she do to change her uncle's demeanor toward her? She wondered if she could bring joy to his life and show him how to be happy.

"It was a lovely service today," she said while forcing a smile. "I enjoyed the sermons."

Reuben grunted, and she racked her brain for something else positive to say.

"Sometimes I consider how blessed we are to be members of this *wunderbaar* community," she continued. "We have many kind and thoughtful friends. It's been so nice seeing everyone help Ruth and her family since her stroke."

"She's gotten more support than I did when Verna died," Reuben barked without taking his eyes off the road ahead of them.

Stunned by his negative comment, Linda swallowed a gasp. "I don't think that's true. I remember many people coming over and offering their love and support. We had meals for days. In fact, I froze a lot of the food and brought it out later."

Reuben snorted. "We remember things differently."

Linda turned her eyes toward the window and hugged her cloak to her body. No matter how hard she tried, she couldn't change her uncle. He'd never see that there were reasons to smile.

"You'll soon learn that life isn't fair," Reuben said while guiding the horse onto their road. "Things never turn out the way you plan them."

"What do you mean?" She faced him.

"I was the oldest son," he began, spitting out the words. "I was supposed to get the big farmhouse and the land. *Mei dat* even told me I would when I was a teenager. But then your *dat* was born, and *mei dat* changed his mind. Matthew was the *boppli*, and I suppose the *boppli* is always the favorite. Everything changed. Matthew got it all when our *dat* died — the farm and the big *haus*. I was left with a tiny *haus* and a tiny piece of land, hardly anything to farm to make a decent living. My brother Caleb didn't seem to care. He had other plans."

Linda's mouth dried as she stared at her uncle, absorbing the anger in his voice and the animosity in his eyes.

"I learned a valuable lesson when Matthew took everything that was supposed to be mine. And then when he died, he left everything to Raymond." Reuben gave her a sideways glance as the horse and buggy approached their farm. "Don't expect too much out of life. If you're prepared for the worst, then it won't hurt so much when it happens. Trust me, because I know firsthand how unfair life can be — even at the hands of family. I never expected to be cheated out of land that was rightfully mine. I never imagined that I would lose *mei fraa* so unexpectedly. We thought she was getting better, and then the pneumonia took her in the blink of an eye. And I never in all my days expected to have to raise Matthew's only *kind.*"

Linda's eyes stung with threatening tears. How could her uncle speak to her about her father that way? It wasn't her fault her grandfather had decided to leave everything to his youngest son. And it certainly wasn't her parents' fault the semi-truck had slid on ice in a bad storm. Linda would give anything to have her parents back, but her uncle only resented them. And he resented her.

"Don't dream big, Linda," Reuben continued, guiding the horse toward the barn. "If you dream big, you'll only wind up with a broken heart." He halted the horse and looked at her. "That's the best advice I can give you." Then he hopped out of the buggy and began to unhitch the horse.

Linda sat in the buggy and watched him work. She was stunned silent. She'd never imagined the depth of her uncle's resentment toward her. Tears splattered her hot cheeks, and her heart hurt as his words echoed through her mind. She needed relief from this pain, and she knew she could only receive that relief through prayer.

While still sitting in the buggy, she closed her eyes and asked God to regenerate her uncle's cold, angry, resentful, sad heart.

Aaron found Trey standing by the deck when he parked behind the bed-and-breakfast.

"Hi, Aaron," Trey greeted him as he climbed out of the truck. "How did church go?"

"It went well." Aaron walked over to him. "A few of my old friends are members of the church district, and we ate lunch together. They were surprised to see me, but it was nice catching up with them."

"That's great." Trey smiled and rubbed his goatee. "So that means you didn't have anything to be nervous about then."

"No, I didn't." Aaron stuffed his keys in his coat pocket. "I actually felt like a part of the community. Everyone welcomed me, except for my brother."

"Solomon is the same, huh?" Trey shook his head. "I'm sorry to hear that, but you have to give him time. You're doing everything you can by showing him you want to be a part of the family and the community."

"I know you're right." Aaron sighed. "It was a little painful to see my friends with their families."

"How was it painful?" Trey asked.

"I just keep thinking about everything I missed by leaving. I could've been like them. I could've been married, raising a family, perhaps running a farm or other business in the area. But I ran away and missed out on that." *Why am I confessing such private feelings aloud to someone I barely know? I may not know Trey well, but it feels good to get all these feelings off my chest.*

Trey gave him a wry smile. "You're not eighty years old, Aaron. You can still have all that. You can meet someone, fall in love, get married, and raise a family. You haven't lost your chance to have the life you want. I'm quite a bit older than you, and I found a way to make a new start. You still have time, Aaron."

Aaron nodded while considering his words. "I suppose you're right about that too."

"You know I am." Trey's expression was serious. "Don't sell God short. He has amazing plans for all of us. I lost my family and thought I'd be alone for the rest of my life." He pointed toward the bed-and-breakfast. "I came here to start a new life, and I met Hannah. I never imagined I'd find someone like her. She had lost her husband and also thought she was going to be alone for the rest of her life. God brought us together. We've built a new life together, and now we're expecting our first child together. God has plans for you, Aaron. You just need to listen and follow his lead."

Aaron was overwhelmed by Trey's words. "Thank you."

"You're welcome." Trey turned toward the deck, seeming to study it.

"So what are you looking at here?"

Trey pointed to the stairs at the far end of the deck. "Hannah showed me where the steps are rotting. I hadn't noticed it before."

"Oh." Aaron stooped down and examined the wood. "These definitely need to be replaced."

"Would you like the job?" Trey offered. "I'll pay you."

Aaron stood and rubbed his hands together. "I'm working on my mother's bathroom, but I can fit it in."

"Great. I'd appreciate it," Trey said. "If you have time, we can go to the home improvement store to get the wood and supplies tomorrow."

"Sounds great."

■ ■ ■ ■

Aaron stood between his father and Manny in his parents' downstairs bathroom the following day as they inspected the new shower.

"What do you think?" Aaron asked.

"It's perfect," his father said. "The plumber did a fantastic job."

"I agree," Manny chimed in. "We've already caulked, so now we just have to paint. *Mammi* should be able to use the shower tomorrow."

"That's right." Aaron patted his nephew's shoulder. "Are you ready?"

"Absolutely. I'll go out to the truck and get the supplies."

"I'll go with you," *Dat* said. "We'll carry it in together."

Manny and Aaron's father left and Aaron examined the shower again.

"Aaron?"

He turned toward the doorway and found his mother watching him. She was leaning on a walker and peering into the bathroom. Her skin was pink, and her expression was bright. He saw hints of the strong woman he knew when he was a child.

"Mamm." He walked over to her. "Are you

all right?"

"*Ya.*" She nodded and smiled. "*D-danki* for g-going to ch-church yes-ter-d-day."

"*Gern gschehne.* I enjoyed it. *Danki* for inviting me to go." He made a sweeping gesture around the bathroom. "What do you think?"

She took a shaky step into the bathroom, and he reached for her arm.

"Are you sure you're all right?" he asked.

"*Ya.* Let me w-walk." His mother moved the walker as she shuffled slowly to the shower stall, then nodded. "*G-gut. G-gut.*" She reached out and touched the door. She pulled it open and peered inside.

"You see the safety bars?" Aaron stood beside her. He pulled down the showerhead. "You can sit on the seat and hold this if you don't want to stand. It has a nice, long hose." He turned it over. "Look here. There are different settings for the water flow. You can have it coming out really fast or slower. There's even a massage setting if your shoulders or back are hurting."

Mamm nodded, and he made a mental note to have Becky or Jocelyn show his mother how to use it.

"We just need to paint." He pointed toward the walls. "We're going to freshen it up a bit. I also installed those safety bars for you over by the commode. It will make it easier for you to get up and down."

"D-danki." She cupped her hand to his cheek. "You were always a *g-gut b-bu.*"

"Actually, that's not true." He blinked. "No, I wasn't always a *gut bu.*"

"Ya, y-you were." *Mamm* nodded with emphasis. "Y-you were j-just a l-little l-lost. You h-have a *g-gut* h-heart."

He frowned. "I don't deserve those compliments, but *danki, Mamm.*"

"Will you st-stay?" She spoke the words slowly, concentrating on each one as she said it. "You can m-move into one of t-he sp-spare rooms up-upstairs." Her eyes were full of hopefulness. "Will y-you c-come h-home?"

"I don't know." He hated the disappointment in her expression. "I have to talk to my business partner and see how things are going."

"S-sell y-your b-business to him." She touched his hand. "I w-want my f-family b-back to-g-gether a-gain. Please, Aaron."

"All right, we're ready to paint." *Dat* had returned, carrying a gallon of paint and a bag of supplies. "Ruth. What are you doing in here?"

"Hi, *Mammi,*" Manny said as he put another bag on the floor. "It's *gut* to see you walking again."

Aaron was thankful for the distraction. He didn't want to break his mother's heart, but he also didn't want to make a promise he couldn't keep. He didn't know where he belonged. He hadn't even felt he could accept his *dat*'s invitation to stay upstairs during this visit — not when Solomon's behavior toward him never seemed to improve. He felt stuck between two worlds, and his heart felt as if it were being tugged by each of them. Part of him wanted to go back to Missouri to get away from his brother's hate and distrust, but another part of him wanted to stay in Pennsylvania to be with his family and to get to know Linda better.

In fact, he realized one reason he'd been paying Trey and Hannah to stay at the bed-and-breakfast all this time was to ensure he would see Linda as often as possible.

Mamm squeezed Aaron's hand. "P-Pray about it."

"I will." That was a promise he intended to keep.

The three men spent the day painting. When they finished, Aaron packed up and headed outside.

Manny sat on the tailgate while Aaron loaded the supplies into the bed of his truck. "*Mammi* is *froh* with the bathroom."

"*Ya,* she is. I'm grateful for your help."
Aaron hopped up on the tailgate next to
him. "I was thinking of replacing the floor
in the bathroom while we're at it. Would
you like to help?"

"Sure." Manny shrugged. "I like working
with you."

"I like working with you too." Aaron
thought of the deck at the bed-and-
breakfast. "The owner of the Heart of
Paradise Bed-and-Breakfast asked me if I
would work on his deck. He's going to pay
me. Would you like to help? I'll split the
money with you."

"Sure." Manny's eyes lit up. "That would
be great."

"You have to ask your *dat* before I can let
you do it."

"I'll ask him."

"Great." Aaron jumped down. "Well, I'll
see you tomorrow."

"*Gut nacht.*" Manny hopped off the tailgate
and helped Aaron slam it shut.

"*Gut nacht.*" Aaron climbed into the truck
and thought about his mother's request as
he drove back to the bed-and-breakfast.

Questions and possibilities swirled
through his mind. Should he move back to
Paradise? Should he join the church? He
thought about his family and how much he

enjoyed feeling as if he belonged. He cherished his time with his oldest nephew. If he moved back, he could open a construction business and hire him. He could also spend more time with his father. He could do more for his mother, and he could get to know the rest of his brother's children better. If only he could fix his broken relationship with Solomon . . .

Aaron steered into Trey and Hannah's driveway and his thoughts turned again to Linda. He longed to know Linda better. He knew she was right when she said their relationship was inappropriate because he wasn't a baptized church member. He had no right to want to spend time with her. But he felt a strong attraction to her. It wasn't just a physical attraction; he also wanted to be her friend.

As he climbed the back stairs to his room, he couldn't avoid the feeling that God was leading him back here. But how would he know if he was reading God's plans correctly?

The questions continued to haunt him as he sifted through his mail. And for the hundredth time, he wondered what had happened to his letters.

Linda stepped into the kitchen at the bed-

and-breakfast and was surprised to hear voices out on the deck. She opened the door and found Aaron and Manny cutting boards.

Manny looked up and waved. "Hi, Linda!"

Aaron put down the saw and then waved as well. "Good morning."

"Hi." She stepped out onto the deck. "What are you doing?"

"We're repairing the deck steps." Manny pointed to where boards had been removed. "They were rotting away, and Trey asked Aaron to fix it."

"Oh." Linda fingered the ribbons on her prayer covering. "That's *gut.*"

She watched them work for a few moments, enjoying the view of Aaron as he held the saw and cut the wooden planks down to the correct size. His talent and precision mesmerized her. She did a mental head shake, reminding herself again that she had no right to be so attracted to someone who wasn't a baptized member of the church.

After the piece was cut, Aaron looked up at her with a questioning expression, and she realized she'd been staring at him. She felt silly as she quickly tried to think of something to say.

"It's nearly eleven. Would you like me to

make you lunch?" she offered.

"That would be fantastic." Aaron tented his hand over his eyes as he looked up at her. "I'm starved."

"I am too." Manny lifted his hat and ran his fingers through his brown hair.

"I'll fix something for you." Linda reached behind her and opened the door. "I'll call you when it's ready."

She hurried back into the kitchen and pulled out a cookbook. She found a recipe for macaroni salad and began to pull the ingredients together. Once the macaroni was in a pot of water, she pulled what they needed to make sandwiches. When the macaroni salad was ready, she set the table, complete with a fresh pitcher of iced tea.

She walked over to Hannah's suite and found her lounging on the sofa and reading a book.

"I've made macaroni salad and have all the fixings for sandwiches. Would you like me to make you something?" Linda offered.

"Oh, no, thank you." Hannah shook her head. "I'm not feeling very hungry right now. And when I'm ready, I think we have something in our kitchen I can eat. I don't need much."

"All right." Linda smiled. "Just call if you need anything."

"I will. Thank you, Linda." Hannah looked down at her book again.

Linda went through the kitchen and stepped out onto the deck, where she found Trey helping Aaron and Manny. "Lunch is ready."

"Great!" all three men said at once. Trey hoisted himself up on the deck since the new steps were only partially finished. "I just got back from the bank." He stepped past her into the kitchen. "Is Hannah in the suite?"

"Ya." Linda said, following him inside. "I just checked on her, and she said she wasn't hungry."

"Oh." Trey looked concerned. "I'm going to go see how she is. I'm worried that she's not eating enough." He disappeared into the hallway.

Manny and Aaron came in and stared at the table.

"I hope you like macaroni salad," she said, wondering if they were disappointed. "It was the only thing I could think of to make quickly."

"You just made macaroni salad?" Now Aaron looked impressed.

Linda nodded. *"Ya,* it's easy."

"Danki," Aaron said.

"I love macaroni salad too." Manny

washed his hands at the sink. "We've worked up an appetite."

"I'm sure you have." Linda pointed to the spread on the table. "I also have lunch meat, bread, mustard, and mayo." She snapped her fingers. "I forgot the chips. Would you like chips too?"

"I can get them. Just point me in the right direction." Aaron had come to stand behind her, standing so close that she could smell his soap mixed with aftershave and earth. Her pulse skipped at his closeness.

"They're in the cabinet over there by the pantry." She pointed across the kitchen.

Manny sat down at the table. "This looks great. *Danki,* Linda."

Aaron fetched a bag of chips and placed it on the table before washing his hands. He then sat down beside Manny. "Are you going to join us, Linda?"

"Ya." She sat down across from him.

After prayers, they began filling their plates with macaroni salad and making sandwiches.

"How is the bathroom project coming along?" Linda asked while squeezing mustard onto her turkey sandwich.

"It's going well," Aaron said. "The shower is installed and we've painted. Now we're working on replacing the vinyl flooring."

"That's *wunderbaar.* I know your *mamm* is enjoying it." Linda cut her sandwich in half.

Manny nodded. "She's really *froh.* She told *mei mamm* that she felt much more comfortable using that shower this morning than she had using the tub, even with Becky or her aides helping her. She said we did a great job."

"You like working with your *onkel,* huh?" Linda asked Manny.

"I do. I've learned so much." Manny bit into his sandwich.

Aaron gave Manny an adoring look, and Linda smiled at the admiration between the uncle and nephew. She longed to have a similar relationship with her uncle.

"Have you talked to your business partner lately?" Linda asked Aaron.

Aaron nodded while chewing and then wiped his mouth with a napkin. "I talked to Zac last night. He said we're still busy, but everything is going fine. He told me to take my time coming back. He's been sending me my mail, so I'm keeping up with everything I need to."

"That's *gut.*" She hoped that meant he planned to stay for a good, long time.

"I'm going to send that package to him tonight," he said as he picked up a chip. "I

341

told you I'd picked up gifts for Zac and his family at Peter's store. I'm going to mail them out instead of taking them back with me when I return to Missouri. He's being so patient and understanding."

"I'm sure he'll appreciate that." Linda lifted a chip from her plate and tried to hide her disappointment. There it was again, talk about returning to Missouri.

"How's work for you?" Aaron asked.

"The hotel is fine," she said. "It's busy as always."

Linda told them about one of their more interesting hotel guests while they finished their sandwiches. Then she brought out a plate of cookies for dessert, and as they ate them, they talked about how nice the weather was getting and how happy they were that spring was just about here.

When the cookies were gone, Linda carried the dishes to the counter. Manny and Aaron picked up the condiments and utensils and brought them to her.

"You don't have to do that." She shooed them away. "You can go outside and work. I can handle the cleanup."

"I don't mind helping." Aaron stood close to her again. "I've told you before that you don't have to wait on me."

Manny smiled at Aaron as if there was a

secret between them. "I'm going to go on outside."

Aaron nodded at Manny, watched him go, and then looked at Linda. "I want to tell you something."

"Oh?" Her mouth dried as he looked down at her. "What is it?"

"My *mamm* asked me if I'm going to stay here, permanently." Aaron's eyes were intense as they searched hers. "She said I could move into one of their spare bedrooms if I want to come back for good. She wants her family back together again. She was pretty insistent."

"What did you tell her?" Her heart thudded in her chest as she awaited his response.

"I told her I don't know what I'm going to do." He stared at her with intensity, as if he might find the answer in her face. "But I guess I'm considering it."

Linda lost herself in his warm eyes. "Let me know what you decide to do," she whispered.

"I promise you'll be the first to know." He smiled. "*Danki* for the *appeditlich* lunch."

"*Gern gschehne,*" she whispered.

Aaron stepped out the back door, and she leaned back against the sink while trying to catch her breath. She had to work to calm her frayed nerves. She couldn't help but wonder why he'd told her his mother wanted him to move back to Pennsylvania. What did his intense expression mean? Did he want Linda to ask him to stay? She wondered if she should've told him how she felt about him, but she didn't want to appear eager in case he didn't feel the same way about her. All she knew for certain was that she wanted him to stay. She wanted him to move into his parents' house. She longed to spend more time with him.

As she stared at the back door, Linda prayed a simple prayer.

"Lord, you know how I feel. If it's your will, I'd like Aaron to stay."

Sixteen

Linda sat with Ruth in her kitchen while they drank tea together. "You're looking well, Ruth. How are you feeling?"

"B-better," Ruth said. "H-how are you?"

"I'm fine." Linda smiled, thinking of the sweet moment she'd shared with Aaron the week before. Ever since he'd told her he was considering staying, she'd felt closer to him. Although they'd only made small talk in passing, she felt as if his smiles held more emotion. She kept hoping he'd tell her he was going to stay.

"H-how's the h-hotel?" Ruth asked, her words slightly clearer than the last time Linda had seen her.

"It's *gut.*" Linda clasped her warm mug in her hands. "We really miss you. Carolyn is home with her *boppli,* and she's doing really well. Madeleine is working more hours. She's joining this spring's baptism class, and she's so excited. I have a feeling she and Saul will get married after she's baptized. She talks about Saul and Emma all the time."

"That is *g-gut.*" Ruth picked up her mug with her good hand. "M-Madeleine is a *g-gut maedel.*"

"She is," Linda agreed. "I'm so glad Saul and Madeleine found each other. They both have been through so much since Saul lost his wife and Madeleine lost her fiancé. The Lord works in mysterious ways. He brought Madeleine to the community to her *mammi*'s *haus.*"

"*Ya.*" Ruth nodded and then smiled. "I'm s-so p-proud of m-my Aaron. He's s-such a g-*gut* man."

"*Ya,*" Linda said with a deep smile. "He is."

"I asked h-him to st-stay." Ruth's eyes gleamed with tears. "I h-hope h-he d-does."

Linda nodded and her heart swelled with hopefulness. "I know. I do too."

After they finished their tea, Jocelyn took Ruth to her bedroom for her exercises and Linda washed the mugs and the teapot. She then made her way to the hallway and peered into the bathroom where Aaron and Manny were working on replacing the flooring. She stood in the doorway watching Aaron as he knelt on the floor and explained the process to his nephew. She was drawn to his care and patience as he spoke.

Aaron suddenly looked over his shoulder and gave her a soft smile. "How long have you been standing there?" He rose, wiping his hands on his worn jeans.

"I just got here." She pointed toward the kitchen. "I had a cup of tea with your *mamm.*"

"That's nice. I'm sure she enjoyed your visit." He walked over to her and then looked back at Manny. "Want to take a break?"

"Ya." Manny stood and cupped his hand over his mouth as he yawned. "That sounds *gut.* Hi, Linda," he said before leaving.

Linda scanned the bathroom, taking in the crisp-white walls and the brand-new shower stall. The aroma of fresh paint tickled her nose. "You do great work."

"Thanks." He seemed almost embarrassed by the compliment. "The plumber was excellent."

She glanced down at the floor. "I like the new vinyl."

"I tried to get my *dat* to go for bright purple, but he wanted to keep it a neutral tan."

"You did?" She tilted her head with confusion.

His lips twitched. "It was a joke."

A loud bark of laughter burst from her lips before she could stop it, and she was mortified with embarrassment. She cupped her hand over her mouth as her cheeks heated.

"Oh," she finally said as he grinned at her. "Excuse me."

"Why are you covering your mouth? You have a great laugh. I enjoy hearing it." He touched her hand. "I always look forward to seeing your smile and hearing you laugh."

"You do?" she asked with astonishment.

"*Ya,* I do." He stepped over to the shower stall. "Let me show you how this works." He pulled open the shower door and explained the different controls. He emphasized how much safer the shower was for his mother than the tub.

While he told her all about the shower, she kept replaying his compliments in her mind. He had told her he looked forward to her smile and her laugh. No one had ever said anything like that to her. She never imagined that anyone would say something so sweet. She felt as if she were dreaming. Had she finally found someone who could possibly love her despite her imperfections?

"*Mei mamm* said she really likes it," he continued, closing the shower door. "I'm so glad I can do something like this for her."

"What was your most favorite construction job?" she asked.

"Hmm." He rubbed his smooth chin while considering the question. "My company once got a job to work on a mansion. I remember telling my nieces and nephews about it when I first arrived."

"A mansion?" she asked. "What do you mean by mansion?"

"Well," he began, leaning against the counter behind him. "It had six bathrooms and ten bedrooms."

"Oh my goodness." Linda gaped. "How many people lived there?"

He raised his eyebrows. "Would you believe only two people lived there?"

"Oh dear. Why would two people need such a big *haus*? It doesn't make sense."

"Sometimes people who have a lot of money like to buy things they don't need because it makes them feel important," Aaron said.

"Really? So what kind of work did you do on that mansion?"

For the next half hour, Linda stood in the bathroom with Aaron and discussed his most memorable construction projects. She enjoyed talking with him and finding out more about his life.

■ ■ ■ ■

Later that evening, Linda was still smiling when she served supper to her uncle. She was determined not to let his foul mood ruin the wonderful day she'd had, and she tried to forget about their conversation two weeks ago on their way home from church. He was still her uncle — and, she realized, she was all he had. Her cousin Raymond had given up on him.

Reuben frowned into his meat loaf while she tried to tell him about her afternoon.

"You should see the work Aaron has done to Ruth's bathroom," Linda said. "He installed this beautiful shower stall that has a bench for Ruth to sit on so she doesn't fall. He also repainted the walls, and he installed safety bars by the commode. He's also replacing the flooring. It's lovely, *Onkel.*"

Reuben grunted while scooping mashed potatoes onto his spoon.

"Aaron told me about this mansion he worked on. Even though only two people lived there it had ten bedrooms and six bathrooms." She watched her uncle while she chewed. He kept his eyes focused on his food, and she longed for him to look at her

350

the way Aaron looked at Manny. Why wasn't she worthy of her uncle's love? What had she done wrong to deserve his constantly cold moods? She had always tried her best to care for him.

They ate in silence for several minutes, and she couldn't stop her thoughts from turning to the conversation she'd had with him in the buggy. She must remind him of all the things he'd wanted but never gotten out of life, about how her father inherited the house and land he'd wanted. She was convinced that was the reason he couldn't love her, not her scars and limp.

When their plates were clean, she began to clear the table. She couldn't stand the silence in the house. She wished her uncle would allow her to invite company over for supper so the house didn't remain so quiet and lonely all the time. Even though there were two of them there, she sometimes felt as if she lived alone. Would he allow her to invite Aaron over for supper someday? Surely dinner would be lively and fun if she had Aaron there to talk to during the meal. No, she knew how he felt about her spending time with someone who wasn't baptized in the church.

Linda prepared the sinks, dropped the dishes into the sudsy side, and began to scrub them as she wondered what Aaron was doing. She hoped he was enjoying a lively supper with his family, laughing and talking the evening away.

"I never thought I'd spend my last years in a tiny *haus* like this." Reuben's booming voice startled her. Had he been reading her thoughts during supper?

"I always thought I'd have a nice, big *haus* on a productive farm. I spent so many years slaving on my father's farm. I didn't deserve to be stuck in this small *haus* on my nephew's land."

She glanced toward where he stood scowling at her. As his angry brown eyes burned through her, she felt her shoulders hunch.

"I have so much to resent in life." He walked away muttering something she could hardly understand. Something about choices and consequences?

Linda stared down at the frothy water. It must have been torture for her uncle to keep all that inside for so many years.

She thought again about her conversation with Aaron when they'd shared coffee at the hotel. *Was* it true that she allowed her uncle, in his own despair, to beat down her spirit? Did how he made her feel cause her so much discouragement that it made her limp more pronounced?

Suddenly she realized she was slumping.

How could she change her life to make it happier and more rewarding?

Perhaps it was time she made a change. She'd been passive for far too long.

"How are you feeling?" Linda asked Hannah as they sat on the front porch of the bed-and-breakfast the following Monday morning. It was warm enough now to sit outside with sweaters.

"I feel huge." Hannah laughed as she rubbed her protruding belly. "I'm getting close. I can't believe it. Some days it feels like the time has passed quickly and other days it feels like I've been pregnant for years."

Linda chuckled and then sipped her tea. "I suppose I could see that. It all must depend on your energy level. Do you feel ready?"

"I suppose I should feel ready, but I don't." She sighed. "Trey started putting the crib together over the weekend. I'm excited to arrange all the baby clothes and supplies, so I guess that means I'm nesting. They say you do that right before the baby is born, and I did with my other children."

"I've heard that." Linda wondered what it would be like to have her own baby. How she longed to have a home of her own, a family, and a life beyond the little house she shared with her uncle.

"I was hoping Lillian would call me or come to see me before the baby is born," Hannah said, her voice soft and quaky. "I had such a good feeling after seeing her in the grocery store that day, and I can't help being disappointed that she hasn't contacted me. I suppose I was too optimistic, and I'm just setting myself up for more heartache. I'm really kidding myself that she'll become a part of my life again. I can't expect Lillian to forgive me after leaving her the way I did."

"Oh, Hannah." Linda touched her hand. "Don't give up so easily. Lily will come to you. Just give her time. The baby isn't here yet, and I believe in my heart that you'll have your family back soon. You can't give up hope. That's not like you."

"Thank you, Linda. I know you're right, but I'm having a difficult time being patient. I just miss Lily so much."

"I know you do." Linda gave her a sad smile. "She misses you. I could see it in her eyes."

"I'm so grateful for your friendship, Linda." Hannah sighed. "You really are a wonderful support to me."

"Thank you. I feel the same way." Linda looked out toward the road as a horse and buggy passed by, and her thoughts turned to her uncle and her growing frustration with him.

"What's on your mind?" Hannah asked, her words breaking through Linda's thoughts.

Linda turned toward Hannah and found her friend looking at her intently. "Why do you ask?"

"You seem pensive today. Do you want to talk about it? Of course, you don't have to tell me if you don't want to."

"No, I will." Linda sighed and stared toward the road where another horse clip-clopped past while pulling a buggy. "You know I live with my *onkel.*"

"*Ya,* Reuben. I know him from church."

"He has never been very kind to me. In fact, he's always made me feel bad about myself." Linda shared about her limp and scars, how her uncle had always treated her, and that she'd taken the job at the hotel to prove she was worthy of his respect.

"Linda, I had no idea." Hannah touched Linda's arm. "I didn't even realize you had a limp. I've never noticed it. And I'm so sorry I never knew that you had a difficult home life."

"Danki." Linda smiled. "The limp usually shows up when I'm tired, anxious, or at home. I realize that now. I never shared this with anyone until Aaron asked me why I was different when I was with *mei onkel.* He noticed that I seem to turn in on myself when Reuben is around. My shoulders hunch and I limp. It's almost as if Reuben has made me doubt myself and who I could be."

Hannah considered this. "You know, I've never seen Reuben smile. He seems like a very unhappy man."

"He is very unhappy. He's very dissatisfied with how his life turned out, and he's angry." Linda placed her teacup on the table beside the bench. "I've tried to be kind to him and draw him out of his sadness, but it doesn't work."

"I hope you don't blame yourself for the way he is," Hannah said.

Linda shrugged. "I don't know. I know he's hurt that *mei dat* inherited the *haus* and majority of their father's farm he wanted, and I remind him of my *dat.* He looks at me with such anger. Somehow, I think he sees his own resentment reflected in my eyes, not the love I've tried to show. I don't think he realizes that I do care for him. He's my family."

"Oh, no. I'm so sorry."

"He treats me like this tremendous burden though I've been taking care of him for years, even before my *aenti* Verna died. Now I make most of his meals, wash his clothes, clean his house, and do all the things around the *haus Aenti* Verna did as well." She sighed. "I even put most of my money into the household. I keep some back just in case I do move out someday. I have a small savings account. Of course, he tells me I'll never move out. I'll just live there alone after he dies."

"That's terrible," Hannah said with a gasp. "I'm sorry he says things like that to you. He's so very wrong." She touched Linda's shoulder. "Don't listen to him."

"I try not to, but his words get to me sometimes. I try to tune him out, but his hateful comments get through."

"How do you handle that? Don't you get upset with him?"

"*Ya*, I do. A few times I've wanted to speak up and tell him he's wrong about me. I'm not as worthless as he makes me feel, but then I remember he's my elder and I have to respect him. After all, he did take me in and raise me, even if he didn't want to."

"That's true, but he shouldn't treat you

that way. You're a *wunderbaar maedel.*"
Hannah took a sip of her tea.

"Danki." Linda considered her words.
"Deep down I don't think he means what
he says, and I try to keep that in mind."

"That's a *gut* plan. Don't let him break
your spirit."

"I try not to."

"You do need to stand up for yourself too.
Don't let him treat you like a child. You're a
grown woman, and you can make your own
decisions. I know you're respectful to him,
but he has to respect you too."

Linda nodded. "Thank you, Hannah."
Hannah was right, and Linda had to find
the strength to stand up to Reuben. "I appreciate your encouragement."

"You're welcome." Hannah was quiet for
a moment. "I want to ask you something."
She turned toward Linda. "Do you like
working here?"

"Ya," Linda said with a nod. "I love it
here."

"I know I'm going to be exhausted from
the sleepless nights and long days with a
baby," Hannah said. "Would you like to
keep working here?"

"Of course I would." Linda lifted her
teacup. "I'd love to work here for as long as
you'll have me."

"I'm so thankful you said that." Hannah rubbed her abdomen again. "My life is about to get crazy."

"*Ya,*" Linda agreed. "It will be crazy, but it will be a blessing."

Aaron stepped into the kitchen at the bed-and-breakfast Friday morning and found Linda standing at the counter writing on a notepad.

"*Gude mariye,*" he said as he picked up a donut from a box on the counter.

She looked over at him and smiled. "*Gude mariye.* Would you like some breakfast? You're our only guest right now, so I decided to wait for you to come down and see what you'd like to eat."

"What if I take you out to breakfast?" He stuffed the rest of the donut into his mouth and wiped his hands on a paper towel.

She studied him. "You want to take me out to breakfast?"

"*Ya,* that's right." He tossed the paper towel in the trash. "Can you take a short break? I'll have you back here soon."

"Well, I don't know. I have to do some cleaning, and I need to get groceries to cook for the guests who are arriving this afternoon." She glanced down at the notepad. "I have quite a few things to pick up. I have to make an Amish meal tonight. The new guests wanted it first thing."

"What if we went to breakfast and then did your grocery shopping together?" he offered, hoping to convince her to go with him. "Would that help you get your work done in time?"

Linda nodded. "*Ya*, it would."

"So it's settled. We'll have breakfast and then we'll take care of your shopping." He pulled on the coat he'd brought from his room. "Are you ready to go?"

"Let me just go tell Hannah." Linda disappeared into the hallway. She returned a few minutes later with her purse and pulled on her coat. "Okay. Let's go."

"Great." He held the back door open for her. "I've been hoping we could talk."

"Oh?" Her eyes were full of curiosity. "Why did you want to talk?"

"We haven't had much time together lately. It seems like we've both been busier with work than ever." He walked beside her to the truck and then opened the passenger door for her.

After they were in the truck and on their way, he asked, "Do you have any particular restaurant you like?"

"No." She shook her head. "It's a treat to go out to eat. Whatever you choose is fine."

"All right." Aaron decided on his favorite place. "How have you been?"

"Fine." Linda looked out the window. "Spring is here. I'm so *froh.* I love this time of year. I'm working in my garden at home as well as in the garden here. It's too much for Hannah right now, but we use home-grown vegetables in our meals at the bed-and-breakfast whenever we can."

"That's nice." Aaron remembered how his mother and Becky enjoyed working in their gardens. "Becky, Ruthie Joy, and Katie have been working in their garden and *Mamm*'s too. *Mamm* sat on a chair outside and watched them yesterday. She pointed and gave some advice. She's a *gut* supervisor."

Linda chuckled. "That's *gut.* How is your *mamm*?"

"She's doing better. She's walking more and more." He saw Linda studying him in his peripheral vision. "She's using the walker, but she's getting a little more steady. It's such a relief to see her up and around. I know she enjoys being outside."

"Have you made a decision?" Her voice was soft and she sounded hesitant.

"Have I made a decision about what?" he asked.

"Are you going to stay?"

He slowed to a stop at a red light and

turned toward her. Her expression was hopeful, reminding him of how his mother looked at him when she asked him to stay.

"I don't know," he said. "I still haven't decided what to do."

"Why?" she asked. "What is holding you back from making a decision?"

"I guess it's my *bruder*," he admitted with a sigh. "Solomon still won't talk to me." The light turned green and he accelerated through the intersection. "I don't feel like I can stay unless my whole family accepts me back."

"Oh." She seemed disappointed.

"I've been doing all I can to show Solomon I want to be a part of the family," Aaron said. "Manny and I have finished working in the bathroom, and we're doing some more work on *mei mamm*'s screened-in porch. We've replaced the door, and we're going to replace some screens as well. And we still have the back ramp to build. Once that's done, we're going to paint the whole outside of it."

He paused before going on. "I don't know what else I can do to show *mei bruder* that I'm not going to hurt *mei mamm* again. It seems to be impossible. It's as if Solomon's heart is frozen solid, and he has no feelings at all."

"Have you prayed for him?" Linda asked.

Aaron steered into the parking lot at the restaurant and parked up close to the building. When he turned and faced her, he said, "No, I can't say that I have."

"I believe prayer is the best medicine. I've been praying for *mei onkel,* and it has made me feel so much better."

He touched her soft hand. "I will try that."

"It works." She smiled. "Hannah suggested that I pray for *mei onkel,* and it's doing wonders for me. It will help him too."

"*Danki,* Linda." He wrenched his door open. "Let's go have some breakfast. My stomach is starting to rumble."

SEVENTEEN

Linda stepped into the kitchen while Aaron held the door. "*Danki* for breakfast and helping me with the food shopping."

"*Gern gschehne,*" he responded with a grin. "I enjoyed spending time with you."

She set the bags on the counter, and he put the rest of the bags beside hers.

"What are you making for the guests tonight?" he asked.

"Hannah asked me to make chicken pot-pie, corn, potatoes, shoofly pie, chocolate cake, and a fruit salad." She counted the items off on her fingers. "That's what Hannah always likes to make for the guests. That gives them the flavor of a typical Amish menu."

"I'm sure they'll enjoy it." Aaron pulled his keys from his pocket. "I have to get to my *mamm*'s *haus*. You should come by to visit her again. I know *Mamm* would love to see you, and I can show you how the bathroom turned out. I hadn't finished the flooring when you were over the last time."

"I'd love to see it." Linda didn't want him to go. She wanted to ask him to stay and spend the day with her, but she knew that wouldn't be proper. It seemed as if their visits were always too short. "I'll come to visit soon."

"Promise?" He grinned at her. "You made me promise to come to church, so now it's your turn to promise me you'll visit *mei mamm.*"

Linda laughed. "You're right. I promise you that I will come and visit your *mamm.*"

Aaron cupped his hand to her cheek. "I'm going to hold you to that promise." His tone was warm and the look in his eyes was intense.

She closed her eyes and tilted her face into his touch. "I will keep it," she whispered.

"Linda?" Hannah's voice rang out through the house. "Are you back?"

"Ya." Linda's eyes flew open. "I'm in the kitchen."

Aaron's hand dropped to his side. "I better go. I promised Manny we'd finish the back ramp today."

"Oh, hi, Aaron." Hannah stepped into the kitchen, moving slowly. "How are you today?"

"I'm fine, thank you." He smiled at her. "How are you feeling?"

Hannah blew out a deep sigh. "I'm doing all right. It's getting harder and harder to even walk around." She shook her head. "I'm hanging in there, though. I'm trying to keep moving. I know that's the best thing to do at this stage." She looked at the counter. "Do you need help putting away the groceries?"

"Why don't you sit and supervise me?" Linda suggested. "I can put everything away."

"That sounds like a *gut* plan." Hannah smiled and sank gingerly into a chair at the table. "I'll stay right here for the moment."

"I need to get going." Aaron jingled his keys. "I'll see you soon."

Linda smiled up at him. "*Danki* again."

Aaron waved and then disappeared out the back door.

Linda began to unpack the groceries, only leaving out the nonperishable ingredients she'd need when she started cooking for supper.

"Did you have a nice breakfast?" Hannah asked.

"*Ya,* we did," Linda said while she worked. "We ate at the Bird-in-Hand Family Restaurant. I had pancakes with syrup. They were so *gut.* We had a really nice talk too."

"That's *gut.*" Hannah's voice seemed curious.

Linda looked over her shoulder at Hannah, who was grinning. "What are you smiling about?"

Hannah shrugged. "I guess I sense something between you and Aaron."

"What do you mean?" Linda faced her, leaning back against the counter.

"There's an attraction there." Hannah held up her hands to illustrate her point. "I can actually feel the electricity between you."

Linda inspected the toes of her shoes while the tips of her ears burned.

"You don't have to be embarrassed, Linda. I've fallen in love before. Twice, to be exact."

"Love?" Linda's gaze moved back to Hannah.

"Don't you have feelings for him?" Hannah asked.

"*Ya,* I do." Linda slipped into a chair across from Hannah. "But I'm struggling with my feelings. I feel so torn. I look into his eyes and I feel emotions I've never felt in my life. I'm so *froh* when I'm with him. I feel confident, and I feel complete. I had no idea love could be this way. It's more extraordinary and amazing than I ever dreamed it would be."

Hannah grinned. "I know what you're saying. I've been there."

Linda's smile faded. "But the problem is that I'm not supposed to fall in love with a man who isn't a baptized church member." She shook her head. "This isn't how it's supposed to happen."

Hannah lifted her eyebrows. "You're talking to someone who understands that problem completely."

Linda felt embarrassed again. "I'm sorry, Hannah. I wasn't thinking when I said that."

"You don't need to apologize." Hannah rested her elbows on the table.

"His *mamm* asked him to stay," Linda said.

"What did he tell her?"

"He hasn't decided." Linda frowned. "I've prayed that God's will be done, and he knows what's in my heart. But it's hard when I'm so afraid Aaron is going to leave. I'll be where I am now — all alone. And to make it even worse, I'll also be heartbroken. I don't think I'll ever find someone else like him."

"Don't give up hope so easily, Linda." Hannah touched Linda's hand. "You've waited a long time to meet someone like him. I don't think God will take him away so quickly. Just have faith."

Linda nodded. "Do you think he'll stay?"

"He might. I can tell by the way he looks at you that he really cares for you."

"Do you think so?" Linda felt her smile light up with excitement and hope.

"*Ya,* I do. I think you need to follow your heart with Aaron. He's a *gut* man. I know what he's done for his *mamm,* and I also know how he's struggling with his family."

"How do you know about all that?" Linda asked.

"Aaron has been sharing his struggles with Trey, about his *bruder,*" Hannah said. "Aaron is working through it the best he can. But he has a really *gut* heart, and I think he'll treat you well. He's been through a lot in his life, just as you have with losing your parents and living with your *onkel.* I think you're kindred spirits."

"But I don't want to leave the community." Linda spoke slowly. "I'm sorry, Hannah, but I'm not ready to leave the church."

"You don't have to leave the church, Linda. I'm only telling you to not to give up on him. He's been here more than three months now. That tells me he feels like he belongs here. I would imagine it's starting to feel like home again." Hannah tapped the table. "I have a *gut* feeling he's going to stay. He just doesn't know it yet."

"I hope you're right," Linda said, putting all her hope into those words.

Aaron ran his paintbrush over the wood on the outside of the enclosed porch while Manny painted nearby. They had finished replacing the screen door, repairing the stairs, and building the additional ramp for his mother. The April sun was warm on his neck as he moved the paintbrush back and forth.

"You've been driving a car a long time, *ya*?" Manny asked while he worked.

"*Ya,* I have." Aaron stopped, balanced the brush on the paint can, and took a drink from a cold bottle of water. "Why do you mention it?"

"I would imagine that you don't remember how to hitch a horse to a buggy or guide the buggy." Manny's grin was taunting Aaron.

"Are you challenging me?" Aaron asked his nephew.

"I don't know." Manny shrugged as he dipped his brush in the paint can. "Do you want to be challenged?"

"I'll take that challenge." Aaron set the bottle of water down, put the cover on the

370

paint can, and wiped his hands on a rag. "Where do you keep your buggy?"

"I'll show you." Manny started for one of the barns, and Aaron followed him.

As they moved past the back porch, Aaron spotted Linda helping Becky hang laundry. He waved at Linda, and she gave him a curious wave in response.

"You can use my *dat*'s buggy." Manny pointed inside the barn. "I'll go get the horse."

Aaron looked at the buggy and the technique quickly came back to him. Manny brought the horse, and Aaron hitched it without any help while Manny watched.

"See?" Aaron asked his grinning nephew. "I hitched it just fine, and you had no faith in me."

"I want to see you guide it now. Show me that you remember how to be Amish."

Aaron laughed. "You really don't think I can do it?"

Manny leveled his gaze at him as a smile tugged at the corners of his lips. "I guess we'll see."

"All right." When they took the horse and buggy outside, Aaron glanced toward where Linda and Becky turned to watch them with interest. He'd been trying all afternoon to think of an excuse to visit with Linda. Now

371

was the perfect opportunity. He could take Linda for a buggy ride. If he played his cards right, it could turn out to be a nice, romantic visit for them.

Aaron walked over to the women. "Do you want to help me prove my nephew wrong?" he asked.

Linda looked confused as she stared at him. She glanced at Becky, who shrugged. "I don't know," Linda said. "What do I have to do to help you?"

"Do you think I remember how to guide a horse and buggy?" he asked her.

She still looked baffled as her eyebrows drew together, and he couldn't help but think she was adorable.

"I suppose you can." Linda leaned forward. "Why are you asking me these strange questions?" Her expression became concerned. "Are you okay, Aaron? Do you feel ill? Has the sun gotten to you?"

Aaron laughed. *"Ya,* I'm fine, Linda. I'm not ill or *narrisch."* He pointed toward the buggy. "Manny thinks I don't remember how to be Amish. He wants me to prove I can drive that horse and buggy as well as I drive a truck. Do you want to come with me?"

"Oh." Linda hesitated and glanced at Becky again as if to ask for permission.

"Go." Becky waved her off with a smile. "I'm eager to see how this turns out."

"Okay." Linda handed Becky the pair of trousers she was holding.

"Great." Aaron clapped his hands together. "Let's go prove Manny wrong."

As Linda walked with Aaron to the waiting buggy, she noticed how handsome he was in his blue T-shirt, and she had a difficult time keeping her gaze off him. His unruly, blond curls peeked out from under a tan baseball cap.

"Do you need a wrap?" he asked. His adorable smile was back.

"No, it's warm enough today."

"Do you know what you're doing?" Manny asked with a teasing expression.

"You're going to feel *gegisch* for asking." Aaron opened up the passenger side door and held out his hand to Linda.

She took his strong hand and climbed into the buggy, smoothing her black apron over her blue dress.

"We'll see about that," Manny commented.

Aaron climbed in next to Linda and shut his door. He inspected the inside of the buggy.

"Do you need help?" she offered, keeping

her voice low so Manny wouldn't hear.

"No, no." He shook his head. "I was just thinking that it's been a long time since I've sat in one of these. Once again, I feel like I've stepped back in time."

"Does that feel *gut* or bad?"

He faced her and his eyes were sentimental. "It's actually pretty *gut.*"

Her heartbeat thundered as she again hoped he was going to stay in Paradise. She couldn't bear the thought of saying goodbye to him and watching him walk out of her life forever.

"All right." He took the reins in his hands. "Let's show my nephew how wrong he is about me." He nudged the horse to move, and they began their journey.

"Where are we going?" she asked.

"I haven't figured that out yet." He guided the horse onto the road. "Wouldn't my nephew be shocked if we didn't come back?"

Linda laughed. "It would at least surprise him."

Aaron moved the buggy close to the side of the road so a car behind them could pass.

"I had forgotten how slow you travel in a buggy. You can't just run up to the store for milk in a hurry." He smiled over at her. "Our trip to the restaurant in Bird-in-Hand was much faster in the truck."

"That's true, but you miss how *schee* the scenery is when you're moving fast."

"Not always." He gave her a serious expression. "I'm enjoying the scenery next to me right now, and it was just as *schee* in the passenger seat of my truck."

She gave him a shy smile and then looked out the window. She still wasn't used to receiving his compliments, but she never grew tired of them. The sweet and sincere way he told her she was pretty caused her heart to soar. She wondered if his feelings for her were as strong and deep as the ones she had for him.

Another car passed by, and Aaron laughed.

"What's so funny?" Linda asked.

"I was wondering what the tourists are thinking when they drive by a buggy and see a guy in a T-shirt and wearing a baseball cap in the driver's seat." Aaron grinned at Linda, and she laughed. "They must be wondering if the Pennsylvania Amish changed their clothing guidelines."

They continued down the road for a few more minutes.

"Do you think we should head back?" Linda asked.

"I was enjoying the break, but I suppose you're right." He guided the horse down a side road to turn around. "*Danki* for riding with me. I like how this feels."

"What do you mean?" she asked.

"You and me in a buggy together." He gave her a sideways glance. "We should've done this years ago when we were teenagers."

Her mouth dried as she took in his attractive profile.

"Don't you agree?" He looked over at her. "We missed a great opportunity."

"There's no time like the present," she said softly.

"You're so very right." He nodded in agreement.

After Aaron steered the buggy back up the driveway to where Manny was waiting with Junior, he hopped out and opened the passenger door for Linda. Aaron then gave his nephew an I-told-you-so look.

"You won." Manny shook Aaron's hand. "Can you unhitch the horse now?"

"Of course I can," Aaron told him.

Linda chuckled to herself as she made her way back to where Becky was hanging a second load of laundry. *"Buwe,"* she quipped with a chuckle. "They are so *gegisch.*"

She hung up a dress and then realized Becky was watching her. "What?"

"Do you have feelings for Aaron?" Becky

asked with curiosity in her eyes.

"Why would you ask me that?" Linda reached for another dress to avoid Becky's probing stare.

"You seem to enjoy being with him, and it's obvious that he enjoys being with you. He was determined to get you to ride in the buggy with him."

"Oh, I don't know about that." Linda shrugged. "He's very nice. We've been getting to know each other."

"That's *gut.*" Becky hung up an apron while she spoke. "I was wrong about what I thought about Aaron when he first arrived. I originally believed it wasn't *gut* for our family when he came back. My *dochder* showed me how wrong I was. She helped me realize that our family needs Aaron. He's not only helped Ruth with her recovery, but he's also been a blessing to my *kinner.* I'm hoping Solomon will see that he needs his *bruder* too." She faced Linda. "I've been hoping Aaron will decide to stay, and you could be the reason he decides to come home for *gut.*"

"*Danki.*" Linda picked two more aprons from the laundry basket and handed one to Becky. She hoped Becky was right, not only that Aaron would decide to stay in their community permanently, but that she could be one of the reasons.

Aaron helped Manny stow the buggy in the barn.

"You proved me wrong, *Onkel,*" Manny said with a smile. "You do remember how to be Amish."

"I remember a lot of things," Aaron said. "*Danki.* That was fun. I hadn't been in a buggy in a long time."

He watched his nephew turn toward the barn door and then freeze in place like a statue. His eyes widened.

"What's wrong?" Aaron looked over his shoulder and found Solomon glaring at them from the doorway. He kept his expression calm despite his instant anxiety. "Hello, Solomon."

"Knowing how to handle a horse and buggy doesn't make you Amish," Solomon groused. "All it proves is that you can command a horse, and just about anyone can do that."

Aaron sighed. "You're right. I get your point. I'm certainly not Amish."

"Don't you ever take my buggy out again without my permission," Solomon barked.

"It was my fault," Manny said. "I prompted him to use it, so don't be angry with him. You can punish me."

"You can go now, Manny," Solomon instructed. "You've done enough. I need to speak to Aaron alone."

"Ya, Dat." Manny shot Aaron an apologetic look before leaving the barn.

"We were only goofing around," Aaron explained. "Go easy on him."

"I'm not going to punish him. My issues are with you." Solomon leveled his eyes at Aaron. "You're doing great work on *Dat*'s *haus,* but you need to take a step back from my family. Manny is getting too attached to you, and it's not *gut* for him. I think it's time for me to pull him away from you. I need him working with me, not playing games with you."

"He's a great *bu,*" Aaron said. "And he enjoys working with me. I'm teaching him a lot, and you may be glad I did someday if you need some work done on your *haus.*"

"If I need work done on my *haus,* the *haus* that I built, I can do it myself. You are not the only one who can do something besides run a dairy farm. I'm going to tell him tonight that he is forbidden to help you anymore. You're on your own." Solomon turned and started to leave the barn, and Aaron's blood boiled.

Aaron made a quick decision — he'd hit the issue of their broken relationship head-on with a direct question.

"Solomon!" Aaron called after him, and Solomon turned. "What's it going to take for you to forgive me? It's been three months, man."

Solomon shook his head. "If you want me to forgive you, then you would have to rewrite history, and that's not going to happen."

Solomon stalked out, and Aaron felt the last of his hope evaporate. After moving outside, he glanced to where Linda still worked with Becky. He wanted more than anything to be a part of his family again and ask Linda to be his girlfriend.

Yet at that moment he stood cemented in place, feeling lost and lonely, as he turned to watch his only brother walk away.

EIGHTEEN

Linda dried the last dish and set it in the cabinet. She was hanging the dish towel over the oven-door handle when she heard the familiar crunch of tires and hum of a truck engine in the driveway. Her pulse quickened as she stepped toward the front door.

"That Aaron Ebersol is here," Reuben grumbled while peering out the front window. "Why is he coming here? Doesn't he remember it's inappropriate for an *Englisher* to date an Amish *maedel*?"

"He's not trying to date me, *Onkel*," Linda said. "We're just *freinden*."

Footsteps sounded on the porch steps.

"It's wrong," *Onkel* Reuben barked while wagging a finger in her face. "Do you know what the members of the community will say about you when they hear you're seeing an *Englisher*? You'll be shunned, and that would bring shame on this family. You're not to see him. I'll tell him myself."

A knock sounded on the door.

Linda gasped as tears stung her eyes. "*Onkel,* please don't. Just let me talk to him." She felt her shoulders droop as she swiped her hands across her eyes.

Reuben swung the door open. "What do you want?" he snapped.

"Good evening, Reuben," Aaron said. His gaze was steady and calm, but he frowned. "I was wondering if I could speak to Linda."

Linda hugged her arms to her middle as she stared at Aaron. She ached to speak with him, but she knew she was stuck standing behind her controlling uncle.

Aaron looked past Reuben at her, and his expression was worried. The sympathy in his eyes was almost too much for her to endure. She looked down at her shoes to avoid his gaze.

"You know you don't belong here," Reuben groused. "You're not Amish, and Linda is a baptized member of the church. You're putting her in a bad position by coming here. You should know that already since you were raised Amish. If you had any respect for this community, you'd leave and not come back until you're baptized."

"You're right," Aaron said. "I'm wrong to come here, but I just need a few minutes of

Linda's time. We'll sit out on the porch and talk. I won't stay too long, I promise."

"No, it's not appropriate." Reuben started to push the door closed.

"Wait!" Aaron yelled.

Linda looked up as Aaron pushed his arm out, blocking the door from closing.

"Just give me a minute," Aaron pleaded with Reuben. "I know you want to keep us apart, but I'm begging you, man to man, to just let me talk to her for a minute. Then I'll stay away."

Linda gasped. He couldn't mean that. He couldn't want to promise to stay away from her forever. Had he come here to tell her he was leaving? Her hope sank.

Reuben glanced back at Linda, and she brushed her hand across her eyes again. "Fine," he barked. "You have five minutes."

"*Danki,* Reuben," Aaron said, relief reverberating from his voice.

Linda nodded at her uncle and started for the door, grabbing her cloak before she stepped out into the cool spring evening. She prayed Aaron hadn't come to tell her he was leaving Paradise for good. Her heart couldn't take that news.

Aaron hated telling Reuben he wouldn't come back again, but he couldn't think of any other way to convince him to let Linda come out to the porch. He'd been thinking of her all day long, and he had to talk to her, one on one. She drooped like a wilted flower behind her uncle, and the sight was tearing his heart out. He wanted to take her away from the constant verbal abuse her uncle threw at her. He wanted to save her, the way she had saved him by showing him how to love.

Linda moved slowly past her uncle and through the front door, her shoulders hunched and her walk marked by the slight limp. His broken heart shattered with each step she took. She turned and closed the door behind her and then faced him.

"Why are you here?" her voice was meek, like a tiny mouse.

"I had to see you." Aaron ran his fingers down her cheekbone, not caring if Reuben was looking out the window.

"Why?" Her eyes glimmered with fresh tears. "Did you come here to tell me you're leaving?"

"What?" He searched her face, trying to find the source of her worry. "No, no. I just wanted to talk to you. We haven't been able to talk since we took that buggy ride. I've missed you. It's been three long days since I've seen you except in passing."

"Then why did you tell my *onkel* you would never come back here?"

"I had to think of something to convince him to let you talk to me." He took her small hand in his and led her to the bench. "Sit with me for a minute. Please."

She glanced over her shoulder and took a shuddering breath as if making sure her uncle wasn't lurking behind the door. Her shoulders then loosened up and she stood up a little taller. Her expression relaxed, and her eyes seemed brighter. She sank onto the bench, and he sat down beside her.

Aaron held her hand and looked deep into her warm, brown eyes. "You don't need to be so nervous and unsure of yourself around your *onkel.* You're like a morning glory."

She stared at him with confusion. "What do you mean?"

"When you're away from him, you're in full bloom. You're radiant and confident," he explained as he pushed an errant lock of her hair back behind her ear. "But when you're with him, it's like nighttime. You curl into yourself, and you lose that confidence and grace you have when he's not around. You need to be in full bloom all the time and let the world see the amazing woman you are. Don't let him steal your confidence. You need to stand up to your uncle and be who you are, no matter how he behaves."

She nodded slowly, taking in his words. "I'll try."

"How have you been?" he asked.

"Fine. I've just been working at the hotel and the bed-and-breakfast. Did you finish the back ramp?"

"*Ya.*" He nodded and relaxed back on the bench. "I finished it yesterday." He shook his head, thinking about his last conversation with Solomon. "*Mei bruder* won't let Manny work with me anymore."

"Why not?"

"Solomon thinks Manny was getting too close to me, so he told him he couldn't help me anymore. I think Solomon is hoping I'm going to get fed up and leave."

"Are you going to let him push you away?" Worry overcame her eyes.

"No, I'm not leaving, but I don't know what else to do to get my *bruder* to accept me back into his life. I've been praying, just like you suggested." He ran his fingers over her palm while contemplating the situation. "What else can I do? I need your advice on this. I'm lost, and it's getting more and more difficult to handle his anger toward me."

"When did he tell you Manny couldn't work with you anymore?"

386

"It was right after we took the buggy ride." Aaron shoved his fingers through his curls while irritation nipped at him. "He was furious that I had taken his buggy out without his permission. Manny tried to apologize and explain it was his idea, but Solomon wouldn't listen. He said I had no right to take his buggy, and that's when he said he didn't want Manny to work with me anymore. I asked him how I could get him to forgive me, and he said I would have to rewrite history."

"He wants you to rewrite history?" Linda scrunched her nose as if she smelled something fetid. "That doesn't make sense."

"I know. He's completely irrational."

"You should try again to have an honest conversation with him," she said simply. "Just calmly ask him why he's so bitter toward you. Tell him you're tired of trying to guess why he's so angry. Explain again that you're sorry you left, and you want to start over. See what happens then. Be strong and confident, like you keep telling me to do with *mei onkel.*"

He smiled and touched her face. "So you think I should take my own advice."

"*Ya,* I do." She nodded. "It's very *gut* advice."

At that moment, as he stared into her gorgeous eyes, he was nearly overwhelmed with the urge to kiss her. He wanted to pull her into his arms and kiss her until she was breathless.

But he knew he couldn't. He was already breaking the rules by visiting her. Kissing her would get her into even more trouble if anyone saw them, and he didn't want to make life difficult for her. Since spring had come, it was only twilight right now. For all he knew someone in her cousin's family could be walking nearby.

The front door opened with a squeak, and Linda stood up like she'd been shot out of a cannon.

"It's time for you to come in, Linda," Reuben said. "You've been out here long enough."

"*Gut nacht,* Aaron. It was *gut* seeing you." Her posture became rigid, but her eyes were still tender and affectionate.

Aaron stood. "*Danki,* Reuben, for the opportunity to speak with Linda." He nodded at Linda. "Take care."

As Aaron drove back to the bed-and-breakfast, he contemplated Linda's advice. He knew to his very core that she was right. The only way to get Solomon to talk to him was to calmly sit him down and ask him to explain why he was so bitter. There was no other way. It was time for him to prod his brother along. He would face him tomorrow and find out what he had to do to make things right between them.

As Linda stepped into the house, Aaron's words echoed in her mind. Perhaps it was time for her to stand up for herself, just as Aaron, Madeleine, and Hannah had all suggested. She was an adult, and she deserved to be treated like one. Her body trembled with both anger and fear as she faced her uncle.

"I can't allow Aaron Ebersol to keep coming here to see you," Reuben began with a sour expression. "What if one of Raymond's girls saw you and started gossiping? What if the neighbors saw his truck coming up the driveway at all hours of the day and night? That wouldn't look right to them at all. They'd figure out that he's here to see you, and if they told the bish—"

"I'm thirty-one years old," Linda began, interrupting him. She placed her hands on her hips in an attempt to stop them from shaking.

"I know how old you are," he snapped.

"That means I'm old enough to choose my friends," she continued. "I'm entitled to sit on the porch and talk to a friend when I choose to. I don't need your permission. I'm aware that Aaron isn't baptized, but I enjoy talking to him."

Reuben blinked while studying her. "Why are you suddenly being so disrespectful? This isn't like you."

"I'm not being disrespectful," she said, trying her best to keep her words calm despite her hammering heart. "I'm tired of allowing you to order me around as if I were a *kind*. I work hard to take care of this *haus* and take care of you. It's time you treat me like an adult who contributes to his household instead of a *kind* who misbehaves. We've been sharing this *haus* for a long time. It's time you started treating me with the same respect I've shown you since I was a *kind*."

Reuben gaped.

"I'm going to bed. *Gut nacht.*" Linda moved past him and walked toward her room with her heartbeat pounding in her ears and her hands trembling. She felt guilty for standing up to him, but she had also felt a strange surge of confidence after talking to Aaron. He made her feel worthy of her uncle's respect — and worthy of Aaron's love.

Could he possibly love me? The question sent a tingle of hope through her body.

She stepped into her bedroom, closed the door, and leaned against it. Closing her eyes, she took a deep, cleansing breath. If only Aaron would decide to stay in the community and join the church. With him by her side, she could face any obstacle. She was certain of it.

Aaron spent the next day helping Trey with a project at the bed-and-breakfast. After a quick bite of supper at a local diner, he drove to his parents' house. He pulled into the driveway and, though it was getting dark, noticed Solomon walking toward one of the barns. He closed his eyes and prayed for the confidence and the right words to confront his brother once and for all.

This is it. This is my chance to make things right.

Once he was mentally ready to face his brother, Aaron climbed from the truck and marched toward the barn with his work boots crunching on the rock driveway. He found Solomon sitting at a workbench, working on a birdhouse next to a lantern. Aaron stood in the doorway and watched Solomon work, wondering how a man who could make such a beautiful birdhouse could also hold such a hateful grudge. His thoughts turned to his childhood and the happy memories he cherished.

"Do you remember when I was ten and you were eighteen?" Aaron suddenly asked, his voice echoing throughout the large barn.

Solomon did not look up or turn, but his shoulders visibly tensed. He sat perfectly still as if he were frozen in a block of ice, and Aaron could only see his face in profile.

"I was trying to hitch the pony to the cart," Aaron continued, "and I was so frustrated that I was close to tears. *Dat* told me it was time I learned to do it by myself, and he wouldn't help me and told you not to help me either." He stepped into the barn. "But you did. You disobeyed *Dat* and patiently showed me several times until I could do it on my own."

Solomon kept his eyes trained on the birdhouse.

"Back then you were like a second father. You were patient and nurturing, even though I seemed to constantly get into trouble." Aaron walked over to him. "You knew I had a lot to learn, and you wanted to teach me. I remember another time when you stayed home from youth group to help me get my chores done. You sacrificed your time with your *freinden* for me."

Solomon looked over at Aaron, his face fixed in a deep scowl. "When are you going to get to your point?"

"My point is that we were close once. I looked up to you, like I look up to *Dat.* I want to get that relationship back. I need you to show me how we can do that. How can I get our relationship back to the way it was when we were *kinner*?"

"That was a long time ago, and that time is gone now. I don't want you here, so you need to leave my barn."

"No." Aaron felt a surge of confidence, and he stepped forward and sat down on the workbench facing his brother. He'd finally gotten Solomon to talk to him, and he wasn't going to give up now. "I want to know why you're so bitter toward me. Why are you the only person who isn't happy that I've come back to the community? I know Becky wasn't at first, but she's come around."

Solomon looked angrier than Aaron had ever seen him.

"You really want to know why I'm bitter?" Solomon asked, and Aaron nodded while holding his breath in anticipation of the answer. "You come back here after seventeen years, and you're welcomed like a hero while I was the one who stood by *Mamm* and *Dat* all along." He pointed and gestured with emphasis. "You did nothing but cause

393

Mamm heartache, but she welcomed you back with open arms. I feel unappreciated and ignored when I was the loyal and dutiful son. Not you. Me!"

"You're right." Aaron nodded as his body shook with irritation. "I don't deserve the warm welcome I've received, but I'm sorry for all the pain I've caused. I don't want to live in the past anymore. I want to move toward the future, and I want to be part of this family again. I want to really know you, Becky, and your precious *kinner*. I want to get to know my *freinden* again. I want to be a part of this community. I want to be here." He pointed toward the floor for emphasis.

"Well, I don't want you here. You went off to Missouri and lived your dream. You opened your construction business, and you've been successful and *froh*," Solomon continued. "What about me? I was stuck here helping *Dat* run the farm. What about my plans?"

Aaron shook his head. "I don't understand. What plans are you talking about?"

"I didn't want to be a dairy farmer. I wanted to start a business building houses. Don't you remember I was building my own house when you took off? You weren't the only one *Dat* did woodworking projects with." He held up the birdhouse. "And how do you think Manny learned the basics of woodworking before you even got here? *I* showed him."

He took a long breath before going on. "I was saving money, and I even had a partner who wanted to help me get started. You were supposed to be the one to take over the farm with *Dat,* not me. This wasn't my dream."

"I never knew that. You never told me." Aaron studied his brother as if he were a stranger. "Why didn't you ever tell me?"

"You never asked."

Aaron shook his head with confusion. "Is that why you were always pushing me to be a better person and a better member of the community? So I would be worthy of running this farm with *Dat*?"

Solomon regarded him with a scowl. "It didn't work. No matter what advice I gave you, once you hit your teens, you always got into mischief."

"Now it all makes sense." Aaron gave him a wry smile as everything clicked into place. "That's why you started criticizing me and telling me I needed to act like an Amish person. I remember now. I wasn't just having trouble getting along with *Dat.* You and I were at odds as well. You were trying to mold me so I would be *Dat*'s partner and take over the farm.

"But you were part of the reason I left, Solomon. I felt like I could never live up to you, the ideal son. Why didn't you just tell me you wanted me to take over the farm so you could open your own business? Why did you expect a fifteen-year-old kid to ask if you were living the life you wanted?"

"What does it matter now?" Solomon kicked a stone with the toe of his boot. "It's all history." He met Aaron's gaze and his eyes still smoldered with resentment. "And you just decide to come back one day after seventeen long years and expect me to forget what you did and just move on?" His voice was growing louder. "You ran off and never looked back!"

"That's not true. I wrote letters." Aaron gestured widely. "I just don't know how they disappeared into thin air."

Solomon stared at him with hatred in his eyes. "They didn't disappear."

"What do you mean?" Aaron asked.

Solomon stood, reached under his bench, and removed a metal box. He pulled a key from his pocket, and unlocked the box. He flipped it open, reached inside, and threw the contents at Aaron. "Here. Take your letters and go."

Aaron was too stunned to react. Envelopes

fluttered through the air like confetti and peppered the floor like large rectangles of snow.

Aaron stooped and picked up two envelopes. He immediately recognized his own handwriting. He looked up at Solomon, who now stood and glared down at him. "What have you done?" He stood as well, standing toe-to-toe with his brother. "You've had my letters all these years?"

"*Ya*, I have." Solomon lifted his chin in defiance and narrowed his eyes. "I made sure I intercepted the mail every day for seventeen years. I've kept all of your worthless letters locked away so that no one would ever find them. I wish I had burned them."

"Why?" Devastation mixed with confusion flooded through Aaron and stole his breath. "Why would you keep my letters away from *Mamm*? I don't understand why you would do something so evil and hateful. Why, Solomon?"

"I wanted to shield *Mamm* from any further pain." Solomon's eyes shimmered with outrage. "You have no idea how much pain she endured. *Mamm* cried and cried for months. She was inconsolable, worrying about what could have happened to you. I, on the other hand, learned from reading

397

your first letter that you had merely started a new life, leaving the rest of us behind. How was that going to make her feel?

"Then you return three months ago, and everyone acts as if that pain never happened." He pointed to his chest. "Well, *I* remember, and I will *never* forget. You're dead to me, Aaron."

Solomon scooped up the rest of the letters, then shoved them into Aaron's hands. "Take your letters and go back to Missouri where you belong with your *Englisher freinden* and your *Englisher* business. We don't need you here."

Aaron stood there in complete shock. He was dumbfounded. He'd never imagined the letters could have disappeared at the hands of his brother. He felt as if he were stuck in some surreal nightmare.

"Go on!" Solomon yelled, pointing toward the barn door. "Get out of here and don't come back."

Aaron walked out and stalked toward his truck.

"Go all the way back to Missouri!" Solomon bellowed after him as he stood by the barn door. "We're better off without you!"

Aaron turned back. "At least now I know the truth. You're the one who kept me from making things right all these years. I hope you can find a way to sleep at night when you realize you're the one who caused so much hurt — and you're *still* causing it. I've been trying to make amends for all the pain I caused, but you want *our* family to continue hurting just to punish me. You're the one who is tearing the family apart, not me.

"But fine. If you want me to go back to Missouri, then I'll go."

Aaron climbed into his truck before Solomon could reply and drove toward the road as fast as he dared. He didn't know where he was going; he just needed to drive. He tossed the letters into the passenger seat as tears stung his eyes.

All along he'd wanted to believe, no matter how improbable, that the letters had been lost in the mail. Instead, they had been locked away, almost all unopened and unread. The letters had been dismissed, the same way he'd always felt his family had treated him.

Aaron's heart was crushed. And the truth hit him between the eyes — he didn't belong in Paradise after all.

"No!" a weak voice cried as Aaron's truck disappeared from view.

Solomon's gaze cut to the back porch. He could just make out his mother standing behind the screen door, partially illuminated by a light from the mudroom. She was grasping her walker and sobbing.

"Mamm!" He rushed to her. *"Mamm?* Are you okay?"

"Ruth?" *Dat* appeared from the doorway to the house. His eyes were round with worry. "Ruth? What's wrong?"

"H-how c-could y-you?" Her words were garbled in her tears. "How c-could y-you s-send h-him a-away?"

She turned to his *dat.*

"H-he's g-gone!" She grasped his shirt. "H-he's g-gone! He's n-not c-coming b-back. N-no, n-no, n-no! A-aron!"

Dat looked at Solomon as if to say, *Not now. We'll talk about this later.* Then he took his wife's arm and helped her into the house. "Just calm down, Ruth," he was saying. "I need you to calm down so we can talk about this. Let's go to the *schtupp.*"

Solomon stood on the porch alone as dread pooled in his stomach.

What have I done?

NINETEEN

Aaron drove through Paradise as desolation overwhelmed him. He couldn't comprehend that his brother had betrayed him at the deepest level. How could Solomon keep him from connecting with his mother? With the whole family?

He needed to talk to someone. He needed Linda, but he knew he wasn't welcome at her house. Still, he had to unload his feelings before he went crazy. Within minutes, he was parked near her front porch. He stared at the steering wheel and contemplated what had just happened. His heart felt ripped to shreds. How could he possibly stay in Paradise after learning Solomon's secret?

This changed everything.

Linda was pinning an apron at her sewing table in her bedroom when she heard the pickup truck's engine rattling in the driveway. She knew who it had to be. She went to the front of the house, moving quickly to get past her uncle's bedroom. But his door was ajar, and she could see he was dozing on his bed with a book resting on his chest. She took the time to quietly pull it shut without clicking the lock.

She stepped onto the porch just as Aaron was climbing the steps. He was carrying a stack of envelopes in one hand, and his face was twisted with heartbreaking sadness. When she looked closer at him in the moonlight, she was stunned to see tears trickling down his cheeks.

"Aaron!" she gasped. "*Was iss letz?* Did something happen to your family? Is your *mamm* okay?"

He cleared his throat and wiped his eyes with his free hand. "*Mei mamm* is fine."

"Please tell me what's wrong," she said. "I can't stand to see you like this."

"I tried to talk to *mei bruder* tonight, but my plan to work things out with him blew up in my face." He held out a stack of envelopes. "These are the letters I mailed to *mei mamm* over the years."

She took the envelopes and saw they were all addressed to Ruth. "I don't understand. Where were they all this time?"

"Solomon intercepted the mail all these

years, and he locked my letters away in a box hidden under his workbench in one of the barns."

Linda gaped as she tried to comprehend what Aaron was telling her. "Why would your *bruder* hide the letters from your *mamm*?"

"He said he wanted to shield *Mamm* from further heartbreak." Aaron slumped onto the bench, rested his bent elbows on his knees, and dropped his head into his hands. "I can't believe it. I don't understand how he could betray me like this. I don't understand how he could think *Mamm* was better off thinking I might be dead." His hands muffled his voice.

"*Ach,* Aaron." She sank down next to him and ran her fingers through his hair, keenly aware of the texture of his soft curls. "I'm so very sorry this happened to you. I thought talking to him would resolve the situation. I never meant to make it worse."

"You didn't make it worse." He straightened to look at her, his eyes gleamed with fresh tears. "You just helped me find the truth. Now I know for sure that I should go back to Missouri."

Her heart constricted and tears blurred her vision. "No, don't say that. You don't mean that."

"Yes, I do, because it's true." He sat up. "I thought I could come back here and fit in again, but the truth is that it's not meant to be. I don't belong here anymore. Not when my brother hates me so. That kind of hate poisons everything. As long as I'm here, my family will never be able to heal."

She couldn't believe her ears. "That's not true. You know your parents want you here. You and Manny have bonded, and your nieces and Junior love you too. I could see love in their eyes that day we went skating. They need you." She paused. "And I need you," she whispered as her voice quaked.

He took the letters from her hand. "Solomon threw these at me and told me to go back to Missouri. He's right. I should go." He met her gaze. "I came to tell you what happened, but also to say good-bye. Your friendship means a lot to me, Linda, and I'm going to miss you."

"Don't go," she pleaded with him. "You can't let one person hold you back from getting what you want. You told me the same thing about *mei onkel.* You already know how your *mamm* feels. She's begged you to stay. She even offered you a place to live. Why would you walk away from that?"

"*Mei mamm* just doesn't understand that it's not meant to be. It's not that simple. I

404

can't pick up where I left off or turn back time. The damage was done when I left the first time." He shook his head. "Maybe Solomon is right. Maybe I don't deserve my family."

Frustration surged through her. "Everyone deserves a family. You even told me I deserve to be *froh.* Why wouldn't you deserve that too? You're a *gut* person with a warm, loving heart, Aaron. Any family would be blessed to have you in it."

Aaron examined the envelopes, and she knew in her heart that his mind was already made up. She was speaking to deaf ears, and she was going to lose him. Her greatest fear was coming to life before her eyes. He was going to break her heart, and there was nothing she could do to stop him. Everything she'd dreamt of was evaporating, and it was shattering her soul.

"I'm sorry, Linda." His voice trembled with anguish. "I have to go. I can't take the heartache any longer."

"Don't let him push you away, Aaron." Tears trickled down her hot cheeks. "I can't let you go."

"I have to go. I don't have a choice. I hope you'll understand." He leaned over and brushed his lips across her cheek. "I'll miss you."

Linda cupped her hand to her cheek where his lips had been.

"Good-bye." Aaron gripped the envelopes and headed for his truck. He climbed in and drove off, and she felt him take a big piece of her crushed heart with him.

She sat on the porch alone for several minutes until her tears stopped flowing. She stepped back into the house and found her uncle scowling at her from his chair.

"What were you doing on the porch with that Aaron Ebersol again?" he demanded. "He promised he wouldn't come back here. I don't care how old you are, Linda. I won't stand for this. You are too old to be acting like a disobedient teenager. It's time for you to learn your place in this *haus*."

Linda stood tall and held her hand up to silence him.

He winced as if she'd hit him. "What does that gesture mean? Are you trying to tell me to be quiet?"

"Ya," she said with confidence. "I am asking you to be quiet so that I may have a chance to speak."

"Fine." He stood. "What do you have to say for yourself?"

"I will no longer allow you to treat me badly," she began. "I love you for taking care of me when I was a child after my parents died. You took me in and I appreciate that. I know you had no choice, but still, you and *Aenti* Verna opened your home to me. And when I was old enough, I started helping around here."

She took a deep breath as he stared at her. "The tables turned when I got older," she continued, "and I have taken care of you for a long time. In fact, I've been cooking for you, cleaning this *haus,* and taking care of your laundry for years. You treat me like I'm worthless, and I forgive you for making me feel that way. I also forgive you for resenting me for a decision your *daed* made. I will no longer allow you to make me feel bad about myself or make me feel like I'm nothing. Despite your insults, I know I add value to this family, and I am worthy of love, even if you think I'm not."

He blanched again, and his tired eyes suddenly glimmered with tears. "You're right."

"What?" Linda swiped away the tears that trickled down her cheeks.

"I've thought about what you said last night, and you're right." His expression softened. "I don't treat you right, and I'm sorry."

Linda gasped. *Have I finally gotten through to him?*

"I do love you, and I'm sorry for taking

my frustrations out on you. It's not your fault." His lower lip quivered. "I've treated you badly for a very long time, and I'm sorry. I just didn't know how to overcome my resentment toward your *dat,* a resentment I've carried since before you were born. And I've only been worse since losing Verna." He paused. "You look a lot like your father, you know. He had the same deep-brown eyes, and I see him when I look at you. I should never have resented him for inheriting the farm instead of me."

He took a ragged breath. "I loved your father. He was my baby brother."

Reuben stood and walked over to her. Then he took her hands in his. "I'm sorry, Linda," he repeated. "I'm so sorry."

"Danki." She forced a smile despite her heartbreak over losing Aaron. "I hope you understand. I've decided that I need to stand up for myself and take control of my own life."

Reuben swiped a tear from his cheek. "I do understand. And I promise to do better. You've taken very *gut* care of me, and I appreciate you. I just never took the time to tell you."

"We can talk more tomorrow. Right now I need some time alone." She sniffed as tears stung her eyes again. "I'm going to finish my sewing. *Gut nacht.*"

Linda made her way to her room, gently closing the door behind her. She sat at her sewing table and tears began to flow like a waterfall. She covered her face with her hands to drown out the sound of her shattering sobs. Her world was crashing in around her. She'd finally found someone to love, and she believed he loved her too. She thought maybe they would be together, but, instead, he was leaving her. Ironically, she'd lost Aaron, the man she loved, just as her uncle had finally acknowledged her worth. While she was grateful to have Reuben's admiration, she wanted more than anything to have Aaron's love.

Now he was going to go back to Missouri and take her heart with him. She didn't know how she was going to go on. How would she face tomorrow when she had lost so much tonight?

She brushed her cheeks with her hand and willed her breathing to calm. Closing her eyes, she whispered another simple prayer. "God, this must be your plan. I trust you, but please, please, heal my crushed heart."

Aaron tossed and turned all night long in his room at the bed-and-breakfast. He couldn't stop thinking about the pain in

Linda's beautiful face when he told her he was leaving. He felt a hole in his heart when he thought of leaving Linda and his parents. Yet he believed Solomon's final words were a sign that leaving was for the best.

Finally, at five in the morning, he pulled himself from bed and began packing his things. He was putting the last of his clothes in his bag when a knock sounded on his door. He pulled it open and was stunned to find Solomon in the hallway.

Solomon held his hat in his hands, a strange expression on his face. "I need to talk to you. May I come in?"

"Of course." Aaron made a sweeping gesture toward the room.

Solomon closed the door behind him. He was gripping his hat and seemed upset, not angry. "*Mamm* heard our argument last night. She was standing on the back porch." His eyes were overcome with regret. "She had a breakdown after you left. She won't get out of bed, and she refused to take her medication this morning."

Aaron gasped as concern surged through him. "Oh no."

"*Mamm* is devastated, and she wants you to come back." Solomon paused to clear his throat. "She says it will kill her if you leave. She says she needs you here."

Solomon sank into the desk chair. "I was wrong, Aaron. I thought I was protecting her by hiding those letters, but I had it all wrong. I never should've kept the letters and I should've welcomed you home. Instead, I let my resentment take over all these years, and it was only when I saw *Mamm* so upset by what I had done . . ." His eyes misted over. "You're *mei bruder, mei* only *bruder.* It's the Amish way to forgive, and I was too prideful and stubborn to forgive. And I've only made things worse for everyone, especially *Mamm.*"

Aaron studied Solomon's face, finding honest regret there. He was telling the truth, and it rocked Aaron to the core. He didn't know what to say or how to react.

"I'm here to apologize and beg you to stay." Solomon's eyes softened, pleading with Aaron. "Please stay, Aaron. If you can't stay for me, then please stay for *Mamm.* She needs you here. The whole family needs you, including *mei kinner.* Manny hasn't stopped talking about you and how much he misses working with you."

Aaron felt his emotions swirl as if they'd been stuffed in a blender and turned on the high setting. He opened his mouth to speak but he couldn't find the right words.

Solomon stood. "I'll give you some time

to think about this." He went to the door, grabbed the knob, and then looked over his shoulder. "Last night while I was trying to fall asleep, I remembered the parable of the Prodigal Son. I've been like the other son, and I never even realized it. We Amish are taught to forgive, and I've gone against everything I've been taught. Becky and Ruthie Joy tried to make me realize how wrong I've been, but I was too stubborn to listen. I'm truly sorry, Aaron. You don't need to forgive me, but I need you to think about *Mamm.* She's in bad shape, and I think you're the one she needs the most."

Solomon disappeared through the door, his footsteps echoing through the hallway as he descended the stairs.

Aaron sat down on the corner of the bed. He stared at his packed bag and tried to sort through the sudden change in events. Now Solomon had asked him to stay, but he was still confused. He didn't know where he belonged.

His stomach growled and he realized he was hungry.

Downstairs, Aaron found Linda cooking breakfast. He stood in the doorway as she scraped hash browns from a large frying pan onto a platter. He enjoyed looking at her beautiful profile as she worked.

Linda must have sensed his presence. She looked over, and her pink lips formed a scowl. Her normally bright eyes had dark circles under them, evidence that she hadn't slept last night either.

"I didn't expect to see you here on a Saturday," Aaron said.

"Hannah asked me to come in because she hasn't been feeling well. I was surprised to see your truck in the driveway this morning. I thought you were leaving." She placed the platter on the table and then turned back toward the counter, where she began to crack eggs into a large bowl.

"I was going to leave this morning." He walked over to her and fought the urge to touch her arm. "I assume you saw my brother here this morning."

"*Ya,* I did." She began to beat the eggs. "He asked to see you, and I told him where to find your room."

"He asked me to stay for *Mamm,*" Aaron began. "He said *mei mamm* heard our conversation last night when he told me to leave. She won't get out of bed or take her medication."

"I'm sorry to hear that." Linda's voice was soft and quaky despite forced indifference. She kept her eyes trained on her work.

Aaron wished she'd look at him. He

needed to look into her eyes, and he needed to know what she thought about the whole situation. Instead of looking at him, she dropped the yolk into the pan. He watched it sizzle a moment before trying again.

"Solomon apologized to me for hiding the letters," he continued. "He said he was wrong to have treated me so badly, and he wants me to stay too." He touched her arm and she took a step away from his touch. The rejection hurt him deep in his soul. "Linda? Will you look at me?"

She looked at him then, and he found anguish in her deep-brown eyes. "What do you want me to say?" she whispered.

He blanched as if she'd hit him. "I want to know what you think. I don't know how to feel. Solomon has treated me like an enemy ever since I came home. Now he is begging for my forgiveness and asking me to stay. I'm so confused. What do you think I should do?"

She shrugged and looked back into the frying pan. "I think you should forgive him."

"You do?" he asked.

"Ya." She moved the eggs around with a spatula. "I told my *onkel* that I forgive him last night, and it made things much better. He apologized to me and admitted he's been treating me badly for years. We're go-

ing to work on repairing our relationship. He actually told me he loves me."

Aaron smiled. "That's *wunderbaar*, Linda. I'm so happy for you."

"That's why Jesus tells us to forgive. It helps repair relationships. If you forgive Solomon, then it will repair your relationship, and you'll have your family back."

"You're right," Aaron said. "You're so wise, Linda."

Linda looked at up him, but the light was still gone from her eyes. "Why are you standing here talking to me? Go see your family. They need you."

"You're right." He smiled at her, hoping to see her smile too. But when she didn't, he said, *"Danki."*

He rushed up the stairs and grabbed the letters.

Aaron hurried into his parents' house and found Solomon and their *dat* standing in his parents' bedroom. His mother was lying in bed with her eyes closed. Her skin was pasty white, and sweat beaded on her forehead. He hoped she was okay. The fear of losing her flooded him, causing his body to quake and stealing his breath.

"Aaron." His father walked over to him, his eyes glistening. "You're still here."

Aaron glanced at his brother, who looked anxious. "Solomon told me *Mamm* needs me."

His mother opened her eyes and smiled. "A-aaron."

"I have something for you." Aaron held up the letters. "I found my letters."

"You d-did." She struggled to sit up, and his father took her arm and helped her, placing two pillows behind her back. She examined the letters with a curious expression. "Wh-where w-were th-they?"

"I had them," Solomon confessed. "I hid them from you all these years."

"Wh-what?" *Mamm* gasped. "Wh-why w-would you d-do that?"

"I don't understand," *Dat* chimed in. "How could you do something so terrible? Those were your *mamm*'s letters. That's so unlike you, Solomon."

"I thought I was helping." Solomon shook his head and stared at his shoes. "I saw the hurt Aaron caused when he left, and I thought maybe if she could forget about him, *Mamm* would heal. I realize now that I was completely wrong. I'm sorry. I'm so very sorry, *Mamm*. I've apologized to Aaron, and I've asked him to stay."

Mamm's eyes locked with Aaron's. "W-will y-you s-stay, Aaron? P-please?"

416

"Aaron, we want you here," *Dat* chimed in. "We want our family back together. It's been too long. Our hearts have been broken since you left, son. Now that you're home, your *mamm* and I feel like our hearts have finally healed, and our family is complete again."

"Please, Aaron," Solomon said. "You need to stay. Even if you never speak to me again, you need to be here. My family wants you here too. Manny, Ruthie Joy, Katie, and Junior have been asking for you ever since you left last night. They heard you were going back to Missouri, and they've been beside themselves. Even Becky is furious with me."

Aaron analyzed his parents' hopeful expressions. And he had never seen his brother look so humble. He knew in his heart that he needed to stay. He was finally home, with his family, where he belonged.

"Ya," he finally said, his voice quavering with emotion. "I'll stay, and I forgive you, Solomon." He reached out to shake his brother's hand. "It's *gut* to be home."

Aaron saw the relief in Solomon's eyes as he grasped Aaron's hand in his.

"P-praise J-Jesus!" *Mamm* exclaimed. "*K-kumm,* Aaron." She waved him over as tears trickled down her cheeks. "I've p-prayed

417

f-for th-this f-for a l-long t-time."

Aaron hugged his mother.

"Excuse me," Becky said from the doorway. "What's going on? Jocelyn is here to see Ruth."

Mamm patted Aaron's arm. *"D-danki."*

Aaron nodded. "I'll be back soon." He squeezed her hand. "I promise."

Aaron followed his father and brother out of the bedroom as Jocelyn came in.

"Solomon," Aaron said as his mind moved through the logistics of relocating, "I'll let you explain everything to Becky. I have a lot of things to work out. I need to call Zac and discuss selling my half of the business to him. I need to go back to Missouri to get my things, and I'll need a place to stay until I can find a *haus.*"

Dat placed his hand on Aaron's arm. "You take it one step at a time. Just go call your friend and then figure out when you're going to go back to Missouri. As for a place to stay, don't you remember we've said you can stay here?"

"I have room too," Solomon offered. "Also, we have plenty of land. You can build a *haus* right here."

Aaron smiled at his brother. *"Danki."*

"Gern gschehne, bruder." Solomon smiled.

Aaron's thoughts turned to Linda. "I need

to take care of something more important first."

TWENTY

Linda was cleaning up the breakfast dishes when she heard Hannah call her name. The urgency in Hannah's voice caused Linda to drop the dish she was holding into the dish water and rush down the hallway.

"Hannah?" Linda burst into the suite and found Hannah leaning against a chair. *"Was iss letz?"*

"My water just broke." Hannah puckered her lips and then blew out a deep breath. "Would you please find Trey? *Dummle!"*

"Ya!" Linda rushed out through the kitchen and raced outside to the barn. "Trey! Trey!"

"Yeah?" Trey appeared, wiping his hands on a shop rag. "What's going on?"

"It's time," Linda said, gasping for her breath.

"It's time? Oh! It's time!" His eyes flew open and he tossed the shop rag on the ground outside the barn.

420

"You need to get Hannah to the hospital. Her water just broke. I'll take care of everything here." Linda followed Trey back into the house.

"Andrew is at a sleepover at a friend's house," he said. "His friend's mother is supposed to bring him home later today. Would you please stay and take care of him? I don't know when Amanda will be home." He stopped. "Would you call her at work? The vet's name is in the address book by the phone in our bedroom."

"*Ya,* I'll call Amanda, and I'll stay for Andrew," Linda said. "It's no problem at all. I'll let *mei onkel* know you need me to stay late. You just go."

"Great." Trey suddenly stopped and faced Linda. "Do me a favor. Call Lillian too. Her number is in the same place."

Linda gave him a knowing smile. "I will."

She helped Trey gather up Hannah's things and then carried them to the car. Trey helped Hannah into the passenger seat before putting her suitcase in the trunk.

Linda leaned into the car and touched Hannah's hand. "Don't worry about anything here. We'll be fine."

"Danki," Hannah said, sounding a bit breathless.

"Thank you, Linda," Trey said as he

moved to the driver's seat. "I'll call you."

Linda waved as they drove off, then made her way back into the house and down the hallway to the family's suite. She found the address book, called Amanda, then located the number for Lillian. She knew Lillian lived with her grandmother, Barbie Glick, who was Hannah's former mother-in-law. Linda dialed the number and hoped someone would hear the phone ringing in their barn. After several rings someone picked up.

"Hello?" a masculine voice said.

"Hello, this is Linda Zook," she began. "I need to speak with Lillian Glick, please."

"Oh, Linda, hello. This is Eli," the man said. "Let me see if Lillian is home. Hang on one moment."

Linda sat down on the edge of the bed and waited until Lillian came to the phone.

"Hi, Linda. This is Lillian," she said.

"Lillian, hi," Linda said. "Trey asked me to tell you your *mamm* went into labor this morning. She's on her way to the hospital now to have the *boppli*. He thought you would want to know."

The other end of the line went silent.

"Lillian?" Linda asked. "Are you still there?"

"Ya," Lillian's voice was unsteady. "Do you

know which hospital?"

Linda told her.

"*Danki* for calling," Lillian said. "Good-bye."

"Good-bye." Linda hung up the phone, hoping Lillian would make this an even better day for Hannah.

Lillian hung up the phone and stared at it. Her mother was having the baby, and Lillian was going to have a baby brother or sister. She was nearly overwhelmed with the urge to go to the hospital and be with her mother. All the past hurt and disappointment that had plagued her since her mother had left the community suddenly evaporated. She was ready to go see her. Her mother needed her, and she wanted to be there with her and her siblings. Lillian needed her family back in her life.

She called her grandparents' driver and asked him to come right away. Then she rushed to the house and found her grandmother in the kitchen.

"Lily?" *Mammi* regarded her with concern. "Is everything all right?"

"*Ya,*" Lillian said. "Linda Zook just called. *Mei mamm* went into labor. She's having the *boppli,* and I want to go to the hospital to be with her. A ride is coming to get me."

"Oh." *Mammi* looked surprised.

"I have to go. I'm ready to see her again." Lillian's lower lip quivered. "I'm ready to forgive her. I hope you understand."

Mammi crossed the kitchen and hugged her. "Of course I understand. Call me and let me know how everything goes."

"I will. *Danki.*" Happiness engulfed Lillian. She couldn't wait to meet her new brother or sister.

Hannah cuddled her newborn baby against her chest as tears blurred her vision. She couldn't believe it. She was holding a brand-new baby.

"She's beautiful," Trey whispered in her ear. "She's perfect, just like you."

Hannah gazed up at her husband as pure elation overcame her. "I'm so happy."

"I am too." He kissed her head. "Have you decided on a name? I know you were considering both Heather and Melissa."

Hannah was surprised. "You're going to let me choose? I thought you wanted to name her Grace after your mother."

Trey shook his head. "No, I want you to decide. I'm happy with whatever you choose."

"How about Heather Grace?" Hannah asked. "I love the name Heather, and Grace will be for your mother. What do you think?"

"Heather Grace Peterson." Trey nodded. "It's perfect."

A knock sounded on the door, and a nurse poked her head in. "Excuse me, Mrs. Peterson. You have visitors. Your daughters and your son are here."

"Please send them in," Trey said. "Thank you."

"My daughters?" Hannah gasped. "Both of my daughters are here?" She looked up at Trey. "Did you call Lily?"

"I asked Linda to call her." He touched her cheek. "I had a feeling she might come."

The door opened, and Amanda and Andrew walked in, followed by Lillian, who had a tentative expression on her face.

"Hi, *Mamm,*" Amanda said. "Linda called me, and I went to get Andrew on my way to the hospital."

"Thank you, Amanda," Trey said.

Andrew rushed over to the bed. "Oh, let me see."

"This is your baby sister," Hannah held the baby out. "Heather Grace, this is your big brother, Andrew."

"Oh, Heather," Amanda grinned down at the baby. "Look at you." She looked back at her twin, who was lingering by the door. "Get over here, Lily, and meet our sister."

Lillian smiled as she walked over to her siblings, who were studying the baby. "Hi, Heather." She gazed at the baby and then looked at Hannah. "Congratulations, *Mamm.*"

Hannah swiped the back of her hand over her eyes as tears began to sprinkle down her cheeks. "Thank you. It's *gut* to see you."

"It's *gut* to be here." Lillian looked at the baby. "May I hold her, *Mamm*?"

"Of course you may." Amanda gently took the baby from Hannah and then put the baby in Lillian's arms. She smiled at her mother.

"Hi, Heather," Lillian said. "I'm your big *schweschder,* Lily. I'm going to teach you *Dietsch* and tell you all about your Amish family."

Hannah held Trey's hand and smiled. She finally had her family back together. She closed her eyes and thanked God.

Linda was dusting the front room when the back door slammed. She rushed to the kitchen expecting to find Trey there. She stopped in the doorway when she saw Aaron instead. Her expression clouded as disappointment and regret coursed through her. She couldn't stand looking at the man who had broken her heart.

"Hi." He took a step toward her. "I was hoping you were still here."

"Are you going to pack now?" she asked, folding her arms over her chest in an effort to protect her already fractured heart.

"I've already packed," he said. "But I won't be gone long. I do have to go to Missouri, but then I'll be back."

"I don't understand." She searched his expression for answers. Was he toying with her emotions?

"I'm going to need your help." His lips twitched as he took another step toward her. "I'll need a tutor to help me remember *Dietsch* when I get back from Missouri."

She tilted her head and looked up at him. "Aaron, you're not making sense."

"I probably will need a refresher course on the language so I'll be able to understand the bishop during the baptism classes."

She gaped as he smiled. "Baptism classes?"

"That's what I said." He touched her cheek as affection overcame his eyes. "I'm going to go to Missouri to pack up my things and take care of some business. I need to call Zac and see if he wants to buy out my half of the company. Once all that is settled, I'll be back. My parents said I can stay with them until I have my own place."

427

"You're moving here?" she asked, her voice trembling with excitement.

"I am. I worked things out with *mei bruder. Mei mamm* is going to be okay. Her nurse came to see her today, and she's already doing better. I know now that my family needs me, and I want to be here. I want to be with them again."

His expression softened. "I owe you an apology. I'm sorry for saying I was going to leave. I could never really leave you. God brought us together. You've been my best *freind* since I came back here. You were there for me when I needed someone to talk you. You've guided me through all these confusing emotions while I've been here, and you've given me wonderful advice. Your friendship has been a blessing to me."

She nodded as tears inundated her eyes.

"I've learned so much from you, Linda. You taught me how to forgive *mei bruder.* You've shown me what's really important in life. I can't thank you enough." He gazed down at her.

"I know I can't officially ask you to be my girlfriend until I'm baptized, but I was wondering if you would take a rain check." He smiled as he cupped his hand to her cheek. "Would you wait for me to be baptized and then be my girlfriend?"

She nodded as happiness swelled inside of her and her heart hammered. "I will on one condition."

"What's that condition?"

"You have to take your *Dietsch* lessons seriously," she teased. "I can't spend my time translating things for you."

"Can you translate this?" he asked. "*Ich liebe dich,* Linda Zook."

Before she could respond, he leaned down and brushed his lips over hers, sending her stomach into a wild swirl. She savored the feel of his lips on hers. When he broke the kiss, he left her breathless. He leaned his forehead on hers, and she stared into his warm eyes.

"So did you translate it?" he whispered.

"Ya," she whispered in return, her voice trembling. "I love you too, Aaron Ebersol."

She smiled then, silently thanking God for bringing happiness and love into her life. He'd heard every simple prayer.

EPILOGUE

Linda stepped out onto Saul's front porch and shivered as the autumn breeze caught her cloak.

"Do you need my coat?" Aaron offered, taking her hand in his.

"No, no." She shook her head. "I'm fine." She smiled up at Aaron. "The wedding was *schee, ya*?"

"It was." Aaron gave her hand a gentle squeeze and led her to the far corner of the porch.

"Madeleine and Saul looked so *froh.*" Linda sat on the swing. "Even Emma was beaming as they took their vows. I know they will have a happy life. It's amazing how God brought them together."

"You're right." Aaron sank down beside her and moved the swing.

Linda turned toward Aaron and found him staring toward the pasture. He seemed to have something on his mind, and she

430

wondered what he was thinking. She admired how he looked in his plain shirt and suspenders. He had been baptized a week ago, along with Madeleine and the rest of the new members of the church. It seemed like only yesterday that he had come back to the community, and now he was an official church member. Time had moved so quickly.

Aaron had been able to sell his half of the construction business to his partner in Missouri, and he had enough funds to start a new construction business in Paradise. He called it Ebersol Family Construction, inviting Solomon and Manny to be his partners. "*Mei bruder* is finally going to realize his own dream of building houses," Aaron had told her. He had also hired helpers for his father on the dairy farm.

"I want to ask you something," Aaron finally said, looking nervous. "We had to wait until I joined the church to make things more official. Now that I'm baptized, I can ask you what I've wanted to ask you since last spring."

Her heart thudded. She knew he was going to ask her to be his girlfriend, and she held her breath with anticipation.

"Linda, I've loved you since that day you calmed me down and fed me *kichlin* after

that emotional conversation with my *dat*."
He chuckled. "I'll never forget how you ac-
cused me of not knowing how to speak
Dietsch."

She grinned despite her swirling emotions.
"Well, you did take your time using the
language again."

"You are *mei* best *freind*," he continued as
he held her hands in his. "You're the most
amazing, *schee*, loving *maedel* I've ever
met, and I can't imagine my life without
you. Now that I have a *haus* and our construction business going, I can ask you the
question I've been dreaming of asking you
for months." He paused, and her breath
hitched. "Will you marry me, Linda?"

She gasped in surprise, and her eyes
overflowed with tears. Happiness consumed
her as she laughed, "*Ya*, I will. I will marry
you, Aaron."

"I'm the happiest man on the planet!" He
pulled her into his arms and kissed her. "I
have something else to tell you."

"What?" Linda asked.

"I found some land for us, and I want you
to help me design our *haus*."

"Oh my goodness!" Linda cupped her
hand to her mouth. She was certain her
heart might burst with all of the excitement.

"What's going on here?" Carolyn Glick's

voice sounded from behind her.

Linda and Aaron stood and found Carolyn, Joshua, Saul, and Madeleine crowded around the front door.

"Did you two sneak outside to have a private moment together?" Madeleine teased. "We were just looking for you."

"Aaron just asked me to marry him," Linda said as Aaron rested his arm around her shoulder.

Carolyn and Madeleine squealed and then ran over and hugged her.

"We have another wedding to plan," Carolyn said. "That's so *wunderbaar!*"

"I'm so *froh* for you," Madeleine said.

"*Danki.* I want to tell Hannah. Have you seen her?" Linda asked.

"*Ya,* I saw her talking with Amanda and Lillian in the kitchen," Carolyn said. "Let's go find her."

Linda looked up at Aaron, who was being congratulated by Joshua and Saul. "I'm going to tell Hannah. I'll be back."

He stepped away from the men and smiled down at her.

"Take your time."

"You've made me the happiest woman alive," she whispered. *"Danki."*

"No," Aaron said. "I need to thank you for leading me home."

As Linda walked into the house with Madeleine and Carolyn, she couldn't stop smiling. How grateful she was to God for the gift of her community, her wonderful friends, and someone to love.

DISCUSSION QUESTIONS

1. Aaron is stunned when Saul calls and tells him his mother had a stroke. He struggles with his decision to go home because he thinks his family has forgotten him. He has moved on with his life, but he feels he must go home and face his painful past. Have you ever had to face a difficult family situation? What Bible verses helped you with your choices? Share this with the group.

2. Aaron feels God is giving him a second chance with his family. Have you ever experienced a second chance? What was it?

3. Linda finds encouragement in Ephesians 4:32: "Be kind and compassionate to one another, forgiving each other, just as in Christ God forgave you." What does this verse mean to you?

4. Linda has always felt unworthy and unloved after losing her parents and hav-

ing to live with her miserable uncle. Think of a time when you felt lost and alone. Where did you find your strength? What Bible verses would help?

5. Solomon believes he's shielding his mother from hurt when he hides the letters Aaron sent her. In the end, it's painful for everyone when they learn the truth. Do you think Solomon's intentions were justified? Have you ever found yourself in a similar situation? If so, how did it turn out? Share this with the group.

6. Linda finds the courage to stand up to her uncle because of Aaron's encouragement. Have you ever had to stand up to someone who hurt you? How did this situation turn out for you?

7. In *A Hopeful Heart, A Mother's Secret,* and *A Dream of Home,* Lillian is convinced her mother is being selfish and is betraying her by leaving the Amish community. In this last book, we finally see Lillian forgive her mother. Do you agree with Lillian's choice to forgive? Share this with the group.

8. Which character can you identify with the most? Which character seemed to carry the most emotional stake in the story? Was it Aaron, Solomon, Linda, or someone else?

9. Linda grows as a character throughout the book. What do you think caused her to change throughout the story?
10. What did you know about the Amish before reading this book? What did you learn?

ACKNOWLEDGMENTS

As always, I'm thankful for my loving family, including my mother, Lola Goebelbecker; my husband, Joe; and my sons, Zac and Matt. I'm blessed to have such an awesome and amazing family.

I'm more grateful than words can express to my patient friends who critique for me, including Janet Pecorella, Lauran Rodriguez, and, of course, my mother. I truly appreciate the time you take out of your busy lives to help me polish my books. Thank you to Stacey Barbalace for all your help with my research.

Special thanks to my Amish friends who patiently answer my endless stream of questions. You're a blessing in my life.

Thank you to my wonderful church family at Morning Star Lutheran in Matthews, North Carolina, for your encouragement, prayers, love, and friendship. You all mean so much to my family and me.

To my agent, Sue Brower — you are my own personal superhero! I can't thank you enough for your guidance, advice, and friendship. I'm grateful that our paths have crossed and our partnership will continue long into the future. You are a tremendous blessing in my life.

Thank you to my amazing editor, Becky Philpott, for your friendship and guidance. I'm grateful to Jean Bloom, who helped me polish and refine the story. Jean, I hope we can work together again in the future. I also would like to thank Kerri Potts for tirelessly working to promote my books. I'm grateful to each and every person at HarperCollins Christian Publishing who helped make this book a reality.

To my readers — thank you for choosing my novels. My books are a blessing in my life for many reasons, including the special friendships I've formed with my readers. Thank you for your email messages, Facebook notes, and letters.

Thank you most of all to God — thank You for giving me the inspiration and the words to glorify You. I'm grateful and humbled You've chosen this path for me.

Special thanks to Cathy and Dennis Zimmermann for their hospitality and research assistance in Lancaster County, Pennsylvania.

Cathy & Dennis Zimmermann, Innkeepers
The Creekside Inn
44 Leacock Road (or PO Box 435)
Paradise, PA 17562
Toll Free: (866) 604-2574
Local Phone: (717) 687-0333

The author and publisher gratefully acknowledge the following resource that was used to research information for this book:
C. Richard Beam, *Revised Pennsylvania German Dictionary* (Lancaster: Brooksire Publications, Inc., 1991).

ABOUT THE AUTHOR

Amy Clipston is the award-winning and best-selling author of the Kauffman Amish Bakery series. Her novels have hit multiple best-seller lists including CBD, CBA, and ECPA. Amy holds a degree in communication from Virginia Wesleyan College and works full-time for the City of Charlotte, NC. Amy lives in North Carolina with her husband, two sons, and four spoiled rotten cats. Visit her online at www.amyclipston.com Facebook: AmyClipstonBooks Twitter: @AmyClipston